LUKA'S ESCAPE

A STORY OF DESTINY AND COURAGE

TRICIA BULIC

First published 2025 by Tricia Bulic

Produced by Independent Ink
independentink.com.au

Cover design by Joe Therasakdhi
Edited by Lucy Czerwinski
Internal design by Independent Ink
Typeset in Adobe Garamond Pro by Post Pre-press Group, Brisbane

ISBN 978-1-7640370-0-6 (paperback)
ISBN 978-1-7640370-1-3 (epub)
ISBN 978-1-7640370-2-0 (kindle)

To my friend Trevor Barrow for supporting and encouraging me on this wonderful journey.

SLOVENIA
CROATIA
HUNGARY
SERBIA
Trieste
Koper
Venice
Rijeka
Omišalj
Pula
ADRIATIC
Ravenna
BOSNIA
AND
HERZEGOVINA
Zadar
Falconara
Marittima
Ancona
Split
Ploče
MONTENEGRO
Dubrovnik
Pescara
SEA
Bar
ALBANIA
ITALY
Durrës
Bari
Brindisi
Vlorë
TYRRHENIAN SEA
Strait of
Otranto
0
100 km

CHAPTER 1

2016

"Leave me alone woman!"

Roko's legs wobbled from side to side as he tried to get out from the sunken chair.

"Where are you going Roko? It's your birthday!" his wife, Maria queried as she saw him trying to stand.

His fingernails scraped the edge of the walking frame that was just outside his reach, and he cursed as he tried to grab it.

"I'm old enough now! You can celebrate. I'm going to bed!"

Rounds of raucous laughter came from the other room as the family birthday lunch threatened to become dinner.

Roko snorted as he drew another deep breath. One leg shuffled forward as the other one struggled to join in. Maria looked away as if to spare him from what he knew so well.

The slow shuffle to the bedroom had used most of the energy he had left. Relief washed over him as he entered the room they had shared for almost sixty years.

"I made you chamomile tea."

"It doesn't help. I don't know why you worry."

"It must help because you snore like a pig when you drink it. I should know!"

His face reddened and the pace of his breath increased. And then suddenly it was gone. Any strength he had to lash out at his wife had left him a long time ago. What was left was for basic survival. All I am good for now is eating, drinking and shitting, he thought to himself.

Maria had felt the back of his hand more than once in the past, but he had appreciated her more as they had grown older. She was a good wife, a good cook and a good mother.

He went over to the handbasin in the small ensuite and splashed his face. When he looked up to the mirror, the creases that draped around his eyes and face said it all.

"You are old Roko. He told his reflection. If there is room, God can take me now. I don't want any more birthdays."

Maria's shrill voice interrupted his moment of self-pity.

"You have new pyjamas on the bed. Don't look for your old ones. I've thrown them in the rubbish."

Sighing, he grabbed the new flannelette pyjamas as Maria finally left him in peace.

He pulled the covers back and took a deep breath as he sank into the side of the bed. With another deep breath, he lifted one leg up and across before shuffling onto the mattress. On the nights when he couldn't be bothered, he would just fall asleep in the chair.

He hated this time of the evening. Despite the comfort of the soft bed, the same images would play over in his mind and the nightmares would shock him awake in a lather of sweat.

Disbelief. Anger. Tears.

He could still sense the lifeless body he held, adrift in the middle of the Adriatic Sea almost sixty-three years ago.

The chamomile tea gave him temporary relief but the nightmares that followed were permanent.

1953

"Race you to the water!"

Roko had the head start on Luka as they sprinted to the sea. The burning cobblestones on the path meant their feet barely touched the ground. They almost hit the water together, but Luka had easily caught his bigger friend and went in first.

"You are getting too fat to run!"

"Better than having arms and legs like Baba's pasta!"

Luka lunged at his friend, but Roko caught him and easily pushed him under water.

"Race you to the jetty!" Luka called as he lurched from the salty water.

Luka was lithe and agile on land, unlike his taller heavier friend, and the hard ground gave Luka an advantage but, in the water, they were evenly matched. The sparkling blue of the Adriatic Sea disturbed by their frenzied strokes.

"Ha! I won!" Roko attempted to scale the iron ladder onto the jetty first but within seconds, Luka had grabbed his swim trunks and pulled down hard.

He crashed back into the water as Luka, laughing hard, scurried up the ladder.

The friends lay on the warmed rough wood of the jetty to dry in the sun. It felt as though they had been competing since they were born. Luka had the wiry frame of an athlete with tufts of black hair in lines on his otherwise bare and shallow chest. Roko was the complete opposite. Lots of hair over his big body.

But they both knew that what Roko lacked in shape was well and truly made up for in strength. Luka had never beaten him in a wrestle.

"I'm glad its summer again."

"Me too. I want to do this forever."

The smell of salt in the air brought the fishermen to life and with the lapping sounds of crystal blue waters against the boats, it was time to celebrate summer.

Summertime in Zadar, on the pristine coastline of Yugoslavia, was breathtaking.

The sandstone pathways that led to the towering walls of the old city were bathed in light. The huge battlements cast their gaze across the Adriatic Sea, waiting and watching for the next challenge. But beauty has a habit of distracting, and the years following the end of the war had not delivered the promise of hope and respite from conflict.

Yugoslavia was still in a struggle to find its identity after losing over one million lives in World War II.

There were sordid and grisly tales of the many insurgencies that were brought upon families and communities and a government that had weakened, then failed its people. Stories of brutality, including abductions, rapes and killings from groups like the "*Ustashas*" would be spoken in quiet behind closed doors.

Its citizens were thrown into gaol for the smallest of things with the guards playing cruel jokes on the many innocent captives. People whispered that the guards would sometimes call out a "lucky person's name" in the morning, saying they would be freed. And when that person was taken out by the guards, they would never be seen again.

The people of Zadar would still endure constant surveillance, monitoring of movements and nightly visits to test allegiances.

Dozing in the sun, their breathing seemed in rhythm with the lapping water when Roko sat up with a start.

"What time is it!" He looked around wildly before realising that it was later than he had thought. "Papa will kill me! I was supposed to help move the goats to the next field today!"

Roko got one leg into his trousers and then with a couple of hops, managed to get the second one in before trying to tie the cord at his waist. Luka stifled a giggle as he saw the wide-eyed look of fear that had appeared on his friend's face.

"Tell him it was my fault. I made you stay longer. We can make up a story. How about when I grabbed your pants, you hit your head?" Luka tried to find the right excuse that would help his friend avoid the inevitable, but they both knew that Roko's father wouldn't believe it.

"I'll come with you, Roko."

"No. That'll just make it worse. See you, Luka."

Roko's head hit the edge of the wooden table as he fell. The familiar shock of pain swept over him as he forced himself not to cry. His father swung his leg back and kicked Roko with full force behind his knees.

"You eat the food that I have worked hard to get and look how fat you are!"

Kick.

The shock of pain hit him in the ribs.

"You are lazy; no good to me!"

Another kick.

"Why can't you be like your brother!" He felt himself being lifted off the worn linoleum floor before a final slap across his head threw him down again. Roko's brother had followed in his father's footsteps and enlisted in the army.

He felt his Mama's eyes on him. She always watched but never moved from the corner chair. She would be next if she did, and she'd had her share of beltings for him.

Silence and wringing hands.

Roko was breathing hard as the cool hard floor gave some relief to the pain as his father stepped over him to leave. The door slammed shut on another belting.

"Get up Roko. I will heat frijole soup for you before he comes back." No mother's comfort or sympathy.

"Why don't you stop him!" Tears streaming down his face.

"Why can't you just learn to do as you are told!" Her eyes fixed and face unmoving.

His mother's strength to the outside world, showed a fierce will and determination but behind closed doors it was always different.

His father ruled. And with an iron fist, for both.

"I didn't mean to forget about the goats." His croaked reply barely heard.

Roko swayed each time he tried to stand. His legs gave out from under him until he could barely sit up. One hand went to his forehead to try to keep the throbbing at bay. He was sick and dizzy. His mother stood to stir the pot on the wood-burning stove, her back to him.

"Luka is trouble for you, Roko. He should take his duties more seriously. Then maybe you wouldn't always be in trouble.

You should be more like your brother. He knew how to deal with your papa. You must do the same."

Yes, he knew, thought Roko. That's why he joined. To get away from the black eyes and bruises. How weird that his brother thought that fighting in an army was safer than being at home.

He dragged himself along the floor until he reached a chair to steady him. The first breath that didn't cause a sharp pain would be the one he would use to lift himself up. The heating of the soup seemed to take as long as his struggle and he didn't notice her dead-eyed gaze until he was juggling to keep hold of the edge of the table and the chair.

The drops of blood from his nose stained the watery broth as he tried to take a first spoonful. He pushed the bowl away just in time as everything went black.

Luka decided it would be safer to walk the long way home from the jetty. The shorter route would take him past Roko's house and the last thing he wanted was to face his friend or his friend's father after the likely beating.

The longer path passed by the small stone dwellings of the village that peppered the rocky hill beyond the gates of the old city. Like soldiers standing ready to charge on an enemy if the order from the ramparts was given. There wasn't much distance between each of them and if there was, it was soon occupied by a garden, pigs or goats. Handshake agreements between families over the years were the only proof of any ownership and if you left anything unclaimed or unoccupied, it was quickly taken. Grapevines draped along rickety fences and olives trees clung to the sedimentary rock base beneath.

Passing the village church and graveyard till the familiar smell of sticky sweet dough teased him away from the path to home.

"Teta Ana!"

The old woman was bent over in the small vegetable patch that sat alongside the small grey weathered stone dwelling on the far side of the village. She grabbed the small of her back as she slowly stood up and turned to see who was calling. Her eyes needed to adjust as a broad smile came across her face when she saw her favourite boy had come to visit.

Not only did his call alert his aunty. In moments a sharp bray and flashing gums from her "Moro" as he trotted around from the back of the house. The alluring eyelashes and saucer-like eyes hid the probability of a nip if you came too close. A quick scratch behind the oversized ears and the mule was subdued in an instant.

"Luka! Why didn't you come to see me for a long time?"

"It's only been three days aunty. Have you missed me that much?"

Her smile changed to laughter with a spontaneous deep sigh to complete her feeling of joy. This boy filled her heart, and she loved the same game they played each time he would visit. Although this time, somehow it was different. She sensed he was troubled.

"Come inside dragi. Tell me what you have been doing. I have warm fritter with honey for you."

Luka caught the smell of sweet pastry and started salivating at the thought of the first bite. Warm honey dribbled down his chin as he sank his teeth into the doughy ball. Her bright eyes watched him take every bite.

"Tell me what is wrong, Luka."

He sat back as if deep in thought. "Roko's father beats him." Luka found it hard to speak the words.

Worry lines appeared on her forehead as she wiped her hands on the front of the apron. The small stool next to the wood stove creaked in protest as she sat and it took its familiar hiding place beneath the folds of her dress.

"You can be his friend, dragi. There is not much else you can do. This is family business." Her loss for anything more helpful made her sadder for him. She knew what he was talking about. The whole village knew.

"But he will kill him one day. Everyone around here knows it."

Her deep sigh only confirmed that this was probably the truth.

"What does he want to do when he finishes school? Maybe that will give him a chance to get away."

"We both want to go to university. He thinks he might study science, but his father wants him to work on the farm with him."

"What about the army?"

"He wouldn't last a day. His brother couldn't wait to enlist. And we all know why. They saw what the army did to their father every day."

Roko's brother had joined the Yugoslav National Army at the demand of their father and once the boy had left the village, he wasn't seen or heard from again. University would not have been an option for him anyway. He was thick-headed like his father.

"What about you Luka. What will you do? Do you still want university?"

"University is the only way I can get away from here and do something for myself." Luka replied.

There was silence for a moment as the old woman dribbled more honey over the next batch of deep-fried pastries.

"Your Tetak used to say that wherever your heart is, is where you should be. When he was alive, we would sit and talk about this village, the war and how many of our friends were lost because of the fighting. He, and your father, spoke out against the war and fighting, and they took them away." She looked out of the kitchen window, lost in the past.

When she returned to the present, she realised that she had been speaking as though they were both dead.

"I am so sorry Luka." Her hands now brushing across his hair. "Your father and uncle, wherever they are, were both honourable men who only wanted what was best for their people. War and fighting were never the answer for them."

Luka could only remember his father as a twelve-year-old did during that time. His uncle was a much older man and someone that his father always seemed to follow. Luka rarely saw him and would only see his father briefly at night after the long days at work were over. Even then it was only to ask about school and to make sure that all the chores were done for their mother. His younger sister, Mira seemed to get the better of their father and would prattle away regardless of whether he was listening or not.

She had only been seven years old when they came in the middle of the night and took his father away.

"What do you want!" He could hear his father yell. "I have nothing to hide! We are hardworking people who don't want any trouble!"

He remembered peering through the crack in the door trying to keep Mira quiet. His mother visibly shaking behind his father.

The man in uniform with a coal sweeper's moustache leered at them. He was known around the area as Dragan. A captain with the police but also suspected to be supporting the "Ustasha" in their vile campaign to assert control over parts of the country. The paunch that hovered over his low-slung belt was under constant caressing by one hand, while the other hand kept finding its way to his groin. As if sensing their discomfort, he kept stroking himself and smiled at the power he had over them. His two henchmen, one was called Matej and the other they didn't know, just stood in the doorway.

"We don't want trouble either Marko." Leering, sniggering. "But you and your moron brother have been talking too much. We are hearing bad things. And you know what happens to people who dare to speak out!"

Luka could just make out his father take a step back as the captain's face inched closer to his and he said almost in a whisper, "We make them disappear".

Just then Mira broke free from Luka and ran into wrap herself around her father's legs.

"Leave him alone!! You can't take Papa! I won't let you!"

The rest had become a blur to Luka. Mira screaming as the captain tried to grab hold of her. His initial shock at her reaction, momentarily catching him off guard. Then his father launching himself with fists flying at the man, only to have the henchmen react. The last Luka saw of his father was him being dragged from their home, flanked on either side by two of their own people. The captain did not take his eyes off Mira.

"One day I might come back for you, pretty one. When you are older. But not too much older" he ran his tongue along the yellow-stained teeth.

"She will be pretty like you, Mara ..."

His mother was inconsolable while she tried to shelter Mira.

"And now we will we go and find your uncle."

Luka could just remember the man they called Matej. He thought he could have been a policeman. Luka never forgot how he came back the next day to apologise and said if ever there was anything he could do, they just needed to ask. Luka knew he would never be able to disobey his captain. But his words made little difference at the time.

Luka's aunty was still brushing her hardened hands through his hair. The front of her apron now wet with his tears.

"We will never forget them, dragi" she said, wiping her eyes.

Standing up to leave, he realised how much he towered over her, and saw that the years were catching them both. As he hugged her, she remembered when his small arms could only grab her hips, and he would bury his face into her soft belly. She now found her head against his chest. She smiled and sighed at the beating of his heart.

"Sometimes, all you can do is what you believe is right. Be a friend to him, Luka. That's what he needs now."

It would be a week before Luka saw his friend again. Roko breathed hard with each step he took as he walked towards Luka. Every now and then, he grabbed his side as if to extract a sharp knife that was causing the stabbing pain. As he drew closer, Luka could see the mottled patches of purple and blue colouring the skin around his eyes. One eye was barely open while the other was like someone had thrown a red web across the eyeball.

"Hey."

"Hi."

Roko's head stayed down to spare his friend from the grotesque result of a beating.

"Was it bad?" Luka regretted the words as soon as they came out. He only needed to look at Roko to see that it must have been terrifying. "Sorry. That was a dumb thing to ask."

"Yeah. It was."

"How was your mama?"

Shrug. "She did nothing. As usual."

"Did the goats get moved?"

"I hate goats."

"I know."

"I want to leave Luka. I've had enough. He's a bastard! He never leaves me alone and I'm never good enough. My mother is too scared to do anything, and she sticks up for him all the time. I can't stay here."

"Then why are you staying Roko! He will only kill you, the way he keeps bashing you!"

"Where will I go? Where *can* I go? It's impossible. I hate it here! And I'm scared Luka. Really scared."

"It's okay, we'll think of something Roko. Just try to keep on his good side for now. Look after the stupid goats and just say yes when he asks you to do something."

The school bell didn't have the chance to finish ringing before the swarm of kids jostled through doorways, and with each other, to get away. Luka and his friends, Tom, Josip, Bruno and a new kid, Sam would hurry to change into swimmers and head to the beach. Roko would only join them when he wasn't herding goats or whatever else he needed to do to avoid the risk of another beating. He had listened to his friend and so far, there had been no more beltings from his father.

The warm, crystal-clear waters were like a tonic. After the sea had worked its magic, they would tear through the large gate into the old town kicking the football between them. A collective gasp, followed by laughter as the ball whistled passed someone's head or hit a shop window.

The threat of a broom to the back of the legs or clip across the head, from a shop owner or a passer-by was always the motivation to get away quickly.

When they finally reached the square, Tom found two rocks and after placing one on the ground in front of a wall, took ten paces and set the other down to set out the goal line.

He started bouncing around, swapping feet and lunging from side to side at an imaginary strike.

Around the square, the thousand-year-old stone walls held the red terracotta tiles up to the sun. There were mulberry trees with the occasional olive tree, to provide shelter from the heat of the day in summer.

"Hey Tom! Luka yelled just as he lobbed the ball into the air off the side of his bare foot. Tom lunged to take a header and missed, just as Josip bounced it off his chest. Bent backwards, he rolled it down his front to the top of his foot, tapped it once in the air, then struck it hard sideways between the rocks of the goal line and into the wall.

"Just like Bozsik!" Bruno ran after the ball and deftly manoeuvred it between his feet as he went.

Jozsef Bozsik was one of their favourite players and had represented his national team, Hungary, at three World Cups and had won an Olympic gold medal the year before in Helsinki.

The ball never ran smoothly across the uneven surface, but this only made the game more interesting. One minute they thought they had a clean strike and the next, the ball would bounce off a cobbled stone and their' foot would find clear air.

"Ha! You missed!"

"I would have got it if the stones were flat!"

"You play more like Bozsik's sister than Bozsik!"

They all laughed.

"I'm going to take a break. Does anyone want a drink?" Luka walked towards the shady trees and tried to get the old water pump going.

The fountain, that sat in the middle of the square, had been destroyed in the war, but the locals had fixed the old pipes and the hand pump, which heaved and shook each time the handle moved.

The boys took turns drinking and splashing their faces before sheltering under one of the large trees in the middle of the square.

"So, what are you going to do when you finish school Luka?" Sam was the first to ask.

Luka shrugged. "Don't know. I wanted to go to university but I'm not sure I can."

Bruno let out a deep breath.

"Papa wants me to work with him on the boat. He says that one day it will be mine. But I don't really want to be fishing for the rest of my life."

"Well, I know I'm going to be a civil engineer." Tom said confidently as he dribbled the ball around. "Things will change. You'll see."

Josip shrugged. "You think they will change, but they won't for us, Tom. I heard my papa say that unless you are a member of the Communist Party, you will spend two years in the army whether you like it or not."

"Who would want to fight. I'm going to apply to study anyway and see what happens." Luka sprang towards Tom, intercepted the ball and dribbled it around the boys.

"And if you miss out?"

"Then I'm going to escape!"

"Shh! Don't say that Luka! If anyone hears you talking like that, you will end up in gaol, or worse!"

"But they won't catch me …"

"You think you can outsmart them? No chance! They will come to your house in the middle of the night with a sack for your head and drag you away." Bruno spoke before he realised what he had said.

"Sorry Luka, I forgot."

"That's okay. I won't let them do that again."

They sat in quiet thought.

Sam was shuffling around. He'd only just arrived and now his newfound friends were talking of leaving.

Tom picked up the ball and started to walk off.

"Let's go. We shouldn't be talking like this. It's stupid and one of us will get hurt," he said.

"Hey!" Josip yelled out to him.

Tom ignored him and kept walking.

"Good luck, Mr Civil Engineer! You don't have a chance at getting to university! Nothing will change. You'll see!" he called as they stood to leave.

"Are you coming Luka?" Sam asked.

"Nah. You go. I'll catch you later."

Luka sat beneath the tree, unsettled by everything that seemed to be happening around him.

His best friend, Roko, was in real danger from his father's beatings and was desperate to get away and the only thing that seemed to be clear, was that if you weren't a Communist Party member, then it was unlikely that you would be accepted into further study. This meant that serving for two years in the army was the only option for them.

Luka had never thought of leaving, even though deep down he knew his future would be away from Zadar. He didn't imagine he would be thinking about this so soon.

But how could we get away, he asked himself. How could we avoid being seen or even worse, captured.

The memories of the night his father was taken were still present, but the thought of leaving his mama and Mira was difficult for him.

But what option is there for us, he thought, other than escaping.

It was the least he could do to help Roko.

CHAPTER 2

Roko sat at the kitchen table as his mother prepared dinner and frequently glanced sideways at the clock on the wall.

It was getting late.

Then in the distance, they both heard stumbles and the scuffing of boots along the gravel path.

Roko looked to his mother, but she kept her head down.

He watched the tightly wound braid of hair stuck to the back of her head and thought there seemed to be more whisps of grey hair appearing along the nape of her neck. Her apron a permanent fixture as she moved from one daily chore to the next.

The steps grew louder.

Suddenly, the door flew open and Roko's father lurched into the kitchen. Blazing eyes and stubbled face with the shirt beneath his suspenders hanging loosely from his trousers.

"What are you looking at fat boy! And what is that stink! Have you shit your pants again or is it this bitch's cooking!"

They both froze.

The alcohol-fuelled rages didn't come often but when they did, they were terrifying.

His father grabbed the pot handle and threw the pot against the wall. The hot contents spilling red across the floor.

"How many times do I have to tell you that I don't eat vomit!"

His mother became a pale statue standing at the bench. Unmoving in fear and keeping her head bowed. Her knuckles turning white around the knife she held in her hand and her other fist clenched. There were no words that could change what came next. And with each beating, it seemed as though his father had dreamed up new ways to hurt them each time.

"Get down on the floor!"

Her eyes darted sideways. Her irises disappearing into the dilated pupils.

Out of the corner of his bloodshot eyes, Roko's father caught him about to stand up from his seat.

"Stay there! Don't you dare move boy. You are going to watch, and you might even learn what to do with that small dick. If you weren't so fat, you might be able to see it." His father laughing.

Dread and panic took hold as she tried not to wet herself. That would just make him angrier. She turned slowly and went to her knees on the hard floor, then lay on her back. The warm sauce seeped through her clothes.

"Turn over! Do you think I want to look at your ugly face?"

As she slowly rolled over, the folds from her dress stuck to the sticky floor and started to tighten around her waist.

"Pull it up!" he ordered.

Roko was desperate to look away from what was unfolding before him and he quickly found a spot on the floor to hold his gaze. As if sensing his son's embarrassment, his father turned to him, grabbed the back of his head and smashed Roko's face into the table.

"I told you to watch!!"

Roko couldn't stop the tears as his father laughed even harder.

Stumbling and almost slipping in the wet his father bent down and tore his mother's garments till she was naked. The stillness of her body suggested that her mind had already gone elsewhere to avoid the pain and humiliation.

He was sweating now and began to reel.

"Spread your legs."

Ripping the suspenders from his shoulders, he started grappling with the drawstring of his pants, becoming frustrated that he couldn't untie the knot.

Then he stopped suddenly and looked across at Roko.

A smile spread across his face as he swung his leg back and kicked the motionless body on the ground. Right between her legs.

"This is where he came from, and I'm going to make that thing pay for giving me a useless son! How old are you boy?" He looked across at Roko as he thought of a new way to inflict pain on his wife.

"Seventeen." Roko gulped. Hardly able to focus as his head wobbled from the swelling and pain of his broken nose.

"Seventeen! So, I have had seventeen useless years from you!" His father roared, "then your mother will know seventeen times, how much I have had to put up with!"

The kicking stopped intermittently as he swaggered about. Then a deep breath, before the heavy work boots found their way past flesh and bone again. His maniacal laughter just added to the cruelty.

Then, he stopped suddenly as if his energy had run out. His head swayed around, and his eyes looked around wildly.

The grunt that followed seemed to signal that he was finished, and he stumbled into their small bedroom and slammed the door shut.

Roko held the side of the chair as he moved to kneel on the floor next to his mother.

She was breathing slowly but didn't move as he pulled her dress over her.

He reeled as he tried to stand.

His head was exploding as the bile rose from his stomach. Swallowing hard, he took a couple of tentative steps before he staggered out of the door.

Luka had been more quiet than usual as his mother started to clear the table after the evening meal was over.

"Have you started your application for university yet, Luka?"

"No mama." Luka glancing at her briefly.

"Well maybe you shouldn't waste your time applying. University may not be the right thing for you anyway."

"But you said that I should apply." He screwed his face in confusion as he looked toward her. "If I get in, I will be able to do something more than just work here. You said that I should go."

"I know what I said but there is a lot to do here, and I am getting older. You could help me work the land. It will be yours one day, anyway."

"Maybe you should do one year in the army. Then you can come back here."

"No! Mama!" He was becoming exasperated at where this conversation seemed to be leading.

"Listen Luka. It may not be possible for you to go to university. There is a good wage in the army, and you can learn many things there as well. You will also be able to come home and visit sometimes."

"Roko's brother joined the army, and he never comes home!" Luka pleading with his mother.

"Maybe it is different for him," her voice softening. "Maybe there isn't anything for him at home"

"I don't want Luka to go anywhere!" Mira cried.

"Go to your room Mira. This is a conversation between us. There is nothing for you to know yet."

"But."

"No. Go to your room now."

Luka's little sister dragged her doll by the hair across the floor. The broken eye with its fixed stare looked eerily on as she sulked back to their room, slamming the door shut behind her.

An uncomfortable silence fell across the room.

Luka clenched his fists and his teeth at the same time, not knowing what to say that would improve his situation.

"I don't want to join the army, Mama." Tears started to flow. It was the best he could do.

"If your papa was here, he would say the same, Luka." She tried to be gentle but firm.

His faced was flushed and cheeks ruddy from crying as he stood and went to the door.

"I'm going for a walk, Mama." All was said that needed to be said.

"Don't be late back. You have school tomorrow." His mother, attempting to bring things back to normal.

"What's the point of school. You don't need a brain to kill people."

As he walked out, she watched the water drain from the concrete basin, and tried to think of what Marko would have done at a time like this.

"How can I help my son who needs a father more than ever now," she muttered to herself.

As he wandered slowly away from home, Luka squinted and saw a large figure seated at the end of the jetty in the distance. Walking barefoot, with his trousers creeping further up from his ankles over the past year, he hardly noticed the stones beneath his feet. As he approached the jetty, he could tell by the shoulders moving that the person was crying only to realise it was Roko.

He hesitated to move closer, wondering if it was better to give him some time alone before stepping loudly on the wooden slats. Roko's head turned slightly in recognition that someone was there. Luka's shoulders slumped in sorrow at the sight of his friend.

"Hi Roko."

"Hey Luka."

Silence.

"You look like shit."

"He'll never stop, Luka." With no air able to pass through his nostrils, he sounded like he had a bad cold.

Luka wavered. "Mama just told me that I should join the army."

"You are lucky she is even interested in you." Roko didn't look at his friend.

Smears of dark stains ran down the front of his shirt with streaks of dried blood to the backs of his hands. His nose sitting oddly off centre from his eyes with pus and congealed blood from his nostrils.

"One day he will kill me Luka. And Mama." Roko started to cry.

Luka put his arm around him and in that moment, Luka knew his friend was right.

The next morning Luka walked straight past the large iron grill of the school gate. What was the point in going if all he was going to do was shoot people?

He scuffed his way along the rocky path, kicking up the stones while catching glimpses of the blue sea beyond.

The walls of the old town stood proudly along the promenade and the local merchants assembled their trestle tables for the market. A fleet of fishing boats chugged into the small harbour before offloading their catch.

He turned the corner to the old stone cottage.

"Teta Ana!"

"Luka. What are you doing here? You should be at school." As he saw the old lady grasp her chest and bend over coughing.

"What's wrong Teta?" He rushed to her side to help her to stand.

"Your aunty is getting old Luka. This cough is only one of many things. Come inside. I will make palacinke for you for breakfast."

Luka loved the warm pancakes his aunty made. She would cover them with crushed walnuts, brown sugar and melted butter, before rolling them into long cigars.

He sat mesmerised as her practiced hands went about preparing the delicious treat. The towering stack was assembled onto a tray and drizzled with honey and more walnuts.

"Mama wants me to join the army."

The tray of cigars almost tumbled to the floor as her body

stiffened, but she caught her balance and set them on the table in front of Luka.

"That was lucky." She replied, pretending she didn't hear what he had said.

He repeated the statement slowly, not sure how he wanted her to react.

"She wants me to join the army, Teta."

"But I thought you wanted to go to university."

"Mama thinks I should stay here and help with the land after I have finished serving in the army."

"But why?"

Luka shrugged.

"Eat the pancakes while they are warm." Her hands moved down to her lap to wipe her hands on the bottom of her apron. She began to wring the material under the table so he couldn't see.

He took a pancake but realised he wasn't hungry anymore.

"I want to go away, Teta."

Her gaze went to the pile on the tray, and she took it in her hands. She stood and then looked around forgetting what she had thought to do next.

She sat back down and could feel his eyes bore into her, hoping that she would say the right thing. The whole village knew what happened when someone tried to leave. Some would be put in gaol and others would be sent to labour camps. Most were never seen or heard from again.

She clasped her black rosary beads with one hand and felt the ache in her heart. Then reaching across the table she took hold of his hands.

"This is a man's decision Luka. You must think very carefully now. Whatever you do might hurt some people. But you might also hurt yourself. Do you want to take that chance?"

"I don't know yet Teta. But I do know that the choice I have been given is not where my heart wants to be."

"Then you must look to your heart, Luka. And don't make your decision in anger."

CHAPTER 3

The last days of warm weather lifted their spirits, and the boys spent every moment they could in and around the sea. Even Roko seemed to be enjoying himself.

They knew that this could be their last summer together, and once school was finished their lives would be torn into different directions. They would make the most of this one.

One day, as they were drying out on the jetty, Sam walked up to them. He seemed to be hiding something beneath his t-shirt.

"What are you hiding?"

"Yeah. Show us."

"Not here. Let's go somewhere private."

They scurried along the jetty and followed him to the pebbled beach below. Once they had gathered between the wooden struts underneath, the new kid slowly revealed his secret.

"Whoa!" Josip's eyes were bulging. "Where did you get that?"

"Shh! Keep it quiet will you. I don't want to get caught." Sam tried to calm their fervour.

"Look at the size of those!"

Bruno was the first to push his hand into his crotch.

"Hey! Does your little man want to stand up, Bruno?"

They all started to laugh.

"Shut up, Luka! At least you can see mine when he does stand up!"

Luka charged at Bruno. Before they could throw any real punches, Josip and Tom grabbed them and dragged them back to the group.

"Stop wasting your time fighting! You don't want to miss what's in here!" Josip's eyes still hypnotised. "Wow! Look at that bush! I saw my sister in the bath once. She didn't have any hair there at all."

"Yeah but these are Italian girls. Their bush is always dark and hairy. Luka replied. "Hey, where did you get this?"

"I saw my stepfather hide them under the mattress. I stole it." Sam gleamed at their excitement.

"Cool." Each of them clearly impressed.

"Italian girls are more beautiful than ours." Bruno commented. "And bigger breasts too!"

They flicked through the pages. Eager to see what else was in the magazine.

"Nada lets the older boys put their kita into her mouth for three kuna."

"Who told you that?" queried Tom.

"I saw her do it behind the big tree at school," Josip said without taking his eyes away from the images.

Tom and Josip grinned at each other. "How much money have you got?"

Silence.

Giggles.

"Why would you want to put yours where every other guy has put his. I want a girl who will only know mine!" Luka chimed in.

"Just like these Italian girls?" said Josip.

They laughed.

Luka thought before he spoke next. "Yes. Mine will be an Italian girl."

They stayed under the jetty till they'd scoured every inch of the magazine.

"Hey, does your papa have any more of these!" Bruno tried to ask without seeming desperate.

"Don't ever say that! He's not my father!" Sam shot back.

"Alright. Sorry, Sam. I didn't mean it." But Sam walked off to leave Bruno scratching his head.

"What's the big deal anyway?"

"Go to the market and get me some fish, Luka. Two cod will be plenty."

When the cooler weather came, Luka's mother would make Bakalar. The dish involved hanging and drying cod after it was covered in salt. Once it had cured, she would boil it in water and mash it through potatoes with plenty of garlic.

"I hate the smell of drying fish!" Mira cried.

"That doesn't seem to stop you from a second helping Mira." Her mother responded.

"I want to go with Luka, Mama!"

"Okay. But only buy fish. And don't steal any grapes either!"

The market was bustling and noisy.

"Fresh tomatoes! Only two kuna a libbra!" Came one cry. The traders used a mix of the Italian libbra, which was equal to one pound, or metric weights.

The villagers would either swap the produce they grew or buy the essential items. It all depended on what little money they had.

"Over here, Luka! I want some crostoli! Please!"

"No Mira. Mama said only fish. I haven't got enough money for that."

They walked by the stall with the deep-fried strips of pastry covered in a thick dusting of icing sugar. The next minute Mira ran past him and hid behind the vegetable stand.

"Hey! Mira! Come back!"

Seconds later, she walked back to him and took his hand.

"What's this?" He felt the grainy residue in his palm and spied the remnants of pastry crumbs around her mouth.

"Mira. Did you take a crostoli?" he whispered as he licked the sugar from his palm.

Mira looked down. Twisting her foot in the ground and glancing away, she grabbed his hand and tried to make him walk on.

"I'm sorry, Luka. I was hungry."

"Don't do it again. I won't be here forever to protect you if you get caught."

"But where will you be, Luka? I don't want you to go anywhere!"

Now it was his turn to look away and move towards something that would distract them both.

"I won't leave you little one." The words catching in the back of his throat.

"I'm tired Luka."

"Okay. We will find a seat and rest. Then we need to get this fish home, or we will both stink!"

Mira screwed up her nose and laughed as they made their way through the stalls and found a seat at the edge of the promenade.

A copy of the village newspaper was left on the bench and Luka had to stamp his hand on the pages as the breeze threatened to blow them away.

A headline caught his eye.

PARTY MEMBER PROTECTS TITO'S HONOUR!

A villager was pardoned by a magistrate this week when he defended the name of President Tito from another man who was protesting the new liberal policy of the government. It is reported that when the villager heard the man protesting loudly about the changes put forward by Tito, he challenged him and began to throw punches. A fight broke out and the men had to be separated by bystanders.

A government spokesman praised the man's efforts in performing his "patriotic duty" to the State.

He went further to say that "any man, woman or child who believes that their duty is to the State, will be rewarded for their efforts and contributions to our nation. If anyone thinks otherwise, they will feel the full force of the law."

The report went onto say how celebrated the "national hero" was upon returning to his village and that he, and his family, would be given privileges afforded only to those who were members of the government.

Luka re-read the last paragraph, knowing full well that you also had to be a friend of, or member of the Communist Party.

He thought about what his mother had said about his chances of being accepted into university and knew then that she was probably right.

He took the newspaper, and Mira's hand, and they walked home.

Luka had finally plucked up the courage to visit Roko's house. "Mama! I'm going out to play football!" Roko yelled as they raced out of the door.

Roko didn't hear his mother call back to him and he had decided that he didn't really care what she said anymore.

They met the others in the square and Tom took the two rocks they used to mark out either side of the goal line and set them up against the high wall.

They took turns, shooting for goal with Tom lunging from side to side trying to save them. Whilst most of the attempted shots made it near the goal, a wayward strike would see the ball sail over the top of the wall and the game had to be abandoned as they scurried around to find it.

Luka sat under the tree and took the newspaper clipping from his pocket.

"Luka! Come and play! We need you in the goals!"

Luka shook his head and kept reading.

"What are you reading?" someone asked.

"Just something."

"Yeah, but what is it?" They all gathered around him.

"It's just an article about someone criticising some government changes. And after reading this, I'm worried that I might not get into university. Mama told me that I would probably have to join the army."

"That's bullshit!" Tom reacted immediately. "I'm going to university. No one can stop me!"

"Are your parents in the Communist Party, Tom?"

"No."

"You've got no chance then."

Tom grabbed the paper from Luka.

"This doesn't say anything!" Tom couldn't see the problem.

"Luka is right. What chance do any of us have? We are small pieces of shit in a small shitty village. No one is going to let us be any more important. Tell me. Who do you know that has gone to university and come back as a professor or a doctor?" Roko challenged each of them to answer, but no one could.

Bruno took the ball from Josip and kicked it as high and hard as he could in frustration. It sailed over the wall.

"I have to leave here." Roko's words seemed to shake them. They all knew about his father.

They had seen the bruises on the outside and felt his shame on the inside.

"I have to leave too." Luka stood next to his friend. "Who knows what will happen if we stay. This is our last year together at school so there won't be any more summers. I don't want to join the army. If I can't do what I want, then I'm leaving."

"You'll be taken away if they find out Luka. You can't risk it!"

"You are the only ones who know what Roko, and I are thinking. If the police find out, then it will only be from one of you."

More silence.

"I won't tell," one said.

"Neither will I. I promise," said another.

"Me neither."

"I want to come with you." Sam took them all by surprise. "This is not my home anyway. Besides, neither of you are smart enough to pull this off."

The jibe at Luka and Roko broke the tension, and they all laughed at the new kid's courage.

"I am not going to force anyone. If you want to come, then

you have to stick with whatever plan we can come up with. No arguments or cold feet. If you are in, then it's all the way."

"What is the plan?" Sam asked.

"I don't know yet. Whatever it is, we'll only get one chance. But I do have an idea."

They arranged to meet in two days at the jetty. It needed to look like they were doing what they always did so it didn't raise suspicion.

"Don't say anything to anyone about this." Luka warned.

Luka, Roko and Sam met at the jetty as planned. Three heads in whispers as Bruno, Josip and Tom ran down the jetty towards them making them all jump.

"Hey. You're not supposed to be here." Luka tried to whisper.

"Why not?" they replied.

"It's better that you don't know what we are doing. Then no one can accuse you of covering anything up."

They looked at each other.

"It won't matter, we're coming with you." Tom said almost in a whisper.

His demeanour had clearly changed after their last encounter and the disappointment in his voice made them all feel sorry for him.

"I think we should go to Italy and look for those Italian girls with the big breasts and hairy bushes!" Josip slapped Bruno on the back, laughing.

"That's the best reason to go, Bruno!"

Luka waited before replying. "That's exactly where I am thinking. And we will go by sea."

CHAPTER 4

The leaves started to turn yellow and brown as the summer days moved away, but the boys barely noticed.

Each day after school they met in the square, and to the casual observer they were just a group of young men playing football.

"Over here!"

"Pass the ball you selfish bastard!"

"Up! Kick it up!"

The wall was pummelled with each stray kick and the ball seemed to groan each time it struck the wall. Tom tried his best to keep goal but gave up as the kicks strayed further away from their target.

When they were tired, they lay around the base of the big mulberry tree in the centre of the square to plan. The tree had its fair share of secrets, from lovers hiding beneath it to the old folk speaking quietly about how their lives had changed.

"So, you think we should go by sea, Luka?"

"Yeah. But I think we will be too obvious if we all go by sea. I think we should split up."

"But how?"

"I think that four of us should go by boat. The other two will go by land. They will be looking for six of us missing. And they will think we are all together. It might just give us some extra time to get away." Luka had thought a diversion would buy them time.

"I want to go by sea, if that means I can get away quicker." Roko staked his claim assertively, followed by Sam, Josip and Bruno. Each thinking they would be less likely to be caught than if they travelled on foot.

"I understand Roko. Tom and I will go by road."

"But we don't have a boat. Or any oars. And we'll need to get food and water as well," Bruno said, thinking ahead.

"I have thought of that. And I think I know where we can get a boat. But we need to be careful," Luka said.

The boys waited in anticipation of his answer.

"We will steal one of the army boats."

"What!" they all exclaimed at once.

"But how can we do that? If we get caught, they will lock us up! Or even worse, we will be sent away!"

"Yeah, and our families as well!"

"I've been watching the boats from the jetty. The fishing boats are always in and out, so it would be obvious if one went missing. And we can't take away someone's job. The skiffs are too small to carry us, and we would never make it across. But the army rowing boats are big enough to carry us and they are only used on some weekends. There are two of them moored alongside each other. Either one will work."

He paused to let this idea sink in.

"But what if we get caught stealing the boat?" Bruno was thinking again.

"We could say we were going fishing. And besides the army only ever uses them in the summertime. Even then, it's not often."

"Yeah. Fuck the army. I'd love to steal one of their boats!" Josip was clearly enjoying the thought.

Already convinced, Roko went straight to the most important question.

"When."

"When the Bura winds come. They will help us get across."

"But they are only weeks away!" Josip cried.

"That's why we must start soon."

Tom was trying to take it all in. "But Luka, if people notice that the boat and six of us are missing, they will put two and two together. This will be too dangerous."

"I had thought about that too Tom. That's why I think we should take the boat and hide it somewhere safe until they give up looking. If the boat is missing but everyone is accounted for, they might just think it's someone from out of town and let it go. That also gives us time to get supplies and plan the route."

"We could hide it at my place?" Sam was eager to help. "We are out about two kilometres away from town, near the water. If a couple of us can row the boat around there, we could find a good spot where no one can see. And I think I know the perfect place."

"Yeah, Sam is right. It needs to be close enough for us to row it there but far enough that no one will stumble across it." Luka agreed. "Let's meet at your place and you can show us the place."

Pleased with their planning, the boys resumed their game and agreed to meet at Sam's over the weekend.

They met at Sam's house on the Saturday. The house could barely be seen from the path, hiding behind the tall oak trees that clutched the rocky ground.

They congregated at the open door and Sam's mother shouted to him that they had arrived.

It wasn't hard to realise that his mother and stepfather weren't too interested in what he was doing, and after quick introductions, they went looking for a hiding place for the boat.

"We can't moor it anywhere along the shore. It's too open," someone said.

"We could put a cover over it?" came a reply.

"Nah. It would look even more like we were hiding a stolen boat."

"We could hide it beyond that point over there." Sam had already considered a potential spot. "The point sticks out and if you go past it, there is a cove. You can't see what's in there from the water unless you go around. There are also some tree branches that hang over the water. It might give enough cover to hide the boat."

They walked beyond, to where Sam had described.

"Mm. I'm not sure it is enough." Luka wasn't sure it would work when Tom spoke.

"We could sink it."

Luka turned to him as the boys started to think about what he had said.

"We could sink the boat with rocks. It looks deep enough. And if we are only hiding it for a short time, it shouldn't get damaged. We just need to make sure we are careful."

Luka started to wade into the water and the others followed.

As they moved alongside the rocky outstretch of land and under the overhanging branches, they could see that Tom was right.

"Great Tom. That is a great idea."

Tom beamed at hearing this. Maybe university was lost for now, but his engineering mind was being put into practice, and he couldn't be happier.

"Now, how do we get it here?" Josip asked.

"We'll need to think about that now we know where we will hide it, but the winds are coming in about five or six weeks, so we need to be ready by then. We should take the boat two weeks before we plan to leave. That way, if the army finds out it's missing, they have time to check that no one has left."

"Yeah. Those lazy bastards will give up looking in five minutes!"

"It's the police we need to worry about. We can't give them any reason to suspect that we are involved in any way. Don't say anything to your families or anyone else."

"Agreed."

"So, what next?"

"We will just act normal for the next two weeks. Keep an eye on the winds. Say nothing to anyone and don't act any differently. We will meet back here in two weekends time."

"Let's go back and play football. Josip, you need to keep practicing or we will lose you to the girl's team."

"Fuck off Bruno! At least I don't run like a girl."

And with that, they sprinted back into town and there was no turning back.

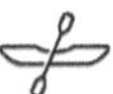

Two weeks seemed like an eternity, and when they finally met at Sam's place again, each could hardly contain their excitement.

"I even looked after the stinking goats."

"Don't look like you are enjoying that too much Roko, your papa will definitely know that something is up."

"Yeah. I can't wait to leave. Wish I could see the look on his face when he finds out. Maybe the police will take it out on him. Prick! So, when do we take the boat?"

"We'll take it at night, when the fishing boats are out and it's a bit quieter in the harbour."

"Yeah. Tom is right. We need to pick a night when there isn't much moonlight as well, so we aren't spotted."

"We've just had a full moon, so it will be better over the next week."

"Good idea."

"Who is going to take the boat? If we all go down there, it will look suspicious."

"You are right Bruno."

"I'll take it." Sam offered.

"I'll go with Sam," Luka replied. "That way one of us can keep an eye out while the other one rows."

They all nodded in agreement.

"But what about oars? If the boat doesn't have any, we will need to take some as well. And if it does, we might need another set anyway. Just in case." Again, Tom had thought of the details.

"There are sets of oars kept in the rowing club and its open during the day. It'll be risky to steal them in daylight, but I don't think we have any other choice."

Tom smiled. "I think I know how we can get away with taking them and not be seen. I've got an idea."

He watched their faces as he started to explain. "We need two oars. Right?"

"Yep."

"Who has a long coat or jacket at home?"

"I do." Replied Josip.

"And me," said Bruno.

"My father had one that I could use as well." Luka could see where Tom was going with this question.

"The weather is getting cooler so it wouldn't look stupid if we were wearing coats in the afternoon when the winds come up. If two of us went into the club and held an oar under each arm, inside the coats, we could easily take them."

The group thought for a moment. "That is brilliant, Tom." Luka then moved to assign the next tasks.

"Tom. You and Roko are the tallest so you should take the oars. Sam, have you got somewhere we can hide them near the boat?"

"I will find a place. There is plenty of forest behind the house."

"Okay, Roko and Tom, it's up to you to you now. But be careful."

Roko and Tom couldn't wait to start planning.

The rowing club sat alongside the harbour and had been in operation since 1908. It housed rowing boats, oars and even a large function room upstairs. All the boats were stacked along the walls on racks and the oars hung in various places according to their length and boat type.

Roko and Tom realised that their task was not as simple as they had originally thought. Luckily, they decided to do a trial run first, for when they entered the club, they had no idea which oars would be suitable.

"Fuck. You said this would be easy, Tom!"

"I did not. Anyway, how hard can it be?"

"I can't tell which ones we should take, can you?" Roko was moving along the seemingly endless rows of oars.

"No. Let's check out some boats outside and see if we can find one that's similar."

"Good idea."

They went out of the shed and walked past the boats that were moored until they found the two army boats. Roko kept watch while Tom grabbed an oar and checked it over.

"Okay, I think I've got the size. With the handle at my shoulder, the blade reaches my knee. Let's go."

Checking to make sure that they didn't look suspicious, they went back inside and located the best fit. They decided to leave them where they were and would come back the following evening when it was cooler. Then they wouldn't look ridiculous wearing long coats.

The next evening, dressed in their long coats, they sauntered down to the rowing club. Trying to act as normal as they could, they whistled at the girls that passed them by as their eyes darted around checking for any soldiers or police. When they were sure they were in the clear, they slipped inside the glass doors.

Roko grabbed an oar and slipped it inside the jacket, holding it under one arm. Tom checked him to make sure that neither the handle or blade were visible before taking the other oar and doing the same.

"Okay?"

"Yeah. Looks okay."

"Let's go. Just keep talking as we walk. That way, no one will give us a second glance."

They confidently walked along the promenade, away from the water.

"Remember those girls in the magazine. Whoa. Amazing!"

"You wouldn't know what to do with them Roko." Then suddenly they stopped. "Shit! Soldiers coming!" Tom just caught the dark olive uniforms in the distance.

Roko took a step sideways.

"Don't turn. It will look suspicious. Just keep walking towards them," Tom urged.

"What if they stop us," he whispered back.

"Don't panic!" Tom hissed.

Just as it looked like they might be stopped, Tom grabbed Roko and embraced him. Roko was still in shock when Tom whispered in his ear, "Kiss me. Now!"

Eyes screwed shut and lips sucked in as far as he could, he pushed his mouth at Tom. Tom's arms embracing Roko as the hard oars ground into their armpits.

"Fucking faggots. Get a room!" The soldiers took a wide berth. Their pace quickened at the sight, as if they might catch something.

Neither boy would let go first, with each an eye open to check if they were safe.

The blade of one oar started to drop beneath the hemline of Tom's coat as he tried to shuffle the handle back in.

Roko pushed Tom away. "Don't get too comfortable or I'll hit you!"

Both looked to the ground, too scared to look at each other out of embarrassment. Then their giggles turned to laughter as they slowly started to walk away.

The next time the boys met, it was near the cove where they would be able to sink the boat out of sight. They gathered rocks that would be used as ballast and set them down near the shore.

"Okay. Sam and I will meet next Friday after school to pick which boat to take. Then, if everything looks safe, we will come back Friday night and take it. Let's all say we are playing football in the square on Friday evening and make sure you tell your parents that's where we are all going. That way, if anyone asks, we have the same story."

"But how will you sink it in the dark?"

"We will have to hide it and come back early in the morning to sink it."

"I can miss school that morning." Josip said.

"Me too," Sam added.

"We can't all miss school. How about Sam, Josip and Bruno meet me here as the sun is starting to rise. Roko and Tom go to school as usual. That way it won't look suspicious."

Roko and Tom had said nothing more about what happened when they took the oars.

"Did you get the oars?" Luka asked.

Roko blushed. "We sure did. They are back there in the woods, covered with leaves. And thanks to our poofter friend Tom, we didn't get caught!"

Roko relayed the story to much laughter from the group.

"You are a hero, Tom. I think we should all line up for a kiss to celebrate."

"Piss off! Thanks to my quick thinking, we made it!"

"Is Roko a good kisser?"

Bruno couldn't outrun Tom, and they wrestled until Tom had him pinned down.

"Help. Someone, help me! I think Tom likes me better than Roko now!"

More laughing until Luka spoke.

"I can't believe you thought of that so quickly Tom! Because if those soldiers had caught you, who knows what could have happened."

"Maybe he was just looking for an excuse to kiss Roko!" Josip wasn't quick enough to get away as Tom and Roko pounced on him as the others laughed.

Friday came slowly, and Luka found Sam waiting for him at the jetty as planned.

"I think this is the one, Sam. Its big enough to carry us and should be safe if the sea gets rough."

Sam looked it over and agreed.

There were two oars in the boat already, but the others would be needed as well. If one broke for some reason, having spares made sense.

"We just need to get it away from the jetty quietly until we are out into the sea."

"Yes, but we can't have too much wind Luka. The sea will be too rough to get it out of the harbour."

"You are right. Let's see if the winds die down tonight. Why don't you come for dinner, and we can kick the ball around till it gets dark."

Sure enough, luck was going their way. The winds died down as darkness fell and they ran out of the door as soon as dinner was finished.

"What's the hurry?" Luka's mother cried out after they left. "Don't be late!"

"We are late for a game," Luka called as they tried slowing their pace down the gravel road.

"We don't want anyone to remember us tonight. Let's look as normal as we can."

Sam slowed down. It was hard trying to contain his enthusiasm for stealing anything, let alone a boat.

They tried to look inconspicuous around the harbour. They sat for a while on the jetty, looking for anyone who might notice them.

The last of the fishing boats chugged out of the harbour and there was silence as darkness fell.

"Okay. Now," Luka whispered.

Sam climbed down into the wooden boat while Luka untied the mooring rope. The waves lapped against the boat as it moved under their weight.

"Get down!" Luka had spied a couple walking along the water's edge. They were clearly distracted by each other, but the boys still waited until they vanished. Whatever they were doing would not interfere with the task at hand.

Once it looked safe, Luka gently pushed the boat away and climbed in.

They took an oar each and deftly manoeuvred the boat, keeping themselves as low as possible.

They kept close to the jetty. Every now and then pushing off the wooden struts with an oar. Then pulling hard on one side, they rounded the end and rowed away.

This was tricky. They were now in the open water and could be seen from the shore. It would have been easy to panic and row hard, but the consequences were well understood if they did. Luka took both oars while Sam lay at the stern of the boat and navigated the way to the cove.

Stroke by stroke.

Luka paused.

"What's the matter?"

"Nothing." Luka looked around before starting again.

The two kilometres or so to Sam's house seemed to take hours, but once they were near the point, both boys relaxed a little.

Luka guided the boat to the cove and once they had decided on the safest place for it to be, they tied it to one of the overhanging branches and swam to the shore.

Standing side by side with arms across each other's shoulders on the shore. A final look.

"See you at sunrise."

"Yeah. See you then."

Luka ran all the way home. Eager to be safely in his bed to avoid interrogation. He had left some clothes in the shed where the garlic was hung to dry and the chickens were roosting. Changing quickly and praying that no one noticed, he went inside.

"How was the game?" His mama asked as her eyes were on repairing socks.

"Great. I'm tired. I'm going to bed."

He quietly shut the door, hearing the gentle sounds from the adjacent bed. Mira was sound asleep. He had avoided the endless questions she would have asked if she had caught him sneaking in.

He smiled as he lay down. The first part of the plan had gone by without a hitch. Now for part two.

Dawn broke and one by one the boys arrived at the cove. Roko and Tom attended school as agreed.

"Try and find some big rocks. But make sure they haven't got sharp edges and aren't too heavy. We need to be able to lift them out again when its time leave," Luka instructed them.

They worked quickly. Before too long they had a selection to choose from and took turns, in pairs, to wade in the water and place the rocks in the boat.

It didn't take long before it was submerged. Once it was out of sight from every angle they could see, they made their way back into town with the football. Sam had agreed to keep an eye on the boat just in case it refloated or even worse, was discovered.

"Now remember. When the army finds out it is missing, there will be trouble. Stick to the story. We were playing football after dinner and then came home. Nothing more than that."

"And if the police get find out?"

"Keep it simple. We were playing football. That's all. They will be more worried that someone is missing. Once they know that everyone is here, they will forget about it."

CHAPTER 5

**ARMY BOAT STOLEN.
POLICE TO INVESTIGATE.**

Luka saw the headline in the local newspaper three days later.

Police will investigate the theft of a boat belonging to the Jugoslovenska Narodna Armija (JNA). A spokesman from the people's army said the boat was reported missing yesterday and the matter had been referred to the police.

The police are treating this very seriously and a severe punishment will be meted out to the persons responsible once they are found. Police believe that this is part of an attempted escape, and they will be visiting every household to ensure all residents are accounted for.

Now they had to wait and hope this would pass quickly.

Sure enough, the police acted swiftly once the boat was reported missing.

They didn't bother knocking when they came to Luka's home.

"Well, we meet again, and the little one is grown up. Even prettier now." The black moustache was as unforgettable as was the man who wore it.

A cleared throat from the older officer with him brought him back.

"You know a boat was stolen from the army?" He caressed a much larger paunch now.

"No." His mother's curt retort as she held Mira tightly to her.

"An army boat. Do you know who might have taken it?"

Luka shuffled his feet.

"No."

Leering. Caressing. Stroking. "How old are you now, pretty one?" He reached to touch Mira's cheek.

"She is ten," her mother replied nervously as she pulled Mira back.

"She's very pretty." He leered. "It won't be long until she is a woman. I might come back and be the first to put a cock inside her."

Luka charged the policeman with his fists raised. "Don't talk about my sister like that, you pig!"

His mother tried to grab him while the policeman laughed. "Your boy has courage and spirit. He would make a good soldier. Maybe after I have fucked his little sister, he can join the army."

They continued to laugh as Luka struggled to free himself.

"You don't want me to take your boy as I did with your traitor husband, do you?"

The huddle tightened. "I see you haven't forgotten me pretty one. Captain Dragan is always at your service ..."

Sweat beads formed on his brow as his tongue lapped along his stained teeth. Again. He took too long to look away.

Then they left as suddenly as they came.

"Bastards. I hope whoever did steal the boat gets away with it and makes fools of them all," his mother said through tears.

They sat and ate in silence while Luka prayed that the other boys could hold their nerve too.

POLICE UNABLE TO LOCATE THIEF. SEARCH ABANDONED.

Two days later, the local paper reported what they had been hoping to read. All the residents had been accounted for and the only outcome that the police could determine was that someone from out of the village had stolen the boat or it had drifted off after being improperly secured.

> Police are satisfied that no one has escaped and have called off the search. They believe it is more likely that someone in the army failed to secure the boat properly and it has drifted off. According to lead policeman Captain Dragan, all houses were visited, and the police could not find any evidence of theft. He hesitated to say that if they do, then the perpetrators, and their families, will suffer the consequences.

Two days later, the next time the boys met, they laughed at how the police made the army out to be idiots.

"Did they give you any trouble?" Luka asked.

"Nah. Papa stood up to them and told them to fuck off. I wish they had knocked him out, but they know what he is like. Besides, we were all home anyway," Roko uttered disappointedly.

"Did they visit you Luka?"

"Yeah."

He said no more than that. He was more determined than ever to get his revenge. They would escape. Then that pig captain would look like a fool.

"We need to decide on a day to leave. The winds are here and if we wait too long, it will be colder. We will leave in the afternoon as the winds come. I have looked at the best route for us to take and think that once we are out of the harbour, we should travel south till we reach the first passageway into the Kornati islands. Then we can turn west and travel by the stars till we find an island to rest."

"What about the army? They patrol the seas."

"We'll travel at night. There is an island on the outer edge of the Kornati. If we can make it there by daybreak, we can rest there during the day and will have a clear run for the next ten hours or so at nightfall. If anyone wants to pull out now, this is your last chance."

They discussed the best days to leave. And after trying to work out the moon cycles, they decided to make their escape in one weeks' time. It would be a Saturday, and they would have some light from the moon if the clouds allowed.

Tom and Luka would see them off and follow them along the shore until they were out of sight. Then they needed to find a ride to take them to Sibenik by road.

They agreed to meet at three o'clock in the afternoon.

"We'll need enough food and water," Roko said.

"Yes. If we can bring food that will keep for three to four days, that should be enough. Has anyone got a big can or tin we can use for water?" Bruno said, already thinking ahead again.

"I have old petrol drums. Some haven't been used in years so we could take one of those," Sam added.

"That will have to do." Roko was satisfied that they had the minimum they would need.

The crew went through the final plan once more and, again, Luka asked if anyone had second thoughts. None responded.

"Let's play football after school each afternoon. If anything changes, we can decide what to do then."

And with that, they parted. Each counting down the days.

Luka sauntered along the path, not really looking at anything but much more conscious of everything. This was a weird feeling, he thought. He was tossing up whether to visit his aunty for what might be the last time.

Passing her home, he saw a solitary candle flickering on the table. He could hear her singing from the window. Moro was nowhere in sight as the mule was probably serenaded to sleep in the back shed.

"O, Marijana,slatka mala Marijana

Tebe cu cekat' ja dok svane dan"

He went in and sang with her.

"Ponoc,ponoc vec je davno prosla

Marijana nije dosla

Na prvi randevu"

She hugged him warmly.

"I love that song, Teta."

"Your uncle would sing it to me all the time."

"You are here very late, Luka. Why?"

"I wanted to see my favourite Aunty to say goodnight." Luka's face started to redden.

"Really, dragi? I think you have more to tell me maybe."

Luka looked away; afraid he might cry.

"I can tell you many things, Teta, but it wouldn't change anything. It's better to sing with you than talk tonight."

She nodded, as if she understood what she was hearing and began to sing again.

When they finished, he turned to leave and then hugged her hard.

"Wait Luka," she said as she moved into the small room beyond the kitchen. The sounds of drawers opening, rustling noises and cupboard doors closing.

"I want you to have this." The round face and stretchy tarnished metal band staring back at him.

"Are you sure, Teta?"

"Take it. He would want you to have it."

Luka slipped the old watch onto his wrist and hugged her once more before he left.

He couldn't look back.

When he arrived home, his mother was clearing the table.

"You are late home. There is a plate of sarma left for you." Luka loved the cabbage rolls his mother made and immediately realised how much he would miss them.

"Thank you, Mama."

Luka ate quietly.

"I'm going to bed," he said as he cleared his plate and placed it in on the bench.

After spending time with his Teta, Luka didn't think he had the energy for any more emotions. Better to get a good night sleep.

"Goodnight my son."

Luka crept into the room he shared with Mira. She was already asleep.

He must have gone through the plan a hundred times or more over the past days. It wasn't perfect. But it would have to do.

He woke early. The day felt like every other, but he wasn't sure how it should feel under the circumstances.

"Arrrgh! Mira!"

The air was forced out of him as Mira bounced on to the bed and his unsuspecting stomach. Winded, he could hardly speak.

"Let's go to the market, Luka! Mama says we can buy crostoli! Please!"

"Okay." He gasped hard for breath. "But we will buy them this time. I don't want to get you out of gaol for stealing again!"

"Ssh Luka! Mama might hear you," Mira pleaded.

"And stop jumping on me. You are getting too big now!"

She giggled. "I can't help it. Your face looks funny every time!"

He had plenty of time before he would meet his friends. Spending time with Mira, while keeping things normal, would also help him relax.

She was starting to look like a young woman but still acted like a little girl.

He tried to push the words spoken by the filthy policeman pig out of his mind. He wasn't going to be here to protect her.

"Hey Mira."

"Yes."

"Has any boy ever said things to you?"

"Like what, Luka?"

"Oh, I don't know. Things about how you look or things that made you uncomfortable?"

"You mean like that pig named Captain Dragan?"

"Exactly."

She stayed quiet for a moment.

"He scared me, Luka."

"I know." Luka could feel the anger.

"Promise me that if anyone even looks at you in a way that makes you scared, you scream. Okay? Scream at the top of your lungs. And run as fast as you can."

"But. I have you, Luka."

Silence.

"I might not always be near you." As the familiar waft passed over them.

"CROSTOLI! Can I have one now please?"

Thank God for crostoli, he thought.

The other boys tried to spend their Saturday acting as normally as they could. They had agreed to use a hike in the woods as a cover to hide some fruit, walnuts and biscuits that they'd hoped would sustain them. Any additional food was taken to make the story more credible or act as a last taste of home.

This day would always prove to be the most be difficult, and except for Roko and Sam, all the boys had last minute doubts.

However, after lunch, when the church bell tolled for one o'clock, they all started to make their way to the meeting point, where the boat had been submerged.

But Luka had one last thing to do and then hopefully, his plan was complete.

"Hey Mira." Luka had stolen into their room as his sister was playing with the wooden doll given to her by Teta Ana.

"Do you want to play, Luka?"

"Sure. But just for a little while. The boys and me are going hiking in the woods today."

"Can I come?"

"No. But you can do something very important for me. More important than anything."

Luka could see that he had her attention. He hated that he needed to deceive her, but it seemed to be the only way he could create a diversion that they may need. Even if it meant a few hours more before they were discovered missing.

"Is it a secret, Luka?"

"Yes. A big one. And you can't tell anyone until I say. You will be the only one who knows."

"Wow …" she whispered. "I promise forever, Luka. I will never tell."

"Ok. Remember that boat that went missing?"

"Yes. Did you take it?" she said louder than she planned.

"Ssh! Two of my friends took the boat, Mira. It's because they want to leave Zadar and I'm going to help them to escape."

"When Luka? But why are they going?"

Luka gave her the minimum amount of information, but just enough for him to know that she was convinced.

"They are leaving this afternoon and I'm going to help them by keeping watch. Anyone that asks, I will say I am waiting for my friends who went fishing. I will be back home when it looks like they are safe. Then I will come home." A lump starting to form in his throat as he spoke.

"Who is going Luka?"

"That doesn't matter Mira. It's better that you don't know the names. Now repeat everything I have told you."

Mira did so. Still enchanted with the big responsibility she had been given.

Luka had hoped that when he didn't return, any search to find the missing boys would be for six in a boat.

"Mama! Where is my football jersey?" It was Luka's favourite. The jersey was red with white stripes on the arms and bore the name of his favourite player, Jozsef Bozsik.

"It is still drying Luka!"

"It's okay, Mama. It will be dry enough."

He ran to hug his mother. She hugged him long and hard and then took his hand.

"What is this for ..." the hesitation in his voice as he saw the roll of paper bills.

"I know that the time will come Luka. Maybe it is already here. There is nothing for you in Zadar and I know you don't want to join the army." Tears streamed as she sucked in a deep breath.

"Take this money. I want you to have it. It is the only way that I can help you. I have been saving it from when they took your papa."

"But ... but, how did you know, Mama?" He swallowed hard.

"Ana and I have been talking. She told me that you want to leave. You are a man now and I can't stop you. But I can give you all I have to try and keep you safe."

The church bell had stopped. It was time for him to leave.

Luka hugged her hard again, then left.

He was trying not to look back, but it wasn't possible. He took a deep breath and started to walk to the cove.

They met as planned with each bringing enough provisions that they hoped would last for a few days. They filled the large can with water and began to raise the submerged craft, one rock at a time.

The boat rushed from its hiding place once the weight was gone, and the boys spent the next little while bailing it out. At the same time, they were checking for any damage.

Once they were satisfied it was safe to use, they gathered on the beach.

Luka went over the route again.

"Head about thirty kilometres south and keep as close to the coast as possible. The Maestral wind will blow from the west. It will be easier to get some distance if you go south first. Stay close to the coast, then anyone who sees you will think you are just normal sea traffic. Once you pass the long island of Pasman, cross in between the smaller islands in the direction of the open sea."

We can find one of the islands to rest but we need to use as much of the night as possible." Luka watched Roko grow in stature as he took the lead.

"Once it's daybreak, we can't risk being seen, so we will stay hiding on the island. Then we will head into open water once it becomes dark again," said Roko.

Luka nodded at Roko's instruction. "Good thinking, Roko. Once you are out of sight, Tom and I will head to Sibenik by land. Then we will try to catch a boat across to Italy as soon as we can."

Glances shared around the group. No movement from any of them.

"What if we don't make it." Bruno hesitated to say. He didn't want to be the one who spoke out loud what they were all thinking, but at least it was said.

"Then at least we tried." Luka knew his plan wasn't perfect and he hoped that by now, if anyone had any other ideas, they would have spoken up or decided not to come.

No one wanted to think about the consequences of failure.

He didn't tell them about Mira. He felt a bit selfish after he had sworn them all to secrecy, but she was also part of the plan. As much as he hated using her, she would add confusion and that might give them more time.

Silently they started to load up the boat. Once everything seemed ready, Luka and Tom hugged each of them and promised they would see them again.

Suddenly Sam started to walk off. "I forgot my other top. It will get cold. I need to go back to the house." Roko was annoyed with him again.

"Here, take mine." Luka reluctantly handed his favourite jersey to Sam. Maybe it wasn't that important anymore, he thought.

"Great! Thanks." Sam said, eagerly putting it on.

"We will keep watch and follow you as far as we can."

They pushed off, each jumping into the boat as it began to float away. The four heads in the boat turning between the shore and sea until they rounded the point.

No turning back now.

CHAPTER 6

"Where is that lazy fat boy!" Roko's father roared as he stomped through the house. "He didn't help me at all today and now he is late. I will kill him when he gets home!"

His mother tried to stay as invisible as she could for fear of taking the beating meant for her son. She was still recovering from the last one and only barely able to walk properly again.

"Have you seen Tom? He was going hiking with his friends and isn't back yet." Tom's mother yelled down from the concrete balcony to her husband below.

"They are probably having fun. Leave them be. They will come home when they are hungry."

Josip and Bruno's families all started to ask the same questions around dinner time.

"It's not like Josip to be late for food."

"Bruno knew I was making his favourite gnocchi. He would never miss it!"

Sam's mother and stepfather maintained their lack of interest in the boy. The move they had made to Zadar was for a new life for them. Sam had tagged along rather than being invited. If he decided that he didn't want to stay, that suited them even better. No alarms were raised.

"Where is Luka. He should be home by now." The thought beginning to dawn on her as she steadied herself with the bench.

Mira turned away. Smiling to herself at the enormous responsibility she had been given to keep her secret.

Begrudgingly, she set the table.

At almost midnight, Tom's father had visited the last of the parents. All except Sam's had expressed varying degrees of concern.

"They said they were hiking. Perhaps they are lost in the woods?" said one.

"What if someone is injured or even worse?" said another.

"We must look for them!"

Tom's father tried to reassure each of them even though his stomach churned. As he walked home, a thought suddenly struck him.

No, it wasn't possible, he thought.

The stolen boat.

Mira sat upright in fright and as she looked across, she could see that Luka's bed was empty and untouched.

"Mamaaaa!" The hurried steps. Arms around her.

"Mama." Sputtering sobs.

"Mira. Ssh. It's okay. It's just a nightmare."

"No it isn't. Luka's bed is empty! Luka said he would come back. He said he was only going to help them with the boat. Mama! They stole that boat!"

Wrestling with her mother's arms before leaping across to her brother's bed.

Sobs into his pillow.

"Tell me what he said, Mira." Gentle, soothing strokes.

The story fell out between sobs and sniffing. Mara's hands were stroking her hair, but her eyes were fixed on the window.

"Did you know, Mama?"

"No. But I did know this might happen one day." Her head still turned away. "We must trust Luka. He is with his friends. We must pray they will be safe."

"But the sea is so big!" The mix of tears and snot hung on her top lip.

"Yes, it is." The ache in her stomach, turning to bile.

"Will you tell the other parents?"

"Maybe. We will see. Now try to sleep ljepotice."

Mira tossed and turned as her mother's arm eventually fell free from her and dangled between the two single beds.

She was caught between thinking about how much she loved her big brother, to feeling betrayed by him. And this made her even more sad.

"Mira. You must go to school today," her mother said gently the following morning.

Neither had slept much.

"I can't, Mama. I'm too sad. I want Luka to come home like he promised."

"I will walk with you. I need to visit Teta Ana. Then I must talk to the parents. Come. Get dressed."

A huddle appeared in front of the church as they walked towards the school.

"Keep going, Mira or you will be late. I need to stop here."

"Okay, Mama." Mira turned to see her mother speaking to the group; their heads turning to look at Mira as she was talking.

"I knew they stole that boat, fucking little bastards! I am going to find them and then I will kill every one of them myself. And then I am going to kill their families."

The tirade could be heard from the streets below the top floor of the police station.

The police station sat just off the main square and looked like every other sandstone building with a red terracotta roof. But with only one difference. Captain Dragan.

"How the fuck did this happen!" he roared.

His two sergeants stood before him in the small office.

Next to them stood Roko's father. His wife had rushed home to tell him what she had heard outside of the church.

"They have all gone. Luka, Roko and four other boys," she had told him.

"What are you talking about?"

"They stole the army boat. Now they have escaped."

He had been humiliated when the police had visited his home to question them about the theft of the boat. Roko had sworn he knew nothing. His father even laughed at the suggestion that his son may have been involved.

"He is far too stupid," he had assured the captain at the time. "Look at him. He is fat and useless."

He had not thought twice about reporting what his wife had found out to Dragan. He hated the man, but it was better to be on the good side of him than to endure his wrath. And this situation would bring out the worst of it.

As the men stood waiting for their orders, the older one shuffled nervously. He was almost about to retire, and he didn't need this shit. Most of all he didn't need any more of the captain.

His reputation for having a raging temper was one thing, but the alarms that sounded for the experienced policeman when the captain went out of his way to speak with young girls, was deafening. He couldn't prove anything, but he had learned to trust his gut.

"What are you waiting for? Go and find them." The two bodies scrambling to get out of the office.

"What will you do?" Roko's father enquired as he waited behind.

Dragan's smoke-stained teeth appeared from his smile. "I will make sure they never forget this."

The school bell rang, signalling the lunch break. Children spilled out of the doorways, jostling with each other to find the best spot to eat their lunch in the yard.

Mira was the last to leave. Instead of going home for lunch, she decided to walk down to the jetty. Maybe she would see Luka, and everything would be back to normal.

The hand caressed his paunch as he leant against the school

fence. They should feel safe knowing that their captain is here, he thought to himself. Eyes watching her every move.

It was after three o'clock when Mara went to the school to wait for Mira.

She waited at the gate just as the final bell rang for the end of the school day.

The children spilled out again. Some went to waiting parents and others walked out together.

As the last of them seemed to emerge, she felt her stomach lurch.

"Where is Mira? She hasn't come out," she asked one of the teachers.

"Oh. We didn't see Mira come back after lunch. We thought she must have stayed home for the afternoon. All of this business must be very upsetting for you both."

Mara felt the cold sensation of blood leaving her face.

"No. She didn't come home." Now she was very worried. "Do you know if she said anything to anyone?"

"I didn't hear anything. I'm sorry. Maybe she went home with one of her friends?"

"Yes. That's probably what happened. I am sorry. With all that's happened." She hesitated before reassuring herself she was overreacting from stress. Mira would be fine.

By five o'clock she had visited all of Mira's friends. No one had seen her after lunch. She wasn't with any of them and hadn't said a thing about where she was going.

By the time she went to her sister-in-law's home, she was frantic.

"Ana, Ana! Mira is gone!"

"What are you talking about? She can't be gone. She must be somewhere." Her hands brushed her apron as she ambled inside.

"None of her friends have seen her since this morning," Mara cried.

"She will be somewhere," she said with a hint of doubt. "She has taken Luka's leaving hard, as have we all. Maybe we give her an hour, then we will look. She will be home. You'll see."

Mara slumped onto the chair, cradling her head in her hands on the table as the tears fell.

The rough hand came around her mouth and, in an instant, her pupils dilated as she tried to let out a scream. His arm wrapped around her waist and her legs kicked as she was dragged along the uneven ground. Everything was blurred in front of her eyes as she fought with her attacker's hand.

As he had stalked his prey, the beads of sweat started to appear in anticipation of the capture. But now that he had her in his grip, the arousal was almost too much to contain.

He needed the time to turn his fantasy into reality and to be able to savour each moment, but he was at risk of losing the moment in the fight to control her.

She felt his hand move from her waist up to the front of her shirt. He grabbed it roughly and spun her around so quickly that she nearly fell. The thin necklace with the tiny gold cross that had been given to her for her holy communion was ripped from her neck.

At the same time, he released his hand from her mouth, and she drew breath to scream. She didn't have time before he struck her with a closed fist to her head.

Her head lolled around. A taste of vomit. Then everything stopped and her limp body slumped away from the hand that still grasped her shirt.

He threw her to the ground. Unconscious.

His eyes darted in all directions. He desperately wanted to take his time with her but knew they could be found at any moment.

He rolled her over, absorbing and cataloguing every inch of her before slowly kneeling over her to fulfil his desire.

Only minutes passed before he spun away, gasping for breath. He had hoped she would wake up during his assault to heighten the pleasure for him, but she remained still.

His hands fumbled with the drawstring of his trousers as he tucked his shirt in. She still didn't move. His eyes darting around in every direction.

Standing over her, the alarms started to ring in his head at the sight of the motionless body.

He grabbed her furthest arm and slowly drew her upper body around. The shade of blue around her lips was in complete contrast to the pale white of her skin. His fore and middle fingers found her carotid artery, but nothing throbbed beneath.

"Shit. Wake up you little bitch! This wasn't meant to happen."

He snatched her up by the arms and shook her, but her head and arms hung lifelessly. He threw her back to the ground, pacing and scratching his head as he surveyed the immediate area.

"No. This can't happen again. I should run." Sweating, mumbling and cursing. Walking around the contorted heap below.

The water was at least twenty metres away and too far to risk getting caught carrying a body, but the forest around them didn't offer a better option.

He spied the old boathouse, trying to stand upright on its rickety stilts and sitting derelict over the water.

"That will have to do," he mumbled. He lifted her from the dirt.

His head spun and his eyes darted frantically around.

Disappointment crept over his face as he lumbered his way to the water. His steps quickened as he became exposed, feet catching the invisible ground beneath the body. He almost tripped twice before crashing into the water alongside of the old building.

He waded out, grateful for the weightlessness that the water gave to help his tiring arms. His head turned from side to side until he let his arms go and she slowly sank before him.

Water rushed up to his waist as he turned and pushed himself towards the shore. His head swinging to help his body move onto dry land.

He bent over. Puffing hard. Still looking around him. Once he had enough breath to take a few steps he looked back across the water. She was gone.

"Let them all suffer. I hope she meets her fucking brother out there. I told them they would pay," he muttered.

He quickened his pace as he looked for a different route to take back to the station. Eyes darting feverishly as he was shaking out his trousers as he walked. Conscious of the squelching sound that was coming from his shoes. Memories came flooding back.

"Dragan! What have you done!"

"Nothing, Father. I mean. I couldn't help it. That girl kept laughing at me and calling me names. I just wanted her to stop." Crying. Sobbing. Hysterical. "I wanted her to stop!"

His muscles started to relax at the sight of the church, and he consciously slowed his gait.

I will be safe here, he thought. Just like the last time.

His shoes clicked their way on the cold tiles to the wooden-terraced compartments. Then he squeezed sideways through the narrow door, and waited.

The latticed window slid open.

"Bless me Father, for I have sinned. My last confession was …"

"How are you, Dragan?" the old priests voice interrupted and spoke softly.

Silence. Waiting.

"I am trying to be a good person, Father."

"That is good, my son. Is it getting easier for you?"

It will never be easier, he thought before answering. I will never forget what they did to me.

"It is easier now than it was, Father."

"Say penance with me, Dragan."

The mumblings of the old priest gave him comfort. They went through the process of confession and Dragan sat for some time after they had finished. Once he heard the door click shut in the room adjacent, he let the images come to life again.

"Hare lip! Hare lip! Looks like a bum Lip!"

The memories of the schoolyard taunts coming back to him as he touched beneath the thick moustache.

He had thought she was the most beautiful girl he had ever seen when she first arrived at his school. Her hair, her eyes, the way she walked. And the way she smiled at him in the first days. She had been the first girl to look at him differently.

Not like the others who turned away in disgust or laughed.

He could deal with them. But she was different.

Until she wasn't.

And she did pay for what she did. Just like everyone else would pay if they ever humiliated Dragan.

He stood to leave, believing he had atoned for his sins, and left his sanctuary to go home.

The grey stone building with its small dirty windows was where Dragan called home.

He scuffed the concrete steps in the cold stairwell till he reached the second floor. He fumbled for the keys and ran a hand along the wooden door in the dark to find the lock.

Click. Darkness.

The small room with a single bed in the corner and white basin fixed to the wall revealed its spartan dullness as the light went on.

It wasn't much different to being in the boy's home, he thought. He had served his time, but the punishment never stopped.

He shuffled to the basin, letting the cold water run as he stared into the square mirror.

"Hare lip! hare lip! Looks like a bum lip!"

Peeling the corner of the dark bristled prosthetic back, his eyes downcast, Dragan revealed the birth defect that had caused more pain than the flaw itself. Humiliation and hate.

"This is the best we can do for your son. I'm sorry. He will have to live with this." The surgeon had told his mother after he had made a rough attempt at closing the flap across the cleft lip, only to highlight the deformity even more.

He splashed his face. Dried it off. Then applied the cream to soothe the reddened area across his top lip.

The nightly reminder.

Turned and sat on the bed. Took off his shoes and lay down.

Lights out.

CHAPTER 7

The Kornati islands lay off the Adriatic Coast between Zadar and Sibenik, to the south. There are eighty-nine islands that range from larger areas of land to rocky islets. The islands cover about a quarter of the area and there were many small coves and bays that were used for fishing and recreation.

The four travellers found themselves on one of the larger ones just after the light started to fade. They hauled the large boat over the pebbled beach and decided they would rest for the night and next day.

Whilst the trip had been uneventful, they were exhausted from the combination of physical exertion and fear of being caught.

"Let's drag the boat out of sight. There must be a place that we can hide it somewhere here."

"Who made you the boss?" Sam snapped at Roko.

"Fuck off Sam. I'm not arguing. Let's just hide the boat."

Sam had needled him at every opportunity, which only annoyed the others when they had to keep the peace. Roko thought he was nothing but a pain in the arse.

"Shut up, you two. We need to work together, not argue. Especially now." Josip tried to calm things down.

They secured the boat and found a sheltered cave to sleep. It would be a long night and an even longer day ahead. The Bura winds hadn't reached their full strength yet. But they would need the strong northerlies to help them cross the almost two hundred kilometres to their destination, the port town of Ancona on the Italian coast.

"There's a boat coming!" Josip raced back to the group who were lazing in the cave. They all heard the engine as it sputtered along.

"Shit! It's coming from the other side. They will see the boat!"

Before they could do anything, the engine slowed.

"Hey!" A voice called out. "Is there anyone there?"

The boys peered around the corner hoping the boat would leave. Instead, it slowly pulled up beside.

"Hello!"

Without warning, Roko emerged from their hiding "Hello." he replied.

"Are you in trouble?" asked the boatman, barely making out the boy against the evening sky.

"No. I am here with some friends. We have been out in the boat and going around the islands. We are going back home tomorrow."

The others revealed themselves and waved to the man.

"Where are you from?" he asked.

Before anyone could stop him, Bruno replied. "Zadar."

"Shut up, you idiot!" Sam hissed. "If he hears that there are boys missing, he might report us!"

The man eyed each of them. "You are too far from Zadar. If the Bura blows, you might get into trouble. Believe me. Dinko knows these things ..."

"Shit," Sam whispered.

"Shut up, Sam. Let me handle this." Roko stepped toward the shore, closer so that Dinko could hear.

"We are going to Italy." A collective groan.

"Italy is far. It will be dangerous to cross."

"Yes. But we have enough supplies. We don't want to make any trouble for you. Please forget that you have seen us."

Caught between fear for their safety if he agrees and greater fear for their safety if he reports them, Dinko relented.

"Okay, I will forget. But hurry off this island as soon as you can. There are patrol boats up and down these waters. I wish you safe travels."

And with that, he turned back to the wheelhouse and gunned the engine.

Relieved as they watched the boat turn away.

Dinko only glanced around once as he navigated through the smaller rocky outcrops.

The road south from Zadar offered the chance to hitchhike with little trouble. They had often caught a lift on the back of a donkey-drawn cart or a truck carting fresh produce.

Luka and Tom had walked to the road after watching their friends from the jetty, making out that they were just relaxing in the late afternoon. Making small talk but always with an eye out to sea.

It didn't appear that the boys had attracted any attention, and the harbour remained relatively quiet. Several smaller boats bobbed in the water as the dinghies and their crew fished quietly.

The ride they eventually got found them sharing the back of

a truck with two goats, a cage of chickens and enough manure to have come from ten times as many livestock.

"I go to Sibenik," the driver informed. "I will not take you any further."

"That is good. Thank you, sir," Luka replied.

The driver grunted as the truck growled and moved away.

They fell asleep for most of the bumpy forty-kilometre trip.

When they woke, the truck was pulling up beside the old fortress known as St Michaels. Luka had known this ancient landmark from previous visits to the town. Once with his family and again with Roko the year before.

"You get out here. I go." The driver pulled away.

From the fortress, they walked down to the harbour to look for somewhere to sleep. It was just getting dark, and they were glad they had decided to take a ride on the truck. At least there was some light left.

There were many types of boats moored along the old stone promenade.

"Let's check these boats out, Luka. Maybe we can find one to sleep in for the night."

"Wait. Look! Here comes a fishing boat."

The chug of the engine slowed as the boat drew nearer to its mooring. Once the fisherman looked as though he had finished for the evening, they moved forward.

Luka kept an eye out if he returned as Tom checked the boat.

"Hey. This one looks okay. He's left the door open!" Tom straddled between the mooring and the gunwale then leapt onto the deck.

The wheelhouse was small with old hessian sacking in one corner. Luka checked the surrounds once more.

"Spread the sacking, we can use it for warmth. I have apples and some cheese." After eating a small amount, they curled up on the floor.

"I wonder where they are now," Tom asked quietly.

"There's nothing else we can do Tom. Let's just pray they are safe. Let's try to sleep."

Luka and Tom didn't have time to move when the large frame barrelled through the cabin door.

"What the fuck? Who are you? And what are you doing on my boat?"

Luka tried to stand but the man pushed him down again.

"Start talking or you'll feel my boot."

"Please, sir. We were only trying to find somewhere to sleep for the night. We have nowhere else to go!"

The man thought for a moment. The young men didn't appear to be the type who would steal, and nothing was broken on the boat.

"How long are you staying here?"

"We don't know, sir. We have only just arrived and are hoping to find some work in the morning." Luka was trying not to give too much away.

Despite his imposing stature, straggled beard and a very bad smell of rotten fish, the man took some pity on them. He allowed them to stand before any more questions.

"Names. And where are you from?"

"Luka."

"Tom. My name is Tom, sir. We have come from the north."

"Where north?" He eyed them suspiciously.

A quick glance sideways between them. Sighs. Shoulders slumped.

"We have come from Zadar."

The fisherman's attention was caught. Four boys on an island from Zadar and now two boys on his boat, he thought. Deciding to keep quiet about his discovery on the island, he considered his options. Again.

"Hrmph! You can call me Dinko. This is my boat. If you want to work, you can work for me, but I won't pay you. You can sleep on the boat, and I will bring you food. I can give you nothing more."

They didn't hesitate. "Thank you, sir," they both answered at once.

How hard can it be to haul fish, they thought.

"I need some help, and you can help offload the fish so we can take it to market. Once you have helped me sell it, you can come back and stay on the boat. And boys ..."

"Yes?"

Pointing a finger, he said, "I am trusting you, but if you try to make trouble, I will hurt you. Understand?"

Furious nodding.

The nuns hurried the group of school children past the open window of the police station in Zadar as the tirade of expletives was again leaping out from up above them.

"Time to find a new route, sister."

"It certainly is. Come, children. Hurry."

More yelling.

"Where is that fucking boat, you morons?" The boss's expectations clearly not met.

"Our investigations ..." the younger officer, Zlatko volunteered, drawing a slight chuckle from his older and more experienced colleague, Matej, who knew exactly where this was headed.

"What investigations? Did I ask you to investigate?" Dragan's red face seemed to explode from beneath his collar.

"B ... but ..."

"I told you to find it. Not stand around playing with your dicks! Who do you think you are? Sherlock fucking Holmes? There's a stolen boat. Six thieves. And a big fucking sea. What else do you need to know?"

"Yes Captain."

Sympathy overtook the enjoyment for the more experienced officer.

"What my young charge was going to say, Captain, was that we have expanded our investigations to look at making another report in the newspaper. Maybe that would jog someone's memory if they happened to see the boys. We will need your permission to do so."

A hint of a smile at a job well done.

"Well, why didn't you say so? Do what you must. Just bring me those boys!"

The older man's arm draped across the younger officer as they left.

"A word of advice my young friend," Matej said, seemingly enjoying his teaching opportunity.

Their eyes met. Eagerness in the younger man. "Yes. Thank you Matej. Anything to help me. Please."

"If you want to avoid a repeat of what just happened, always let me do the talking."

Moments later, a knock at the captain's door.

"What have you forgotten now?" The increased activity not going down well.

"There are two women here to report a missing girl, sir." Zlatko panted at the door. The older officer choosing to stay at the bottom of the stairs rather than risk another outburst. Or a heart attack.

"They are very upset."

The stained teeth broke through the wiry black brush. His voice lowered and softened.

"Send them up immediately. We can't have them upset, now can we …"

A puzzled look came over the young officer at the change in his boss's temperament. Maybe he did have a soft side, he thought.

The women held hands underneath the wooden desk as the captain rummaged through his drawers looking for a notepad and pencil. Anxiety heightened at the time it seemed to be taking to locate, what they thought, were basic tools of his trade.

He slowly opened each of the three drawers on the left side of the desk, looking up at them and shaking his head at the failed attempts.

"It is here somewhere." The curled corner of his mouth unsettled them even more.

"Please, Captain. We just want to find Mira. She is only ten years …" Mara was sobbing harder. The older woman held a stony expression as she clearly saw through his sick enjoyment at the suffering he was causing them.

"A-ha. Found it. It was in the top drawer all the time. I mustn't have looked properly the first time." He leered now across the table.

"Now tell me what happened, Mara."

Gasping to breathe while hearing her own words tumble out, Luka's mother told what she knew.

"I see." Dragan leant back in the chair with the notepad held up to his face. He was impressed at the stick figure drawing in front of him.

"Now help me remember what your daughter looked like. And please don't skip any small detail. We will need a good description of her."

A low, almost silent growl from his throat as the women finished.

"Why aren't you looking for her! She is only a child!" Ana stood, placing her flat hands on his desk.

I will start looking when I am ready, he thought. "If your boy hadn't decided to run away, I would have more men to help with the little girl …"

His cold response caught them both. Mara's swollen eyes caught his as she looked up for the first time.

"My boy is old enough to look after himself. His father taught him very well." Her eyes bore into him.

"Well. I hope his father taught him how to swim. The boat that he stole won't last a day in the open rough seas."

He ducked just as the cup flew towards him. "You filthy pig!" Ana grabbed her sister-in-law and started out of the door.

"Come, Mara. We will not have any help from this animal."

She turned to give him once last message.

"You will go to hell, Captain Dragan. Unless you are already there."

He shifted in his seat. His hand went to his upper lip.

You don't know what hell is like, he thought and went to the open window.

His head cocked to one side. "Matej. Zlatko. Get back up here. Now!"

Their half-smoked cigarettes were flicked to the ground and stamped out as Matej and Zlatko made their way back to the captain's office.

"Whatever you do, Zlatko. Say nothing. The mood he is in will only get worse if you say something dumb."

The afternoons at the harbour in Sibenik were busy with fishing boats returning with their catch. The time of year and the risk of strong winds meant they didn't travel too far from home.

Luka and Tom were waiting as their new boss came into view. The boat pulled in and Dinko threw the line to secure on the T-shaped metal cleat.

"Here! Take these containers!" Dinko called as he leapt onto the deck. "When you have unloaded them, I will drive the truck down. Then we can stack them on the back."

"Why can't we just stack them directly onto the truck? If you reverse it down as far as you can, we can do it in one go."

Dinko hadn't thought of this. Probably because he rarely had help.

"Good idea, Luka. You are already useful!"

Luka smiled to himself.

"What was that for?" Tom caught Luka smiling.

"I'll tell you later."

Once the containers were loaded, Dinko and his new assistants headed the short distance to the evening market.

The town square would gradually fill with people hoping to

find fresh fish for the evening meal. Dinko's catch would be gone in no time.

Arching their backs with grimaces on their faces made Dinko chuckle. "Not so easy, is it? And you are young men! Come home with me for dinner. You have earned your meal today."

They didn't need to be asked twice and went to climb into the bench seat of the old truck.

"No. Get in the back. We will pick Rosa up from the church on the way. She will make a good dinner tonight and we will talk. My wife is a very good cook."

Watching the town go past as the truck lumbered through the narrow streets to the church, Luka and Tom sat in silence against the wooden slats.

The truck seemed to take a deep breath as Dinko got out to greet his wife and carry the supplies to the back.

"Who is this, my husband?"

"These are my new helpers. Tom. Luka. From Zadar. I think they are escaping but we will know later …" Shock on the boys' faces drew an exaggerated wink from Dinko.

"How does he know?" Tom whispered from the back.

"I don't know. Maybe he is psychic?"

"We can't say too much, Luka."

"Tom. He would have reported us by now, if he were worried. Let's see what happens tonight. We can leave tomorrow if anything changes."

They drove out of town, past the grey concrete dwellings that were scattered through the fields. The red terracotta roofs stuck out to add colour to the landscape with rows of olive trees and draping grape vines, as well.

The truck stopped at the end of a gravel road and as they got out, the smell of freshly baked bread, that had been prepared earlier, almost made them faint. They were starving.

"Come around the back. We will wash before we eat."

There was a well in the backyard and Dinko pumped the handle as they tried to wash the smell of fish away. Something told them that there wasn't enough water to remove that stink. Dinko's constant odour reminded them of that.

The warmth of the small room that housed the kitchen and living area, along with the smell of bread was almost too much.

"So, boys, do you like fagioli soup? The beans are from the garden." Dinko watched his wife fuss around them as she served up the thick garlicky brew.

"Eat!" Dinko's instruction was more of a command than an invitation.

Alternating crusty bread with each mouthful of the thick soup, Dinko seemed to have been able to work out how to chew and speak at the same time, alternating from cheek to cheek.

"So, tell me why you are escaping." Dinko didn't mince his words. If his suspicions were correct, these two would know the four boys he saw on the island.

They looked at each other. No point trying to make up a story. They both had the same thoughts. If they were going to get help from Dinko and Rosa, it was better to be honest.

Luka started to talk and when he got to the part about the police taking his father away, Dinko stopped him.

"Wait, Luka. You say that the police took your father? What did this policeman look like?"

"All I remember is his black moustache."

"Dragan." Dinko slumped back in his chair, running his hands through his hair. "I remember him very well from when I used to spend more time fishing near Zadar. He was in the bar sometimes when we went for a drink after."

The lights seemed to come on for Dinko. "Wait. You are Luka? Son of Marko and Mara?"

"You know my parents?"

Rosa took her husband's hand, sensing where he was going.

"Your father saved my life Luka!"

Rosa stood and went to the stove. This was looking like it might be a long evening, so she filled the pot with milk from the bucket next to the backdoor as Dinko started his story. The warm milk coffee and slabs of sweet torta would keep them going.

"I remember many years ago. I think you must have only been very young as I remember your father mentioning he had a son. I was almost finished taking the crates of fish off my boat when I heard yelling. There were two men, your father and I think, his older brother?"

"Yes. Maybe my Tetak."

"They were arguing with some others about something. I think it was maybe about politics or the government. Anyway, it doesn't matter. Then one of the men threw a punch at your uncle and there was a fight. Your father was smaller and tried to stop them. So, a few of us went over and tried to break up the fight when the police appeared. I remember very clearly that one of them called himself Dragan and he had a weird black moustache."

Dinko took a long sip of the warm milky coffee that Rosa had placed quietly before him. Tom and Luka were too engrossed to notice theirs.

"The police didn't bother to ask who was in the fight, they just took all of us and we were thrown in gaol."

"I didn't see Dinko for three days. No one could tell me where he was." Rosa wiped her eyes with her apron.

Dinko patted her on the knee. "And this was the most unusual thing. My wife knows everything about everyone!"

She swatted his hand away. "You were very lucky then, husband."

"Anyway. We were all sitting on the floor in the gaol. Your father told me his name and gave me the best advice I ever heard." The boys leaning closer now.

"He told me that there was one guard who was always playing cruel jokes on the prisoners. He said that if that guard called out a name, and it was mine, I should ignore him. He had heard that any man promised freedom, would be taken away and never seen again."

"And was your name called?" Tom getting in first as Luka's mouth opened.

"The very next day. I sat quietly and didn't answer. Then he called another name. A man I had seen sometimes around the market. He jumped up quickly and left with the guard."

"And?" This time Luka reacted quicker.

"I have never seen the man again, to this day." He went quiet, thinking of what could have been. "And I never got to thank your papa properly."

"What happened then?" Luka asked.

"We were all sent home after three days. We didn't want to hang around. And now the son of Marko is here and needs help."

The irony was not lost on any of them.

Luka and Tom shared their reasons for leaving Zadar as Dinko and Rosa nodded their understanding.

"Now. Tell me about your four friends in the boat ..." Dinko asked after they had finished.

Shock appearing again. There was no question now that the fisherman had divine help.

"What four friends?" they both asked apprehensively.

Dinko was unconvinced. "The four boys I met on the outer island in the Kornati yesterday. They said they were from Zadar and were traveling to Italy to escape. Surely it would be too much coincidence that I meet six boys, the same age, who are escaping from Zadar, at the same time. And they don't know each other?" Dinko looking bemused.

They went over their plan to split up, to confuse the authorities. Dinko slapped his thighs and roared laughing as they went on and spoke of stealing the boat and oars.

"I would buy a ticket to see the look on Dragan's face when he found out!" "Rosa! Remember you said there was talk of a boat stolen from people in the village who had been to Zadar recently. We have the thieves in our kitchen!" Dinko laughed even harder now.

A different energy filled the room as the boys talked about their escape. Rosa was clearly taken by them and for a moment only, felt the loss of not having children of their own.

Her kitchen had a warmth that was long past but for the first time in many years, Dinko also saw the blue in his wife's eyes as she laughed along with him.

They talked about Dinko and Rosa. How they met and made their life together.

"You couldn't even stand up as the priest was giving us his blessing Dinko! I don't even know if we are officially married!"

"You were too beautiful when I saw you my darling, my legs went weak."

"That's because you were drunk. I don't think you will have remembered how I looked."

Tears were streaming from their eyes. The increasing glances from Dinko to his wife made her blush more than once which only spurred him on to tell more stories.

"It's getting late, Dinko. The boys will be tired from such a journey. Not to mention listening to your crazy stories." It was Rosa's turn to wink at them.

"Tonight, you will sleep here. There is no use driving back to the boat. Dinko, show the boys to the shed. There is straw and some blankets. It is warm. I will have a warm breakfast ready before you go. You will need the energy for the day."

Luka and Tom turned back to Dinko as Rosa was leading them out to the shed.

"Were our friends, okay?"

"I only spoke to one of them. A bigger boy. I didn't ask his name," Dinko replied.

Luka thought it probably would have been Roko.

"They will need to be careful with the Bura and rough seas from when they leave. Who can say what they will find. Rest now. We will talk more tomorrow."

The reason the shed was so warm was the four goats, one cow and the chickens that were in residence. And tethered alongside was an old mule. The marks on its back were from the large baskets that were slung across to carry the washing. Rosa would do the laundry for some of the farmers in the village, and in return, she would receive vegetables or fruit and sometimes a couple of kuna, for the larger loads.

The rafters above, where the boys would sleep on the large stack of hay, were adorned with drying cod and legs of salted ham or prsut. The smell was quickly forgotten as tiredness set in.

"Goodnight, boys. Get a good rest."

"Goodnight, Rosa. And thank you again."

Her warm smile came freely.

As she walked through the door, Dinko saw the lightness in her movements as she hummed her way around the kitchen. His lips met the warmth of her forehead as they embraced.

"You would have been a wonderful mother."

"It wasn't meant for us, Dinko."

CHAPTER 8

The boys launched from the island in the evening, and they knew that they would be at sea for however long it took to make land.

The Bura winds had picked up and would help them to keep moving south. But they would still need to row hard through the waves. The open sea, beyond the outer islands, was treacherous at the best of times and travelling by the stars at night would add another challenge.

"Sam. You and Bruno take the first shift rowing. Josip, try and get some rest before we take over. I will keep watch and try to steer." Roko had felt the responsibility and enjoyed taking charge.

I never want to go back, he thought to himself.

They rowed for as long as the blisters on their hands allowed them to before swapping over. The cramps seizing up their legs with greater frequency. Bruno took over the watch while Sam and Roko tried to get some sleep.

The night was clear and there was some light from the moon, but they could barely distinguish the water from the horizon.

Roko dozed.

There was no sound from the oars.

They had stopped rowing. Each of them was exhausted.

In his daze, out of the corner of his eye, Roko could just make out the large can at a right angle against the light of the moon.

"Hey! That's enough! We need to save as much water as we can."

"Fuck off Roko. You don't get to tell anyone what to do out here. I'm thirsty and I'll drink what I want." Sam raised the can again.

The others woke quickly, but not quickly enough to stop the full force of Roko lunging at Sam.

They wrestled with the can, trying not to spill any of the remaining water. The boat started rocking uncontrollably.

"Let go, you fat bastard!"

Roko let go suddenly and Sam fell back into the hull. The can falling from his grip.

Roko was overtaken by a rage he didn't know he had, and his hands were soon around Sam's neck. He just kept squeezing. The others tried to stop the fight while trying to keep the boat from capsizing.

"Enough, Roko. He's had enough."

"Let go of him, Roko. It's not worth it."

Without letting go, Roko lifted the boy and forced him against the boat's frame.

Crack.

The sound of splitting bone seemed to jolt him out of his rage. He let go and the limp body crumbled into the hull.

He could feel something sticky in his hands.

Sam wasn't moving. "Sam! Sam!" Roko shook him. "Come on, Sam. Wake up!"

They went silent.

There wasn't enough light to see the boy clearly, but they knew it wasn't good.

No one dared to speak.

Roko, now breathing hard, fell back in the boat.

Josip was the first to speak. "Shit, Roko. What have you done?"

"Is he dead?" Bruno's hand searched for the throb of a pulse on Sam's neck. "He's still warm. And I can just feel a pulse. I think."

Roko started to shiver. The cold enveloping his body before the nausea started to rise. He heaved his body over the side and the vomit came from his nose and mouth in bursts.

He fell back into the boat.

"Roko. This is bad. What are we going to do." Josip almost in a whisper, not sure how to handle the mood that his friend was in.

"Shut up and let me think!"

"Maybe a boat will come along? We can wave it down and get help?" Josip now desperate to think of an answer.

"And what if it's an army boat or the police? We will all be taken back and thrown in gaol. Maybe worse!" Roko already thinking of the consequences.

Josip and Bruno moved to either side of Sam. Roko sat opposite, head in his hands.

Josip took a hand while Bruno kept his fingers firmly on the boy's neck. Searching for the throbbing pulse that would tell them he was still alive.

Drifting. Wide awake. Staring out at the strip of light across the water. Shaking the boy gently. Each time trying to rouse him. Nothing. The night hours passed. The boys let sleep take them over.

Josip and Bruno were still asleep as the dawn started to break. Roko silently leaned over and touched Sam's hand.

He reeled back from the dead cold flesh, waking the others in fright.

Stunned. Hearts raced. Both stared at Roko who was now lying face down with his arms hiding his head.

"He's dead. He's dead, Roko. Anguished. What are we going to do." Pleading. Imploring. Josip and Bruno sat in utter disbelief at what Roko had done.

Then, to their surprise, Roko took the body into his arms. Drew it up to his shoulder and started to rock Sam's body slowly. They couldn't make out what he was saying but watched as his lips moved next to Sam's ear.

Tears were streaming down his cheeks.

Then Roko looked up at Josip and Bruno.

"Sorry … I am so sorry … Please forgive me."

Roko staggered as he stood and took the lifeless body, with its head lolling to one side and the legs dangling from the other, to the side of the boat.

"Roko! What are you doing?" Both shrieking in disbelief.

"The only thing we can do now."

Splash.

The light caught Roko hunched over the gunwale of the boat, shoulders shuddering as he vomited over the side again. His muted sobs.

Then, as if in a trance, he moved to the wooden seat. He took both oars and began to row.

He rowed in silence. Not a word.

The boys sat and watched. Not able to comprehend what they had just witnessed.

In the light, they could make out the dark stain on the hull of the boat and used a wet shirt to try and clean it off.

The water that was left in the petrol can was starting to taste like the fumes left from its past use and the blisters on their hands from the coarse wooden handles had opened and reopened.

They had no food left and could not see anything but sea in every direction.

The wind picked up again and carried them.

They put the oars down and lay on the hard hull as the movement of the boat began rocking them to sleep.

They lost track of time.

And hope.

Matej scratched his head as they walked away from the station.

"Okay. Now we have six boys who probably stole the boat to escape, and they are somewhere at sea. And a ten-year-old girl who is missing."

"Correct."

"Zlatko. There are only two of us."

"But the captain said that we should keep looking for the boys. He said that the girl will probably turn up. Maybe she went looking for her brother."

"Look at me, Zlatko." The younger office stopped to face him.

"Does it look to you like I have joined the police force yesterday?' Zlatko's head bowed.

"No, sir."

"Something is not right with this. I can feel it."

"So, what do we do, Matej?"

He paused.

"First. We talk to that reporter from the paper and get him

to write more about the boys and now about the missing girl. Maybe someone will know something."

"But the captain said …"

"Fuck the captain! I am not going to end my career with this hanging over my head. Let's go."

Two days passed and the large truck rumbled its way down the gravel road again just before dawn. The boys squeezed onto the bench seat in the cabin next to Dinko; their eyes struggling to keep open.

This is nice, thought Tom, as he stared out at the land. It would be so easy to stay.

As if reading his mind, Luka took a deep breath. They had been very lucky to have met Dinko and Rosa, but he knew they couldn't stay. He had decided that he needed to talk to Tom later that night after dinner. They had to plan what to do next. Where were their friends and were they safe? How would they find out?

The truck lurched to a halt, waking them both from their daydreams. The day's work was the same, only this time they went out on the boat with Dinko, helping to cast the nets and then hauling them back in.

"These are too small, throw them back. They will be ready the next time."

The wind started to come up, so Dinko decided to cut the day short. There would be a wait until Rosa had finished at the church. The same routine for each day. Dinko would fish, then call past the church to pick up Rosa.

Each time after Rosa had finished her work at the church, she would wander into the square and spend the time meeting with the people of the village. They would all share news with each other, and it was one of the few ways they knew what was happening.

The boys discovered how true Dinko's words were when he said that Rosa knew everything about everyone. She seemed to have new stories each evening as they ate.

"The town doesn't need a newspaper with my Rosa. She is expert at finding things out and then telling everyone!" he joked as they headed back to the harbour.

The thin figure standing on the jetty came into view as they approached. Dinko leaned out of the cabin to see who was waiting.

"Rosa?"

Tom and Luka turned from folding the nets to see.

Her hands were wringing. The look of worry appearing on Dinko's face.

"Grab the rope, Luka. Get ready to toss it over the cleat."

The bump of the boat against the jetty nearly threw them off their feet as Dinko wrenched the gears into neutral and cut the engine.

"Rosa! What's wrong?"

She took his hand and walked away. Luka and Tom left to watch.

Her hands moved constantly as she spoke. Every now and then looking past Dinko at the boys.

She was showing him a piece of paper.

"Something's wrong, Tom."

"Yeah. Looks like it."

Dinko turned to face them and started walking. Rosa moved towards the truck.

"What's wrong, Dinko? Is Rosa alright?"

"Let's get these fish to market. I have a friend who will sell them for me. Then we will go home."

His demeanour said they should wait till he was ready to talk and after they had helped offload the fish, the truck was on its way home.

"Boys. Go and wash up. I need to speak to my wife."

Luka pumped the handle as Tom washed. Neither knowing what to say.

They went into the shed and lay down on the straw beds and waited.

"Tom. We can't stay here. We need to find a way to meet our friends."

"I know, Luka."

"Luka. Tom."

Dinko was standing in the doorway.

"Come inside. We need to talk."

Rosa had her back to them, busying herself preparing their meal.

"Sit down."

Hands in their laps. Eyes now widened. Hearts racing.

He unfolded the paper, holding it close as if there was something in it that couldn't be shared before he handed it to Luka.

"I think you need to read this, Luka." Dinko said, pointing to the headline.

GIRL MISSING FROM ZADAR.

Luka held the paper down in his lap as he read.

A ten-year-old girl has been reported missing to the police. She was last seen at school but didn't return after the lunch break. Her mother was waiting for her at the end of the school day but was told by her friends that she hadn't been to class that afternoon.

The deep howl made them shudder as he finishing reading the next line.

She is reported to be the younger sister of Luka, one of the boys who allegedly stole an army boat and escaped.

The paper dropped to floor just as Luka did.

"Mira! Mira! My Mira!"

Tom rushed to his side.

Rosa stood behind Dinko. The tears unable to be controlled from both.

Luka was inconsolable. "This is my fault. It's all my fault." Over and over again.

Tom tried hard to do something, anything to calm his friend.

Then without warning, Luka sprang to his feet.

"I have to go back!" he said as he started to run for the door.

"No, Luka!" Tom grabbed his friend.

Whack.

Tom didn't see the punch as it caught him on the chin sending him backwards to the floor.

"Leave me alone! I have to go to Mama!"

This time Dinko leapt up and took Luka in a bear hug. Wrestling with him until he had no fight left.

"Hush Luka," Dinko said, trying to sooth him. "We will think of something. Tom is right. You can't go back now. The police are looking for you too. This will not help your mama. Come and sit down. Rosa, make some milk. We need to think now."

The reporter had proved to be of some help and the story of the missing girl had spread very quickly. The village was rife with speculation

"I bet she followed her brother," said one villager.

"Maybe he came back for her," said another.

Matej and Zlatko followed up everything that looked like a lead but still came up empty-handed. It seemed as though Mira had vanished into thin air.

"Maybe we should notify the Italian Coastguard about the boys?" the younger officer offered. "Someone has surely seen something by now. A fisherman or a patrol? We can't just wait for someone to tell us. Who knows what the boys will say if they are found?"

"Good idea, Zlatko. By now, they should already have been found."

Captain Dragan stomped his way down the stairs and bellowed from their office tearoom.

"Well! Have you two idiots found anything? It appears the newspaper has been as useless as you."

"Ssh, Zlatko. Don't say anything yet. Let's call the coastguard first. We can report back after we know something."

"Or nothing," his colleague said.

"We are still conducting interviews Captain. Then we were thinking we might start to talk to fisherman outside of Zadar. Maybe someone from the other towns has seen something? We could head south to Sibenik? They may have seen something around the Kornati?" Matej replied.

The boss appeared in the doorway, cup in hand. "Mm. Okay, Matej." Dragan thought that would keep them away from anything that might arise from the other matter. And he certainly didn't want that.

"Go there tomorrow. Hang around the harbour and meet with the fishermen. Arrest anyone that you think is hiding anything."

The humming of an engine roused them awake and Josip was first to peer over the edge of the boat to see from which direction it was coming.

"Look! It's a boat!" Roko and Bruno now trying to sit up. Eyes squinting into the sharp sun. Their skin burned from the sun and wind; their lips peeling and dried.

Josip had no strength to wave and fell back into the boat as the sound got louder.

The boys could barely make out the navy-coloured uniforms with the badges on the shirt pockets.

"Hello." one of the seamen said as the large patrol boat pulled up alongside.

Luckily the sea was relatively calm as the winds had died down and the men in the boat had no trouble securing the rowing boat to theirs so they could climb aboard.

The metal ladder hung down as the seaman climbed over. The other passed him bottled water.

"Drink slowly. He said watching them desperately quench their thirst. Bruno vomited as soon as the water hit the back of his throat.

"Where are you from?" the seaman queried as he passed water to each of them. The other man waited to lift them up and into the larger boat.

"Zadar in Yugoslavia. We have come from Zadar."

The seamen looked incredulously at each other.

"Zadar? But that's nearly two hundred kilometres away! You rowed this boat all the way?"

Heads shaking at the enormity of what they were hearing.

"We escaped," croaked Roko. "We have escaped."

"We are from the Italian Coastguard. You are in Italian waters now, my young friends. You are safe and, you are welcome in Italy."

From the nineteenth century and then through two world wars, Yugoslavia was part of much bigger changes throughout Europe. What could have been construed as internal fighting between fascists and anti-fascists, and communists and anti-communists, was more like an extended struggle to create sovereign states through political experiments and land seizure. The impacts on its citizens were violence, fear, severe distrust in government and a lack of hope.

In contrast, Italy was experiencing a resurgence following World War II. The country was rebuilding its infrastructure, cultural identity in the arts and cinema, and there was an optimism for its people. Italy needed and wanted manpower, skill and experience to help it achieve this. The immigration camps were filled with migrants from other parts of Europe and North Africa, and everyone was welcome.

The boys lay on the deck wrapped in blankets as the patrol boat headed to the customs building in Ancona.

The wooden boat bobbed along behind them.

Its job had been done.

Dinko stayed in the shed that night and kept watch over the boys. Luka had been adamant that he should go back to Zadar. Tom had fought him all the way and was just as exhausted from fighting as Luka was from grief and worry.

No one slept well at all.

Rosa crept in at dawn to see the large frame of Dinko holding the young man in his arms. Protecting and restraining at the same time. He peered up at her, his eyes bloodshot.

"I have made palacinke. Come. You must eat something."

Luka stirred. Tom rolled over.

Then, as if it hit home again, Luka sat bolt upright and looked wildly at Rosa, then at Dinko.

"I have to do something, "he said.

"Yes. We do," Dinko said firmly, "And we will stay here today and try to plan. It will not matter if I miss a day's fishing at this time of the year."

"Rosa. I think you should go into town. Maybe you can find out if there is any more news about Mira or the boys. Luka, it will be better for you to stay here. I know this is hard, but your name is now in the paper, and it will draw attention. It won't take long for anyone to guess that maybe six boys are not in the boat."

"Dinko is right Luka," said Tom. The tension now gone from between them. "There is nothing that we can do now that won't cause more trouble for everyone."

"But Mama needs me now."

"She has your Teta. They are both strong women and have had to deal with a lot since their husbands were taken."

"Maybe we can get a message to her?" Luka brightening at the thought.

"Yes. Maybe. But not just yet. Rosa will see if there is more to know in town."

Rosa took the hessian bag and slung it over her shoulder. "I will see if old Sime can take me into town on the cart. I can say the truck has broken down again."

"Good idea. And don't forget to get the money from my fish yesterday. Give him a couple of kuna for selling them for me."

"He can ask for it," she said walking out the door. "He owes you more than you owe him."

CHAPTER 9

That same day in Zadar, the sun warmed the pebbles on the beach but with the change of season, there was less heat in the stones to burn the soles of your feet. The crystal-clear water still attracted beach goers. More strolling than swimming.

Feet dangled from the jetty surrounded by fishing rods fixed in place by bags of sand. At no further than a bite away, sat the owners with trails of smoke billowing into the air.

Couples holding hands wandered slowly away from the harbour area and disappeared into the forest beyond. Giggles and laughter fading as they disappeared.

Zoran had been planning this day for months. The weight of food and a bottle of wine threatened to tear the frayed handles from the old wicker basket he was carrying. Svetlana took the other handle as though it was an extension of his hand, and he guided them to the place he had chosen.

"Is it too heavy?"

"No, its fine if we walk slowly."

Zoran would have preferred to move a little quicker as his sweaty hands fought to keep hold of the handle.

"I hope you like sardines."

A giggle and a blush.

"I have some fresh bread and cheese as well."

Her long black hair blew back across her face as she turned into the wind to look at him. A sharp flick of her head and it flowed back behind her.

A deep breath and a smile.

A gnarly root from a large tree jutted out to mark the spot that they would stop.

"Let's leave the basket here and walk before lunch."

"What if someone takes it?"

"No. It will be fine." Zoran caught her eye and winked as he put out his hand.

Her hand drifted into his and they went closer to the water's edge.

Zoran picked up a flattened pebble and slipped it between his thumb and forefinger. He drew his arm back as far as he could and flicked the stone parallel to the water.

"It skipped six times! It's my turn now."

They kept moving along the edge of the water looking for the flattest stones to skip.

A small red buoy bobbed in the shallows as Svetlana spied a coloured conch. As she was inspecting the shell, the buoy caught her eye. She moved gingerly over the stones to get a closer look.

The sudden scream pierced through Zoran and his legs struggled to get to her fast enough.

"What is it, Sveta?"

She launched her body at his and wrapped her arms around his neck.

"Look! Just past that red floating thing."

He peeled her off him but only to have her clutch him from behind.

He went closer to inspect and reeled back in horror.

"Go back!"

Her hand went back to her mouth, muffling the sounds of her sobbing.

An old fishing net was attached to the buoy and below the surface there was a billowing red garment that looked like a shirt. From within the shirt, something could be seen caught up in the webbing of the net.

The chewed ends of the fingers were frozen onto the white rotting flesh of an arm. They didn't stop to find out if there was any more and ran back to the harbour for help.

Within minutes, a half a dozen men had approached Zoran and Svetlana on the beach, trying to comprehend what they were saying.

Two men slowly waded into the water where the red buoy could still be seen on the surface. Several moments passed as they looked and spoke to each other, yelling out to the other men on the shore. Another soon joined them and once the signal was given, the netting slowly emerged from the water behind them.

It seemed to breathe out as the water left it, until it lay flat along the shore. It looked like a tourist that had gathered souvenirs along a journey.

"My God. It's a body and I know that shirt." One of the men pointed.

"Yes, me too. It looks like ones that the national football teams wear."

"Is it Poland or Hungary?"

"No. It's definitely Hungary."

They were quickly brought back to the human remains that had been left. Trying not to touch them, they unravelled the netting as best as they could to see what was left. One half of one leg had been savaged, the other still attached and rotting on the torso. An arm was completely gone up to an armpit and the head was missing.

They didn't need to inspect it any further.

"Go to the police," said one of the men. "Tell them what has been found."

The youngest of the men ran back to the police station and once there, bounded up the stairs, two at a time till he stood in the doorway of the captain's office.

"A body," he gasped. "We have found a body. Well, part of a body. Wrapped in nets." He panted even harder.

The captain paled. His mouth drying out in a heartbeat.

"Where? Where did you find this body?" The words came out slowly as he attempted to manage his racing pulse.

"Down near the jetty. There isn't much left. I mean, you can't tell who it is. Just bits of someone."

His pulse didn't back down and he grabbed the arm of the chair to stop him from falling.

It's too soon for her, he thought.

"Matej! Zlatko! Come to my office at once." He suddenly remembered that he had sent them to Sibenik to ask more questions.

"Go back and wait for me. Tell everyone to stay away from the remains. I will find the doctor. No one touches the remains. Understand?"

"Yes, Captain Dragan."

The young man almost tumbled down the stairs as he fled.

The local doctor doubled as the funeral director. Owing to the rare occasion that this type of service was required, he was doubtful that he could offer much under the circumstances.

"But Dragan. I'm not sure that I can do much."

"Well, the least you can do is pronounce death."

"That will take none of my skills from what you have described. Any bystander can tell you that."

"I need the doctor with me. Matej and Zlatko have travelled to Sibenik today. Of all days. You need to attend."

Out of habit, he grabbed his medical bag.

His left leg shook as they drove down to the waterfront. Even placing a hand on his knee, made little difference.

"You seem anxious, Dragan. Surely this isn't your first dead body."

The captain stared out the window as he replied, "No. Not my first but who knows what this might bring."

A small crowd was gathered around the discovery site and like a school of fish, they parted for the two officials, then moved back to their positions to see what would happen next.

Dragan thought everyone would be able to hear his heart, not to mention see it throb wildly under his shirt.

They treaded carefully around the netting before circling in to where the remains lay.

"Do you think they could have been wearing this red shirt?"

The doctor inspected the remains closely. "Maybe. Maybe not. I will need to take them back to see if we can make a positive identification, at least as best we can. However, I would say that it is going to be very difficult to identify who these remains belong to."

"But we do have the six boys who escaped by boat." Dragan offered hopefully.

"Is it one of the boys?' shouted someone from the crowd. They ignored the question.

"Yes, but there is also a missing girl, Dragan. We don't know anything about what has happened to her yet. Or it could be someone completely different," the doctor said, trying to keep the options open.

"Don't worry about the girl. I am sure there could be many reasons why she is gone. Maybe her mother sent her away to work. Maybe she couldn't look after her anymore. And who knows why the boy left as well. Maybe the mother is the reason." Dragan thought of everything he could as a diversion from Mira.

The doctor used a stick to lift and move the netting around; exploring for anything else that may assist as evidence.

Suddenly, the reporter appeared from nowhere and started taking photos.

"Stop. Keep away from here until I say you can take photos. Don't do anything unless I say," the doctor said, not wanting anything to interfere with the investigation.

The reporter froze on the spot.

"Wait. We might be able to use the photos. Maybe someone can help identify the shirt? It could be useful?" Dragan intervening.

The doctor shrugged and nodded in agreement. "Maybe."

"Okay, take the photos, but be very careful. I don't want to see them in your newspaper before I have had a chance to look at them. My men will be at your office first thing tomorrow morning to look at them. If it makes the paper before I see them, I will throw you in gaol. Understand?"

The large wet spots that had appeared in his armpits were nothing compared to the headache that was coming. Dragan would have to stick very closely to the investigation and make sure that it went in a direction that he could control.

"We will need to cut the netting around the remains and carefully transport them back to my laboratory. I will make some calls and see if there is any way of identifying someone from remains. Who knows how long this has been at sea?"

"Yes. I imagine they might have been there for some time in that state."

Looking for every opportunity to cast doubt where he could, the captain went back to his office to start to think of the next steps. He had hoped his men would return from Sibenik with news that someone had seen their escaped boys out at sea.

He needed to find and capture them.

Dinko made sure that Luka and Tom were kept busy for the day.

"When you have finished clearing the shit from the shed, spread it around the garden. There is a barrow in the corner you can use."

Just as they were on the second load, they saw Rosa hurrying in the distance as the horse and cart slowly moved up the road.

"Dinko! Luka! Tom!" She gasped for breath as she approached them.

"There were two policemen from Zadar in the market today. Asking questions about the missing boys!"

"Shit, Luka. We have to leave now," uttered Tom under his breath. Luka stayed silent.

"Did you speak to them?" Dinko enquired.

"Of course! I wanted to know if they knew anything. They said they were hoping one of the fishermen might have seen the boys."

"And?"

"I said you didn't mention anything to me."

"Where are they now?"

"They said they didn't find anything so will go back to Zadar tonight. But I got the feeling they will be back."

"Nothing about Mira?" Luka's fists clenched into balls.

"They didn't mention her, Luka …"

Sensing Luka's angst, Dinko put an arm around him. "We will find a way Luka. Please be patient. I will help you. We just need to make sure it's safe."

They rose early the next day. Luka was noticeably quiet and Dinko decided he would need to keep a closer eye on him. Tom was also anxious for what he might do.

They all piled into the truck; Rosa keen to follow up on anything she may have missed from the visit by the policemen the previous day.

"You can help me on the boat today. We will head out a bit further. The conditions look good for fishing." No argument.

Rosa left them at the harbour and walked into town.

Luka had already decided what he was going to do. He just needed to find a way back to Zadar when the others were distracted. He would find a way after one of the markets and hope he could get a ride before they noticed.

Somehow, he would see his mother.

Matej and Zlatko met outside of the Zadar police station, unsure of how their unsuccessful trip to Sibenik the day before, would be received.

They would check to see if there had been any calls from the

Italians before they briefed the captain on the little progress that had been made.

The girl who took the messages and made the tea, had only one message back from the Italian coastguards.

"Well, what did they say!"

"They said that there haven't been any boats with six boys that have been intercepted or reported as being seen."

"Are you sure?"

"That's what they said."

"Mm. Strange. You would think someone has seen or heard something by now."

The creak of the bottom step was enough.

"Get up here, you two. After your joy trip to Sibenik yesterday, I have work for you to do! Hurry up."

The younger officer passed Matej on the stairs and saluted on entry to the boss's office.

"Yes, Captain!"

He briefed them on the events from the day before. Neither believing what they were hearing.

"Go to the newspaper office first and track down that reporter. He has photos that I want you to show each of the parents. There is a red football shirt that, I am sure, someone will recognise as belonging to one of the boys. Now!"

"But what about the missing girl?"

"Has anyone come forward with any information?" the captain demanded.

Their heads shook.

"Well then, we focus on what we do have now! Find out who belongs to that shirt. And tell that reporter if he prints any of the photos or mentions the shirt, I will see that he loses his job!"

The men turned to leave.

"Wait. There's one more thing. Mention that we have a crucial piece of evidence and hope that will provide a link to identifying the remains."

"Yes, sir."

The reporter buzzed around the large print machine, pushing the letterpress operator to work faster, as the two officers approached.

"Hurry up. We need to get this paper out urgently."

Matej and Zlatko took deep breaths as they looked at the photos. After leaving the reporter in no doubt about his job, or his life, they left him to supervise the operator.

"How much more can these parents put up with. First their boys escape, then a girl goes missing and now we have photos of someone's football shirt that might belong to one of the boys. And all we have are their remains. It's all wrong." the younger officer said, indulging in a moment of hopelessness.

"We do what we can Zlatko. But let's leave the mother of the missing girl to last. This will be bad enough."

Rosa could see Dinko's boat come closer. The market had been buzzing with the news of the human remains that had washed up in netting on the shore in Zadar. Some of the fishermen were there when it unfolded, the story taking life very quickly.

Rosa had heard all she needed to hear before making her way back to the harbour to meet the boat.

Seeing his wife for the second time, waiting for them on the jetty, was all Dinko needed to get the boys to secure the boat so he could find out if there was any news.

Again, they huddled in closely with looks of concern and shaking of heads.

Luka and Tom were unsure of how much more they could take when Dinko approached them.

"We will unload the fish at the market, and I will ask my friend again to sell them for me. Then we will go home."

The boys climbed in the back with the crates of fish, and the truck started to rumble away. The boys exchanged quizzical looks and shoulder shrugs at Dinko's decision.

Luka's heart started to pound. He was more desperate than ever to find a way back home. Once they were back at the house, it would be even harder to get away. He needed to leave from the market. Today.

"Stay here while I find my friend." Low talking between Dinko and Rosa. Luka couldn't make out what they were saying but Rosa had moved from the cabin and now stood with the boys.

Luka's eyes darted around still.

There was a clear path through the trestles, to the left, that looked as though it would take him through the larger fruit and vegetable stands. He would be hidden through parts of it, giving him more time. Once away from the market, he could easily run towards the road and hope there was someone who would give him a lift.

One step. Two steps. Then a large hand clamped down on his shoulder.

"Where are you going?" Dinko had just seen Luka out of the corner of his eye as he was making his way back to them. He lumbered forward and just got hold of the boy.

"Let me go!" Luka wrestled to break free.

"Luka don't be stupid! I can see what you want to do. The police are asking many questions and the last thing you want to do is to be seen."

Luka went limp in Dinko's arms, and the big man held him as he sobbed.

Tom was quickly by his side again.

"Once we have finished taking these containers over to my friend's stall, we will go. Tom. Please stay with Luka." Tom understood what this meant but he didn't think his friend had anymore fight left to leave.

Dinko despaired at what to do. Luka would be recognised as soon as he went back, and he had no doubt would be thrown in gaol or shipped away to a labour camp.

Little did he realise a solution to his problem was about to be revealed.

CHAPTER 10

The customs officer in Ancona finished his phone message to the receptionist at the Zadar police station.

"Signorina, please tell the officers that none of my men have had reports or have seen, six boys in a wooden boat. Yes. We will be sure to let you know if anything changes."

He put the phone down and walked out to the three boys sitting outside his office.

"Okay. We will need to interview each of you. My men will show you where you can shower first, and we will find some clean clothes. Then after you have eaten, we will meet back here. There is a doctor who will check you over and treat the blisters on your hands. Don't worry, we will look after you."

Josip and Bruno looked bewildered at Roko as he sat with his head in his hands.

"What are we going to say, Roko."

"Nothing. Don't say a thing. Any mention of what happened, and they will send us back. Do you want that?"

Both shook their heads.

"Just think that is was only the three of us."

"What about Luka and Tom?"

"Forget about them. All we can do now is try to stay here. Just tell them what we agreed. Everything will be okay if we just stick to the story."

They were quickly back at the place where the customs officer had said they would be interviewed. The long bench sat along a pale grey concrete wall with doors at each end. The windows had wire mesh in the glass. The boys were the only people present.

Even though they had showered, been fed and were wearing clean clothes, each of them still had the shivers.

"I will go first, if they ask," Roko whispered. Remember, there was only three of us."

The door opened and a tall, young officer approached them.

"My name is Paulo and I will be interviewing you today. Now, who would like to go first?"

Roko stood and followed him into the room. The door closing behind him.

A glance between Josip and Bruno at Roko's last instruction suggested disquiet and uncertainty.

The truth was, there had been four of them in the boat.

An hour later, Roko emerged from the room. Josip and Bruno shifted uncomfortably on the bench, both reluctant to go next and neither wanting to tell the truth or to lie.

"Who is next?"

Roko's elbow caught Bruno's ribs.

"You can go next Josip," he said. "I can wait."

"Why me? You go."

"One of you come now. I don't have all day. You. You're next."

Bruno moved slowly into the room. The door closed again.

"Well. What did you say Roko?" Josip whispered, his eyes looking around to make sure no one was in earshot.

"Like I told you. There was only three of us, and we left from Zadar."

"Did they ask you anything else?"

"Just why we left and if our families knew. I just said what we'd agreed. That we didn't really have a choice and wanted to come to Italy."

Roko had nothing more to say about anything. It was like he'd wiped everything that had happened.

Josip sprung up suddenly and ran for the bathroom. When he returned, his eyes were red, and he was holding his stomach. Roko didn't even look up.

When Bruno finally emerged from the office, Josip had made another two trips to the toilet.

"Remember. Only three," came Roko's sharp whisper as he stood up.

It felt as though Josip had been interviewed for much longer than the others and by the time he appeared, they were feeling more anxious about what would happen next.

"Okay boys. Wait here."

The officer strode off. Not a word was uttered as they sat.

Some minutes later, he returned with a much older man wearing a uniform that seemed to have a lot more badges.

"This is the Chief of Customs. We now want to speak with you together. Please follow me."

Frowns and glances between them, the boys followed the men.

"It seems we have a problem. The older man started. Your stories do not match."

Roko could feel his anger rise.

The locals in Zadar were struggling to comprehend all that had happened over the recent weeks.

A boat stolen, boys escaped, a missing girl, a red shirt. And now, the remains of a body caught in netting.

The newspaper hadn't been filled with so much local action since the end of the war, that it was sanctioned to print anyway. The reporter had asked for extra copies to meet the demand for updates.

Matej and Zlatko started the slow process of meeting with the parents of the boys first and showing them the photos. Silently hoping that no one would recognise it so they wouldn't have to deal with the aftermath.

Everyone knew a shirt like it, but no one could connect it to the investigation.

Mara sat looking out of the bedroom window where both of her children once slept.

Her sister-in-law, Ana, was quietly tending to the chores that needed to be done. Collecting and chopping wood for the stove, feeding the chickens and cleaning over the places that had already been cleaned the day before. Trying to keep up a routine.

The two figures that approached in the distance meant nothing to Mara until they came closer and seemed to be heading her way.

Her hands clutching at her apron.

A knock at the door. Her breath caught as Ana answered.

"What do you want?" Her face was drawn with angst.

"May we come in?" Matej asked blandly.

"Why. Have you found anything?" The women had stayed away from everyone. Too many questions and too many sympathetic looks when all they wanted was some hope.

"We need to ask you and Mara some questions."

The old woman hesitated, keeping the door only slightly ajar.

"Say what you need to say here." Ana didn't want their safe space intruded upon any further.

"Ana. Let them in." Came the soft voice from behind.

"But Mara …"

"It's okay. Let them in."

The men removed their caps, scuffed their shoes on the mat and walked past Ana.

"Zlatko. Can you please wait outside while I speak with them?" The experience in Matej told him that things might go awry if it wasn't handled properly.

Annoyed, the younger man turned and left to stand guard outside the door.

He reached into his jacket pocket, removed the photos and gestured for them to sit.

"Can you please look at these and tell me if you recognise anything."

Mara held her hands tightly to her and glared at Matej. She couldn't bring herself to look.

"Please, Mara," he gently urged. Every muscle in his body was tense.

Her eyes slowly dropped to the image placed before her on the table.

She touched it and moved it closer before picking it up to see more clearly.

"It's, it's a shirt. A red one."

"Yes. Have you ever seen one like it?"

"Where was this photo taken?" she stammered.

"Do you know this shirt, Mara." He tried to complete one task at a time to keep her focussed.

"Oh God. Where did you find this? What are you doing to me?" Mara standing in a rage, waving the photo at the policeman.

"So, you know this shirt …" He kept his voice calm and stayed seated.

Ana took the photo and looked at it before taking Mara in her arms.

"Could this shirt belong to your son?"

"No. Luka would never leave his shirt. It was his favourite." Temporary relief washed over her as she tried to create a plausible reason for the shirt's discovery.

"He would never … Have you found Luka? Please tell me!"

Matej got up from his chair and went outside to his colleague before returning soon after.

Hesitating now. "Would Mira have taken it?" Matej now trying a different tack.

"Why would Mira take it?" Ana now confused.

"Maybe she took it to remember him after he left? Maybe she knew where he was and took it to him? Maybe she went with him?" Matej relayed all the possibilities.

Mara's face contorted, trying to recall the sequence of events. When did Luka go? When did I last see my Mira? What did Luka say? The shirt. What did he say about the shirt? The thoughts rolling over and over.

With startled eyes, she looked directly at him. "He wanted his shirt. I said it was still drying. He said it didn't matter. That was the last time I saw him." She grasped Ana's hand. "Where did you find it?" she said, imploring.

"So, you can confirm that Luka had a shirt exactly like this one."

"Yes."

The last words she heard him say were, "This shirt was discovered among fishing nets on the shore, with the remains of a body …"

Moments later, the priest arrived at the house and after hearing of what had transpired went into the house as the two policemen left.

The newspaper print room was a hive of activity as papers were rushed to be printed for immediate distribution.

It was mid-afternoon and even though deliveries weren't due till the morning, the reporter decided to deliver as many as possible that day.

With the ink barely dry, he left piles with some of the traders in the market before heading to the harbour to distribute among the fishermen.

Some would be returning to their villages that evening so the news would be made available before it was expected.

The trip from Zadar to Sibenik by sea took a couple of hours and by the time the last boats arrived, Dinko and Rosa were about to leave.

"That's strange," Rosa said, seeing the wad of papers being carried from one of the last arriving boats when they were almost finished with the fish.

"What is?"

"Wait here, Dinko. I will only be a minute."

The boys had already crawled into the back of the truck. Tom kept his friend close.

Rosa came back carrying a newspaper.

"This has been delivered early. We don't usually get them until tomorrow."

"Open it, Rosa."

The remains of a body found on shore in Zadar. Police investigating.

"Oh God, Dinko."

"Stop reading. Let's get away from here. We need to get Luka home."

Rosa tucked the paper into the top of her dress as they walked to the truck.

"What do we do now Dinko."

"We tell them, Rosa. At least we will be there for them."

The truck rumbled onto the road towards their small home.

Luka had fallen asleep. Partially through the hard work of hauling fish and partially through exhaustion.

Tom stayed alert, watching as his friend slept.

As it slowed, Tom gently shook Luka to wake.

As they stood, Dinko and Rosa were waited at the back of the truck. It was hard to see their expressions as the light of day began to fade.

"I will start dinner. Boys, please wash first. It will be ready soon."

The smell of sardines frying in garlic wafted through to the backyard as they took turns pumping the handle on the well. They would bathe once a week with only their extremities seeing any soap on the other six working days.

As Rosa squeezed the mixture of olive oil, parsley, lemon juice and more garlic over the hot fish, Dinko bowed his head for a prayer of thanks as they took their seats.

Along with the large bowl of fresh salad, boiled potatoes and yesterday's bread, they ate the sardines in silence.

"Are you not hungry, Luka?" Rosa spied him as he picked at his food.

Luka kept his head bowed.

Dinko looked across at his wife as if to let her know to leave him.

"What were you and Rosa talking about back at the market?" Luka not wanting to make eye contact.

Dinko chewed noisily, looking for words.

He wiped his hands on the tablecloth and turned to Luka.

"Luka." Looking for the words but deciding that the fewer he used, the quicker they would deal with the fallout.

"A body has been found in Zadar."

Tom gasped as he looked toward Luka.

Frozen in the moment. Waiting for a response.

"Is it Mira?" Luka said, almost inaudible.

"It doesn't say who. Just that the police are investigating."

Rosa read out the brief article that covered the salient pieces. It promised more news when the police made it available.

"It could be anyone Luka. They don't know."

"But the evidence? If I could find out," Luka said, pleading with Dinko.

"Yes. There is only one person I know who could find that out." He peered over to Rosa.

"Who? Me?"

"Who else knows everything that goes on here?"

Rosa wasn't sure if she felt flattered or insulted. But either way, she would do what she could.

"Luka. I know what you are thinking but we can't go back to Zadar. With everything that has happened, it's too dangerous," Tom said, siding with Dinko. "Let Rosa and Dinko find out what they can. When we have the information we need, then we can decide what to do."

His head went to his hands. He knew they were dammed either way, but he wasn't about to give up.

Tom and Dinko were right. Just for now.

CHAPTER 11

"Pronto. This is Ancona Customs. Can I help you?"

"Yes. My name is Dragan. I am the captain of the police in Zadar, Yugoslavia."

"Yes, Captain."

"Can I speak to an officer in charge?"

"What is it about?"

"Just put me through. This is a matter of urgency." His patience for questions wasn't great.

"Certainly, sir. Please hold the line."

He heard the line go dead.

"Hello, Captain Dragan. Can I help you?"

"Are you the one in charge?"

"I am the senior officer here. My name is Gino."

"Good. My men contacted you recently to enquire if you had seen or found six thieves who we believe stole a boat to escape to Italy."

"Mm. Yes. I am aware of the call," the officer said, reluctant to give up any further information.

"Well, we were told that you haven't seen or found these boys. Is this correct?"

"Yes. We already advised your men of this."

"I'm calling because we now have human remains that were discovered." He let this sink in for a minute.

"That is unfortunate. But how can I help you?" Dragan felt the lack of assistance already.

"Well now. If you did happen upon any wreckage of a boat or suspicious activity that might be linked to this, I would appreciate being notified. It may help with our investigations."

Gino took his time to respond.

"Are you still there?" Dragan's patience wearing thin.

"I will make some enquiries. If you could call back in, maybe a couple of days? I might be able to help you then."

"Is that the best you lazy spicks can do? I have parts of a body on my hands. Six boys who have escaped. A stolen boat. And a big pain in my guzicu!"

"Captain, as I said. I will make enquiries. It wasn't us who lost those boys or the boat."

Click.

Furious with the way he was treated by the Italians, Dragan's face turned a dark shade of beetroot.

There were footsteps on the stairs and had his officers walked into the office a minute earlier they may have been killed or maimed by the chair that was hurled across the room.

The officers waited in the hallway until it seemed safe enough, they moved tentatively inside.

"You better have something to report, or you will both be working nightshift. And with no pay."

"Sir. We believe we know who the shirt may belong to."

"Who?" Dragan asked, his temperament shifting suddenly.

Matej briefed his boss on the outcome of their interviews with all the parents.

"We visited the mother, Mara, last."

"Go on. What did she say?"

"We showed the photos and initially asked if the shirt might have been taken by the little girl."

"And did she?" The images playing back in his mind again.

"Well, she was very emotional but then she remembered that her son Luka was looking for the same shirt on the last day she saw him. That was the day he left, Captain."

"And none of the other parents knew of their boys having the same shirt?"

"No, sir."

And there is no one else missing, he thought to himself.

"Okay. Good work. Tomorrow, we will visit the doctor and try to put everything that we have together. But without any other supporting evidence to the contrary, I think we might assume that they have drowned."

Neither man thought this was good work. As a matter of fact, they both thought that was the worst day of their lives.

"I need a drink, Zlatko."

"Me too. How are we going to deal with this? Telling all those parents?"

"I think the priest will be very busy soon. Let's go."

The following day, the captain and his two officers made their way to the building that housed all things related to illness and death: the doctor, pathologist and funeral director. Apart from some secretarial assistance from his wife and a couple of local men to help with bodies, the multitasking doctor occupied the building alone.

The basement housed the mortuary and a steel dissection table if required. There was a small laboratory where he had access to dental charts and medical records. Most were gathering dust but, at times like this, something may be of use.

The main level was for office space and examination rooms.

The men made their way into the offices and were greeted by the doctor.

"Can you tell us anything more about the remains, doctor?"

"Follow me. I can take you through my autopsy report, but I may have found something that will be of interest to you."

They stood at the door of the mortuary fridge as the doctor slid the gurney out. Body parts were wrapped in individual plastic bags and strewn along the tray. Had it contained a cadaver, rather than having pieces of meat strewn along it, it would have been a little more confronting. This was more like a butcher's fridge.

"I have performed an analysis of all the parts we have here and have been able to take a partial fingerprint from the only full finger. Unfortunately, there are no records here to be able to match it, so it is useless."

All eyes on each part as he rotated and pointed out the features.

"All of what is left would be deemed to be unremarkable. That is, there is nothing to distinguish anything from most of the population."

"Population of who?" Dragan was keen to get moving.

"Young men. This is the body of a young male. It is difficult for me to estimate the age without the teeth or head …"

"A rough guess, doctor?"

"My guess, by the skin and muscle is roughly between sixteen to twenty years of age. There is some evidence of pubic hair left in the base of the torso and hair under the single arm. What is left of the pelvic bone would certainly lead to it being from a male."

"Mm. That helps."

"But this is where it gets interesting. As you can see, the head has been severed or removed from just under the chin. This may suggest a large shark, as you can see by the serrated edges around the neck."

"I would have been happy to just read the report, doctor," Matej said, grabbing his handkerchief to cover his mouth and nose.

"Zlatko, can you please pass me the magnifying glass," the doctor requested.

"You can see that the body is macerated from the time it has spent in the water. The prune-like effect on the hand suggests that it has been in the water for maybe, a short time only. However, there is some peeling evident, which occurs as the water begins to soften the underlying tissue. The skin is pale but there is a bluish tinge which would now suggest that it has been submerged for several days."

"So, Doctor, we now have the body of a young man between the age of sixteen and twenty, who may have been in the water for several days? Maybe up to a week?"

"Yes, I think we can assume this correctly."

"So, we could then say that this is a likely drowning?" Dragan becoming excited at the thought that the escapee saga may have been resolved for him.

"Not necessarily, Captain."

"Please look at the sides and front of the neck." The men craned over the magnifying glass.

"You can see the dark blue areas?" Heads nodded.

"If the body was subject to any trauma postmortem, you would only see faint areas, if any at all, of bruising. That's because there isn't any blood to pool in the traumatised places."

"So?" Zlatko was already lost at the amount of science he was hearing while trying not to pass out.

"So, I think this bruising was caused antemortem, that is before death. There has been available blood to cause pooling from the trauma. The fact that the body may not have been in the water for very long, means that the bruising hasn't changed under the conditions and is still discernible. Had the body been in the water for much longer, it may not have been quite as easy to identify."

"What do you think was the cause of death?"

"Gentlemen, I think your young man was strangled before death. Without the head and eyes, I can't say if it was the direct cause, but it would suggest that there was a struggle or fight."

"Is there anything else we should know doctor?"

"Nothing that provides anything definite but that's my working theory on what we have at hand."

"My men have interviewed all the parents, and we think that we can connect the red shirt through a positive identification by one of them. Let's confirm what we have."

The doctor provided the formal summary as the policemen took notes.

"A young male, approximately sixteen to twenty years of age who appears to have injuries consistent with strangulation that were sustained prior to or were the cause of death. Death may have been due to strangulation, after which the body entered the water. Or strangulation occurred prior to death and the body then entered the water and drowning was the cause of death. Without access to the head or teeth, I can't provide any further comment. The skin pallor and condition would suggest the body has been in the water for several days, which is supported by the maceration and bluish tinge."

"In your opinion doctor, with all of the analysis, could you confirm that these remains could belong to one of the six escapees?"

"It certainly fits the age group and the fact that drowning has been a factor in causation. I would say it is a possibility. Yes."

"Thank you doctor." Turning to face his officers, the captain took a deep breath.

"Men. With the positive identification of the red shirt by one of the parents, along with the doctor's autopsy results, and the fact that those useless Italians don't have any reports of capsizes or rescued boys, I think we can confidently say these remains belong to one of those boys. And it is highly likely that the boat capsized, and they are drowned."

"Luka." Matej uttered quietly.

"Yes." Zlatko had put the jigsaw together.

"But what about the other boys? What can we say to their parents if we have nothing else than a few remains and a shirt?"

"Let's deal with his family. Or what's left of them." Dragan stroked his moustache. "Pay a visit to the priest first and let him know. It is best that he is with you when you officially inform them."

"Shouldn't we wait a couple of days, sir? Maybe there will be more news from Italy? They did say to call back."

"Do you think these body parts can be brought back to life? No. See the priest this afternoon. Visit Luka's family, then work your way around to the others. Then we will decide on what to report in the newspaper. Let this be a lesson to anyone stupid enough to want to escape now."

"Maybe we can also start to focus on the missing girl too?"

"Forget her. I am certain the mother knows something. She will be back and if not, she is earning a living somewhere on her back! Now move!"

Matej started counting the days to retirement as he walked off.

"And don't forget to write up your reports. I want them on my desk by end of tomorrow."

Roko, Josip and Bruno sat facing the officers, Gino and Paulo, in a small room with one desk between them.

There was barely enough room for the five of them. Roko, his body half turned, sat leaning away from the others. Josip in the middle, looking down and Bruno had slid his hands under his thighs to stop them shaking.

The two customs officers had note pads and very serious faces.

Gino cleared his throat loudly, adding to their anxiety.

"It seems we have a problem," he looked down at his notepad. "My officer, Paulo, informs me that he has interviewed each of you and that you signed your statements as true and correct. Yes?"

The boys nodded and squirmed.

"I have read each of your statements and would like to check a couple of things. Is this alright with you?"

More nodding and squirming. The officers were acutely aware of the discomfort in the room.

"There were only three of you in the boat. Can I confirm that this is correct?"

Roko looked up immediately. "Yes. There is only us."

Josip looked to Roko, nodding along with him. Bruno kept his hands under his thighs.

"Bruno? Is this correct?"

"Yes, sir."

Staring at each of them in turn he went on. "And only three of you managed to lift the boat into the water, row across the Adriatic Sea and escape?"

Nodding again.

Considering his next move carefully, he decided not to impart the information he had been given from the police in Zadar to the boys yet. He wasn't yet sure.

His next move would make them think, and then he would leave them alone together to see what happens.

He cleared his throat again. Louder this time.

"Someone is not telling the truth. But I am a patient man. The stories that you gave to my officer do not add up and I think one or more of you, wants to tell us what really happened."

"But we were telling the truth! It's just us!" Roko's cheeks started to burn.

Both officers taking note of how the boys reacted.

"It is getting late, and I think you will need some time to think about what I have said. My officer will show you to your sleeping quarters. You will stay here tonight. Tomorrow morning, we will meet again."

Heads bowed, they walked in single file to the dormitory area. Each was given a blanket and pillow and led to the three iron framed beds they had been allocated. The walls were lined with single beds, but they were the only ones in residence. The room was so big with walls so high that the voice of the officer who gave them instructions echoed around the large space.

It had been a very long day. After the officer returned with a tray of sandwiches and a jug of water, they were left alone.

Roko sat with his fists still clenched. No one touched the sandwiches.

"So, which one of you said something." Roko's fury grew by the minute.

"I said what you told us to. I swear!" Josip felt the tears about to fall.

"Bruno?" Roko moved to sit next to him, the bed creaking under the added weight.

"What are you trying to say Roko? That I told them what really happened out there? That you killed Sam!"

Roko's arm went around Bruno's neck, as Bruno swung heavily into his gut. The boys tumbled to the floor in a mess of fists and feet.

"Stop! Stop it!" Josip lunged at them, grasping any piece of clothing or body part to separate them.

The two sets of eyes looked through the window, watching and waiting.

Then, as if they didn't need any more information to confirm their suspicions, Gino and Paulo were upon them, pulling them apart.

"Enough!" the command was clear and direct. "We will not accept any fighting. If anyone breaks this rule, you will all be sent back. Do you understand?" Gino said, clearly annoyed by their behaviour.

Roko and Bruno nodded as Josip wiped his eyes with his sleeve.

"There is an officer here all night. If there is any more trouble, he will report this to me in the morning. I don't give second chances. Now, get into your beds and rest."

They obeyed the order. Roko, turned away from them in the far bed.

They heard the door click shut and then again as it was locked.

"What do you think?" The younger officer asking in a low tone as they walked away.

"I think they are scared of the bigger boy, Roko," Gino said, considering all of what he had seen and heard.

"Yes, I think so too."

"Could you hear anything that was said?" The senior man hoping to hear that something had slipped in the fight.

"No, but there is definitely something they are not telling us."

"Mm, okay. This is what we will do. We will interview them separately again in the morning. Keep Bruno by himself and the others together. Let's see if we can put some pressure on them. It can't be a coincidence that the police in Zadar are looking for six boys in a boat and somehow, we have three arrive here from the same place, and in the same timeframe." Paulo nodded in agreement as they walked.

"And he did mention something about human remains. This seems to be more than just an escape. Before we meet with them in the morning, I need to make another call to Zadar. I just hope it's a little less difficult than the last one."

CHAPTER 12

The slender fingers of the elderly priest moved along the row of black beads as the two policemen spoke. His eyes closed in silent prayer.

He drew a long breath when they finished, still in awe of how his God continued to act in mysterious ways. He had baptised, christened, wed and buried most of the people who lived in this area. His faith never wavering in the face of so much trouble that had been visited upon them in the past.

Perhaps his ageing years were catching up on him because after hearing from the officers, he suddenly felt very tired.

"Six young men with so much ahead of them. And that beautiful little girl," he sighed. "And Dragan is sure that this is what happened?"

"The evidence seems to point to this. Yes, Father," Matej confirmed.

"And you are sure that the remains belong to Luka?"

"Yes Father."

"Then I must pray for guidance. Meet me here in an hour and we will go together."

They watched him slowly walk to the altar, then kneel in prayer.

"What now, Matej?" asked Zlatko.

"Let's see that reporter and give him the story. Then we can plan our visits to the other parents with the priest."

The reporter sat bolt upright at the old mechanical typewriter. His Smith-Corona was much smaller than the bigger Remington's used by the police, and Zlatko made a mental note to see if he could get one.

"Now just to be clear. We have given you this story but under no circumstances can this be printed until we have seen all the parents. Understand?"

"Sure. Don't worry."

The reporter was far too keen for Matej's liking. "We will come back and confirm in the morning. If all is finished, you can print it tomorrow."

The reporter nodded as he typed.

"You have met our captain, haven't you?" Matej said as they stood to leave. A warning.

The furious click clacks of the keys followed them out of the door.

The priest was waiting for them at the large wooden door of the church.

"Are you ready, Father?"

As if lost in the moment, the priest looked out from the hill where the church was perched. The lowering sun sending long swathes of light across the water.

"Yes. I am ready."

Trying to find the right walking tempo for the situation, they eventually fell into line with the priest. Still in prayer as they trudged along the stone path.

The older woman stood from the table where they sat as they heard the footsteps on the concrete stairs. Both women with eyes on the door.

Peering through the crack in the door, Ana saw the two policemen approach. But as she opened the door wider, a long deep howl came from Mara as she saw that the priest was with them.

Clutching her chest, Ana moved to the younger woman. There was no sound like the grief of a mother about to hear the news she never wanted to hear.

The visitors stood in the doorway, until the priest moved quietly inside.

"I am so sorry, Mara," the priest offered.

Ana looked up, grief-stricken. "Is it Luka?" she said, wanting to take the burden even though her heart was shattering into pieces.

"Yes, Ana. The police and the doctor believe it is."

The only thing they omitted was the bruising found on the neck. The captain's final decision was that it didn't matter.

"They drowned. That's all you need to tell them. Case closed," he had said.

They left the women holding each other as they sat, rocking and sobbing.

The priest and policemen visited each of the families that evening. The same scripted story for all of them along with the devastating news they delivered to Mara and Ana.

"We are sorry to have to inform you that the doctor has

confirmed that the remains are most likely from one of the missing boys. We have informed Luka's family."

And the same responses from each of the parents of Tom, Josip and Bruno.

"But what of my son? What has happened to him?"

"In light of all the available evidence, the likelihood is that none of the boys survived."

The priest sat with each of them in prayer, promising to return the next day.

"Well, it was his own stupid fault for thinking they could escape like that. Sam's stepfather replied. Thank you for coming here to tell us but we won't be needing any prayers, Father."

Matej thought he could hear Sam's mother blowing her nose, as they left.

Roko's house loomed in the distance. This would be their last visit.

"Who is going to help me now?" Roko's father blasted them as they stood waiting to be invited inside. Zlatko wished he hadn't been the one to deliver this kind of news on the doorstep.

Loud sobbing came from within.

"May we come in?" the priest enquired.

"Alright. Come inside. My wife will probably need you."

The priest spoke as Roko's father stood leaning against the kitchen bench.

"This isn't good news at all," he said, as his wife looked to him, hoping that he might show even a small amount of the despair she was feeling.

"I have a lot of work to do around here, and my only other

son is in the army for two years. He won't be able to come back for another year."

The sobbing stopped suddenly, and his wife stood as if a switch had been turned on for the first time.

"Our son is dead. He left because of you. And our other son will never return here. Because of you."

She turned and went to their bedroom and closed the door.

His face was pale and eyes wide as he watched her go. Not knowing how to act in front of the police and a priest.

"Is that all, Father?' It was the only thing he could think of saying.

"Please tell your wife that I will be available if she needs me. If it is alright, I will come back and visit tomorrow. But yes, that is all we have to say now."

As the trio walked away from the house, they heard the door shut again and watched as Roko's father left.

"I guess the tavern might be busy tonight." A shaking of heads.

"God does work in mysterious ways, Father."

The old priest nodded.

"Care to join us for a drink? You look like you could use one."

"Thank you, Officer. Maybe just a small one."

The news broke mid-morning the next day.

**BEACH REMAINS
IDENTIFIED. POLICE
CONFIRM DROWNINGS.**

The reporter had made the press operator start at daybreak

so that the printing would be ready by the time they had been given the green light from the police.

They had enough copies to distribute at the market in Zadar but also to give to the fishermen to take back to their villages.

Stories like this didn't come along every day so the interest had remained high.

Rosa had kept up her surveillance and information gathering, and by the time she had finished helping to clean the church, it was mid-afternoon.

Deciding it was too early to go back and wait to be collected by Dinko, she took a walk along the promenade next to the market. Despite the coolness of autumn, the sun still provided warmth if there was shelter from the sea breeze. Maybe she would hear of more news from Zadar.

There was a pile of newspapers fluttering in the breeze on top of the bench at the end of the jetty. She thought that one of the boats must have delivered them, but the papers were a day early. There must be more news. Rosa untied one of the strings so that she could pull one out.

Several minutes later she sat back on the bench, shaking her head.

"But this is impossible. Luka? How can they say this?" she repeated under her breath.

> Police have confirmed that the human remains found on the beach in Zadar are most likely to belong to one of the six boys who escaped. After reviewing all the available evidence, including the distinctive red and white football shirt that was with the body parts, and performing an autopsy, the doctor is satisfied that there is no other conclusion.

> It is believed that the boy is Luka, the brother of the missing girl. All the families have been notified and are being supported by the church.
>
> The captain of police extended his condolences to the families but has given this warning. "Let this be a warning to anyone who thinks that escape is possible. These families are suffering due to the reckless acts of these boys. We cannot accept further hurt and disruption to our community."

She took another copy and walked slowly back to the church. Not knowing what Dinko and the boys would make of any of this.

The truck rumbled up to the church as Rosa gathered her shopping bags. Dinko sensed that something was awry immediately. She was quiet as she climbed into the cabin.

"Is everything okay, Rosa?"

"I don't know. But I have something to show you when we get home. How were the boys today?" She spoke in soft tones.

"Very quiet. I think Luka still wants to go back, but thankfully, Tom is being a good friend."

"We have a lot to talk about when we get home," she said.

The newspapers were spread on the table in front of them.

"What? I don't understand this. How can they say I'm dead?" Luka read the story over and over, trying to figure it out.

Tom sat wide-eyed. Just letting it all sink in.

Dinko and Rosa didn't know what to say.

Then suddenly, Luka jumped up.

"Oh God, Tom. Remember when we said goodbye to the

others and Sam said he needed to get something to keep him warm?"

"Yeah. Shit, Luka. You gave him your football shirt. The red and white one. Bozsik's shirt from the Hungary national team!"

He slumped back down.

"This means something bad has happened, Tom."

"But how can they say we are all dead if they only have one body?"

"I don't know, but I do know one thing."

"What's that, Luka?"

"That it's not Mira."

Tom's hand found its way to Luka's shoulder. Both boys struggling to come to terms with the situation.

Rosa served up the heated bean soup with crusty warm bread. There were olives and cheese on the table with a decanter of homemade red wine.

The shock of reading about Luka's demise was one thing but then accepting that all their friends had perished, based on one set of remains, didn't make sense.

"But surely someone would have found the boat and then they could say they were all gone. How the fuck can this happen?" Tom said, feeling the frustration and hopelessness of it all.

"These waters are very busy. There is always a patrol boat or fishing boats. I would find it hard to believe that no one saw anything." Dinko was sitting back picking olives from his teeth with his knife.

"Well, I don't believe it," said Luka. If it is Sam's body, then something has happened on the boat and maybe he went overboard by accident. The police have been wrong before. All that captain wanted was for us to be dead!" The anger rising.

"Luka." Tom had paled. "Our parents think we *are* dead." The realisation struck them both.

"Oh no. Mama." Luka stared back at him.

Dinko and Rosa pulled their chairs closer to Tom and Luka. Each with an arm around them.

Dinko had been listening as the boys tried to process all the events leading up to the report in the newspaper. Why had one thing happened and not another? What did the police investigate and had there been any effort made to find Mira?

When he finally spoke, it changed the course of the conversation dramatically.

"But you are not dead."

"We know that Dinko. What's that got to do with anything?"

"They don't know you are alive." He allowed this to sink in.

Tom caught what Dinko was saying. "Of course! Luka! They don't know we are alive!"

Luka still looked puzzled until the penny dropped for him.

Then his face brightened as he started to realise what this could mean.

"If they think we are dead, no one will be looking for us."

"Or expecting to see us." Tom knew where Luka was going.

"We can go back to Zadar. Just to let our parents know we are alive." Luka felt an enormous sense of relief.

Dinko smiled. "And I have a boat."

Rosa hovered over them and gently touched her husband on the face. This is how you can help them, she thought. He smiled back at her knowingly as he took her hand.

"So now we have to think very carefully about this." Dinko was ready to put a plan together.

"And I have to know what happened on that boat. If it is Sam, then where are Roko, Bruno and Josip?"

"We must prepare for the worst as well, Luka. Maybe there was an accident and the boat did capsize."

"One thing at a time boys. Now let's plan for Zadar."

It was late before they eventually went to bed but, for the first time in days, Luka felt some hope. If not for his sister, then at least his mother.

The news of the drownings spread quickly and for those who weren't directly impacted, there was much sympathy for those who were. Food was left on the doorsteps for the parents of the boys and flowers were laid at the site where the remains were found. The whole place was grieving.

"They want what?" Dragan roared.

"The locals have asked for a vigil, sir. They would like to close businesses early one evening and for everyone to assemble on the foreshore in memory of the boys." Matej had lost the bet as to who would approach the captain.

"But these were thieves and anti-government rebels. They are traitors and should be remembered for what they did." The veins in his neck were working overtime.

"The priest thinks this is a good thing, sir." Matej knew that his boss wouldn't argue with God. But he was the only one.

"When and for how long? I don't want this to go on for hours."

"Well, they are also wanting this for the little girl too," Matej said, taking a few steps back, ready to flee if he had to.

Dragan was caught now. To deny them that might create suspicion where he didn't need that at all.

"Find out when they want this bloody thing and just get it over and done with." Better to be conciliatory, he thought.

Matej began to back out of the door. "They have asked if you will be attending …"

"Get out."

A deep sigh as he ambled his way down the stairs.

The priest, two officers and the reporter finalised the main requirements for the vigil with some of the locals forming a working group to help with the smaller details.

The reporter agreed to print posters to be distributed, and the priest and policemen agreed that it should be held as soon as possible.

> VIGIL: In memory of Luka, Roko, Sam, Josip, Tom and Bruno and to pray for the safe return of Mira.

The messages went out the following day for the event to be held in the late afternoon two days hence. Candles and flowers were collected by the working group and food would be available after the service that would be led by the priest. Everyone wanted to play their part.

Posters were also sent out with the boats, again, to make sure that everyone in the region had the chance to attend.

"Mara, you should come to the vigil. Even if we only stay for a short time. Then we can start to plan to say goodbye to Luka. It will be good for you."

"How can it be good, Ana? Luka is dead and Mira is gone.

Nothing is good anymore. I have no reason to live without my children!"

She is right, thought Ana. I don't have any reason to live either.

"Okay. Let's see what happens. You might change your mind on the day."

"I won't Ana. No one will understand and if all it takes is praying, then why aren't Luka and Mira here with me now! It's all I've done since they have been gone!"

CHAPTER 13

It seemed as though the perfect opportunity had landed in their laps when Rosa showed them the poster for the vigil in Zadar. They couldn't believe their luck.

"That's perfect," exclaimed Luka.

"Yes. With that many people, our plan should work out. We can leave here mid-afternoon. That should give us plenty of time once we get to Zadar."

"I just hope you can convince Mama to come to the boat Dinko. She might not believe you," Luka said, still unsure.

"Leave it to me and Rosa. We can be very convincing."

"I just hope my parents can keep it quiet," Tom said, also concerned. "They will go to the vigil to pray for my death. They can't leave happy."

"I am sure they will understand the risk to you both, if the secret gets out. Don't worry now."

Neither boy got much sleep that night. They talked long after they went to bed. And after only a couple of hours sleep, they lay awake and talked again.

Luka couldn't accept that Roko, Josip and Bruno had perished, if in fact the remains were Sam's.

"What if one of the others borrowed my shirt, Tom? We still don't know for certain who it is."

"I know. There must be some way to find out."

"Let's wait till after today is over. Then maybe we can come up with some ideas."

Several of the other men who fished from Sibenik were also going to pay their respects and suggested they go in one boat. Dinko had to quickly deal with any expectations by saying that he and Rosa might take a trip further north, so they wouldn't be returning that evening.

He had hoped that his friends wouldn't see through this as being a highly unrealistic prospect, as Rosa had never really spent any time on his boat and appeared to show little interest.

Luka and Tom hid in the small cabin beneath the wheelhouse as the boat chugged along the coast for the one-hour trip. Conditions were calm but even though they had spent a lot of time on the boat over recent times, the deck was far more comfortable than the cabin. They couldn't see out, but once the boat started to slow, they knew they were close. Both feeling the anticipation in what was ahead.

The boat pulled into the far end of the jetty as they had agreed. There were already many locals assembling at the site. There were flowers everywhere and people seemed to be waiting for the service to start so they could light their candles.

Dinko spied the three policemen talking to the priest and a small group of people. They looked as though they were making final arrangements.

Then Dinko and Rosa opened the small door to the cabin below to go over the last-minute instructions.

"Okay. It looks as though they might be ready to start. Tom, you are first. Keep the blanket over your head and stay low on the deck. When you get to the gunwale, look across and see if you can find your parents. Once you have pointed them out, Rosa will approach them. She will then try to get them back to the boat."

"Oh, and Rosa. Make sure you tell them clearly that there is someone who has news of the boys that wants to speak to them. And them only. If the police find out, then he will be arrested, and all hope will be lost."

Rosa took her husband's face in her hands and kissed both cheeks. She was doing everything to hold back the tears.

"There! Tom pointed to his mother and father with tears already streaming down his cheeks. That's them. My father is wearing the brown trousers with his black suit jacket. Mama is next to him in black with the white flowers."

Rosa double checked to make sure and then started to walk towards them. Dinko was standing next to the boat to greet them as they came back.

Luka could pick out Josip and Bruno's parents but not Sam's. He was surprised to see Roko's mother and father but thought his father would only be there because he wouldn't want to look bad.

"I can't see Mama. Or Teta Ana?" Luka was getting more and more anxious.

As Rosa was nearing Tom's parents, the priest asked everyone to bow their heads in prayer. Dinko watched Rosa as she spoke to Tom's parents. He saw Tom's mother put her hand to her mouth as his father grabbed hold of her.

"Now! Come on!" Dinko whispered urgently. "While their heads are bowed!"

"Dinko, Mama and Teta Ana are not there." Luka was peering frantically over the edge of the boat.

"Wait, Luka. Be patient. I am sure they will come."

The next minute, Tom's parents turned and started to walk towards the boat as they had hoped. Dinko had to hold him back from jumping onto the jetty.

"Wait here, Tom. We want them to come on board. Go into the wheelhouse. You too Luka. When they are here, we can ask if they know about your Mama and Teta."

Rosa was talking gently to them as their sombre faces barely registered what they were told to expect. It was getting darker now.

"This is my husband, Dinko," Rosa said as they shook hands.

"I am sorry for the secrecy, but this is too dangerous any other way. Please come on board the boat so we can talk. But be very quiet. I urge you." Dinko helped Tom's mother as his father followed.

"Hello, Papa." His father turned to see Tom stepping out from the wheelhouse. His mother was just caught by Dinko as it looked like she was about to collapse.

"Tom!" They grabbed their son as he tried to wrap his arms around both at once.

"My boy. My Tom." His mother ran her hands through his hair and around his head. Tears of joy from everyone.

Then her hand flew to her mouth as if she had seen a ghost. Luka stepped out behind Tom.

"My god. Luka? Is it you? But you are dead?" Dinko started to tell them quickly what had happened when Luka interrupted him.

"Have you seen Mama? And Teta Ana? Are they here? I can't see them. I have to see them!"

"Oh Luka, your Mama is so upset. She didn't want to come. I know the priest tried but she refused."

Luka's eyes darted around. This isn't happening, he thought.

And for a split second, he thought he may as well crawl back into the cabin. At least Tom had been reunited, maybe they could tell his mother.

But then something clicked inside him and before anyone could stop him, he leapt over the edge of the boat and ran along the jetty till he could see the sand appear from the water below.

"Shit!" Dinko could only watch the boy run.

Luka jumped from the jetty onto the beach and hid for a moment under the wooden struts. He had clear sight of the vigil, so he could keep an eye out as he made his way to his home. He kept low and moved between places he could easily hide.

Dinko and Rosa lost sight of him quickly.

He crossed the wide cobbled promenade and hugged the tall wall that surrounded the old town. The shadow keeping him hidden to the corner. Once he was past the corner, he could easily move between the houses without being seen.

As his home appeared in the distance, he crouched behind a rock wall and took another look around, hoping that no one else had stayed home this evening.

Crawling along slowly, peering up and over every now and then. All was clear. All he needed to do was to cross the gravel road, and he would be at his front steps.

He looked up at his house. That's weird, he thought it is in darkness. Mama always has the oil lamp burning at this time of night.

He had one more look around, then he sprinted across the road and climbed the steps to the door two at a time. His hand on the knob, he slowly turned it and slithered through the opening, closing it quickly behind him.

"Mama. Mama," he called quietly as he crept through the darkness. Going room to room.

Shit! She's not here. Not imagining where she could be, he went into the bedroom he shared with Mira and sat on her bed, placing his hand on her pillow. "Where are you, Mira. What has happened to you." Tears fell uncontrollably.

What do I do now? His mind raced. Teta Ana! That's where she will be.

He peered out of the kitchen window to check if anyone was outside. Then creeping back through the front door, he walked quickly across the road before hurdling back over the rock wall.

Keeping low, he made his way past the church onto the dirt road to his aunty's home.

He gasped as he saw the light in the distance and almost sprinted without taking another look around. Keep calm, he told himself. I can't just burst into the front door, it will be too much of a shock.

He sat leaning against the wall for a moment, breathing heavily. He checked the time on his uncle's watch.

The watch! Yes. If Mama and Teta are in the kitchen. I will creep into Teta's bedroom and leave the watch on the bed. If I make some noise, she will come and check, then find the watch. I can then come out of hiding slowly.

There wasn't any time to think of a better plan and he was terrified that if he did just walk in, one or both would start screaming. Or maybe worse, they would have a heart attack.

Checking once more, he walked towards the old house. He ran up to the front wall and slowly edged himself up till he was standing alongside the window.

Peering in, he could see them sitting at the table. The sadness in their slumped bodies was almost too much for him.

He took a deep breath, then moved along the side wall next to the garden, till he reached the window into his aunt's bedroom.

Nothing was ever locked in anyone's home, so he was able to hoist himself up and crawl through. Landing as softly as he could, he quickly removed the watch and placed it on the bed.

That will have to do. All I need is to get her thinking.

He crawled under the bed and knocked hard on the wooden floor beneath him.

"What was that? Ana's voice travelling from the kitchen. Did you hear that noise?"

He knocked again.

The scraping of the chair and footsteps told him they were going to look around.

"Grab the broom, Mara," he heard his aunt say.

The door to her bedroom creaked open slowly and the light from the oil lamp spread across the floor.

"Oh my God, Mara! Look on the bed!"

"The watch? But how did it get there? And whose is it?"

"Mara. It was my husband's. I gave that watch to Luka."

"But how? And who?" Mara with the broom raised above her head.

Thinking that the time was right, and they were already shocked at the sight of the watch, Luka slowly slid from under the bed. "Mama. Teta Ana. It's me." He placed a finger to his mouth to try to keep them from screaming out.

"What? Luka!" Touching, holding and sobbing in disbelief.

He had to pull himself away to speak as they sat either side of him on the bed. Holding his mother in his arms as his aunty took out her rosary beads and kissed each of them, in between kissing his hands.

He told them as much as he could with the little time he knew was left. Their heads constantly shaking at Luka's return from the dead.

"God willing this will happen with Mira, and she will come back to us."

"I will try to find her, Mama. I promise. Have the police told you anything?"

"Nothing. Pigs! They were too worried about looking like the idiots they are when it looked like you had escaped."

"I will try to think of some way, Mama, but in the meantime, I will leave you an address of some people in Sibenik who have been taking care of Tom and me. They will let you know where I am and get messages to you and Tom's parents if needed. If there is anything you need to tell me, just contact them. But please be careful."

He stood up with them still wrapped around him.

"God has brought you back to us, dragi. But the remains they found. If they didn't belong to you, then who do they belong to?"

Luka didn't share what he knew about his shirt. Not until he could discover the truth.

"I don't know, but I plan to find out."

And with that, he carefully made his way back to the jetty. He scurried back along the tall wall again and could see Dinko's outline standing near the boat.

He made it onto the sand and hid under the jetty until he had a clear run to the boat.

The people were starting to disperse and were wandering all around the waterfront.

Shit! I'm stuck. Someone will see me.

The flowers had been left along the beach as a mark of respect, and Luka caught sight of a bunch just to the other side of where he was hiding.

Creeping slowly, he took hold and slid them towards him and held them up to his face. He turned and walked towards Dinko, lowering them slightly so he could see it was him.

The relief on his friend's face was palpable.

"Hurry! Get back into the cabin!"

Luka leapt back onto the deck. Tom's arms grabbed his shoulders. Luka grabbed him back. The smiles on their faces said it all.

"I saw her, Tom. I saw Mama. She knows I'm alive."

They headed below as Dinko shifted the throttle into gear and the boat sputtered to life. Rosa slid next to him in the wheelhouse and put an arm around his back.

"You are a good man, Dinko. You have made these boys very happy."

Her arm stayed around him as he steered them south to home.

Evening had turned to dark in Zadar as Mara and Ana held each other tightly after they watched Luka disappear into the evening.

"I can't believe this, Ana. Luka is alive. I had given up any hope. For him and for Mira. It makes me feel like a bad mother. A mother should never give up." She wiped her face with her apron.

"It is a miracle, Mara. Let's just be thankful that he is with us again."

"What do we do now? I can't just sit and wait."

"Let this sink in first. We need to rest. Then maybe tomorrow we can make some plans. I think it would be great to take a trip to Sibenik. We should do it soon." They both smiled.

CHAPTER 14

Two new officers greeted the boys as they finished breakfast. "Roko. Josip. You can come with me. Bruno, please go with my colleague."

"But why can't we stay together?" The butterflies in Bruno's stomach started to flutter.

"Our boss wants us to interview you separately this morning. Don't worry, it will be alright."

Easier said than done, they thought, as they followed the two uniforms back to where they were the day before.

Bruno kept his head down as he went in alone. Sensing Roko's eyes bore into him as the door closed.

The other two boys took their seats in the adjacent office.

"Wait here. The boss will be here soon. He has to make a phone call first. He shouldn't be long."

They were left alone. As was Bruno.

"Bruno needs to keep his mouth shut. I bet it was him who didn't stick to the story. That's why they are keeping us apart."

"Shut up Roko! Don't you think we all know what will happen if we say anything? It won't just be you who gets into trouble!"

"That's bullshit. They could promise him anything! He's in

there telling him now. I'll be sent back and then what?" Roko leapt up and tried the handle, then started banging on the door.

"Hey! Let us out. You can't keep us locked in here."

Moments later, the door flew open. Roko charged at the officer, fists and arms swinging. "You can't keep me here! Let me go!"

The officer did his best to restrain Roko, but it wasn't until another officer arrived that the situation was able to be contained. Roko was directed to sit back down on the chair or risk further trouble if he didn't comply.

Roko buried his head into his folded arms on the desk in front of him. Whilst he didn't want anyone to see his tears, the shaking of his shoulders gave it away. One of the officers stayed with them until Roko settled down.

"Is there anything you would like to tell us Roko?" The officer had been instructed to keep probing the boys.

Roko shook his head. Still buried in his hands.

"That's okay. Take your time to think. We are having a very good discussion with your friend in the next office anyway."

Little did they know but Bruno was sitting quietly alone.

Roko sobbed harder.

The senior customs officer, Gino, had made several attempts to contact the police in Zadar.

"What time of the day do these people start work?" he muttered to himself. "It will be lunchtime before anyone answers."

One more try.

"Hello. Zadar Police. This is Matej speaking." He had heard the phone ring a couple of times but decided that finishing his cigarette was more important.

"Yes. I am the senior customs officer in Ancona, Italy. My name is Gino. Can I speak to your captain, Dragan, please?"

"I am sorry, sir. He is not in the office. Can I be of assistance?" Matej was curious to know why they would be calling back.

"Your captain called me several days ago to enquire about six boys that had escaped from Zadar. He was asking if there had been any reports or sightings of the boys at sea. I would like to speak with him further about this situation."

"Yes. I was the one who had placed the initial call to your people. I can discuss this with you, if you wish."

"Your captain seemed somewhat frustrated in our previous call. However, I was not in a position to discuss anything with him due to investigations that we were making at the time. We have now been able to make some progress, and I hope to have a more reasonable discussion with you."

Reading between the lines, Matej knew exactly what he meant about his boss's frustration. Their heads only just missed the flying chair that seemed to follow that phone call. The captain was clearly unhappy.

"Of course. Please continue." Matej rifled through the drawers at the same time, for a notepad and pencil.

"Before I do start, are you able to provide me the details of what actually happened regarding the escape of the six boys?"

Matej took the Gino through the events leading up to the discovery of the human remains, and then the subsequent outcome of the investigations carried out by the police and the doctor.

"We have reached the conclusion that the boys drowned and that the remains appear to belong to one of them."

"Can you please tell me the names of these boys," came the reply as Matej finished.

Matej obliged. Seeing no harm in sharing the information as it had already been published in the newspaper.

"Well, that is even more interesting," came the next response.

"How so?"

"Well, you say that six boys named Luka, Roko, Sam, Tom, Josip and Bruno all escaped by boat from Zadar. And that the conclusion you have reached by investigating some remains is that they all drowned. Is that correct?"

"Yes, sir. Even the doctor concluded that this could be the only reasonable possibility." Matej anxiously awaited the support from another authority and started to wriggle uncomfortably in his chair.

"Well then. How is it that the Italian Coastguard intercepted three boys in a wooden boat who informed us that they escaped from Zadar some days before? And their names are Roko, Josip and Bruno." He stopped there. Waiting.

Matej's ears could not believe what they were hearing. He slumped back into his chair with the phone's handset still in his hand, his elbow now resting on the desk.

"Holy hell," he whispered.

"Hello. Hello, are you still there?" The customs officer began to realise the impact of his question.

"Yes. I am here. I am sorry but this is a shock. You say you have three boys? Roko, Josip and Bruno? In a boat?"

"That is correct."

"And did they say that there was only three of them?"

"Yes."

"Are you sure, sir?"

"That is what they have said but I think there is more to the story than they are telling us. One of them said four in his interview but then changed it to three. He said it was a mistake, but I didn't believe him. We are still pursuing that line of questioning."

It struck Matej that this could now go a number of ways depending on what he did next. He needed time to think, and he needed the Italians to keep this quiet until he could work it out.

"Okay. I will need some time to review all of this and to report this to my captain. As you may understand, we have informed families and made public announcements. This will need to be handled very delicately." His left leg bounced uncontrollably at the thought of telling the captain. God. What an awful mess.

"Can I please ask that you give me some time? I will call you as soon as we have discussed this. Could I ask that you also keep this between us for the time being?" Matej rummaged in his pockets looking for his handkerchief to mop the sweat forming on his brow.

"Of course. I understand completely." A smile on his face now. That will teach that arrogant captain a lesson. If it wasn't for the Italians, there would be families who would continue to suffer because of the incompetence of the Yugoslav, not the Italian, authorities.

After he finished the call, Gino returned to where the boys were waiting.

"Has anyone said anything further?" he enquired of his officers, as they moved out of earshot.

They reported Roko's reaction and distress from the belief that Bruno was providing them with information.

"Okay. I have received some very interesting information from my phone call. Let's interview Roko by himself. Tell him that we have finished with Bruno. Bring the other two in together."

"Josip." Both boys looked up. "Can you please join Bruno in the next office. My colleague and I need to speak with Roko alone."

Josip stood and looked down at Roko. Unsure whether he could do or say anything, before walking out into the hallway.

Gino and his colleague shut the door behind them. Then Josip heard the click of the lock.

"What did you tell them, Bruno?" he said as he leaned up against the wall, looking at his friend.

"Nothing. I was sitting here alone. I thought they were speaking with you and Roko?"

"They tricked us, Bruno. They know something and now it will be easier for them to make Roko talk. Especially if he thinks that you have already told them something."

"Well. I might have accidentally said something Josip."

"What? What did you say?"

"When they asked me to say how we escaped, I accidentally said the four of us, not three. Then when they checked that with me, I realised my mistake and changed but they kept asking why I said four and not three. They kept confusing me, Josip."

He sat down next to Bruno, leaning close to his face. "What were you thinking? Now this will fall back on all of us if they don't believe it. And Roko is really losing it." Josip leant back in the chair with his arms behind his head.

"What do you think he'll do?" Bruno faced him.

"I don't know. But we can't do anything more but save ourselves and hope that he is not sent back. I am getting really worried for him. And for us."

The reaction in Zadar was equally concerning. Matej leaned back in his chair reading over the notes he had taken from the phone call. He scratched his head then shook it in disbelief.

He did not intend to say anything to the captain or his colleague. He couldn't trust what either might do.

No. This needed to be thought through very carefully, and right now the only person he could trust was himself.

The first thing he would do was try to retrace their steps. There might be something they missed in the initial investigation.

CHAPTER 15

Luka and Tom were too excited to sleep after they returned from Zadar. The reunion with their parents was almost too much for them.

"I wish we could have just stayed there, Luka."

"Me too, Tom. But there will be time for that. We need to find out what happened to the boat and the others. And who belongs to the remains," Luka said, settling down into their haystack beds.

"And then, I need to find Mira."

"I will help you Luka. She must be somewhere." Tom's eyes were closing quickly.

Luka heard the rhythm of Tom's snoring moments later. He lay awake thinking for the next hour until, he too, started to snore. The beginnings of a plan started to form.

Daybreak saw them already up and helping Rosa in the kitchen. She was covered in flour as she kneaded the dough for the day's baking.

"There was a time that I only needed to make one loaf, and it would last two days. I now make two loaves, and they only last one day!" she laughed joyfully.

"We have to feed our young adventurers, Rosa! I can already see

that they have been making new plans since our trip yesterday."
Dinko was clearly enjoying the new lightness in their moods.

The trip to Zadar had been much more than he could have
ever hoped to be able to give to the boys. And their families.

"So, let's hear what you have dreamed up overnight. I could
hear you talking till very late!" Dinko was keen to join in any
action that was ahead.

They all sat at the kitchen table, talking over one another as
they recounted the details of the previous evening.

A new day was beginning. And the hopes of Luka and Tom
were rising.

The fence that surrounded the schoolyard in Zadar, where Mira was
last seen, seemed to have fresh flowers strewn along it every day.
The locals seeming to want to keep their hopes alive for her return,
especially after the news about the boys drowning had been spread.

Dragan was leaning against the streetlamp across from the
school gate again. He had returned several times since that day,
lost in the memories and savouring every moment.

"Why are you standing here again?" An old lady had been
watching him for some time unsettled by his frequent appearance
over the recent days. "I have seen you here before. Unless you
have any police business, there is no need for you to be watching
these children. You should have been here to when that child
disappeared. It's too late now to take an interest"

This made him smile.

But I was here, you stupid old woman, he though as he walked
off.

She decided to tell one of the other policemen about this.

Captain Dragan's reputation for violence and having an eye for young women was well known to locals. And after Mira went missing, everyone was keeping an eye out for anything that looked suspicious. Policeman or not.

She marched up to the police station as soon as he turned his back.

"Is anyone here? I need to make a report," she shouted from the bottom of the stairs.

Zlatko appeared from the tearoom.

"You can make your report to me. What is it?" He was feeling impatient after his tea break had been cut short.

"I don't like it that your captain is standing around the school so much. I have been watching him, and I think he is looking at the young girls!"

Matej stood quietly listening to the conversation from the top of the stairs. Out of sight.

"But madam, he is the captain of police! He is probably wanting to keep a close eye to make sure it doesn't happen again." Zlatko was taken aback at the old woman's accusation.

"Rubbish! Everyone knows what he is like. I am near the school almost every day. I have seen him many times leering at the young girls playing. I'm just sorry I wasn't there the day that poor Mira went missing!"

"Are you accusing the captain, madam?" Zlatko said, now incredulous.

"I'm not saying yes or no. But it looks very suspicious to me." And with that, she stormed off.

Zlatko scratched his head, not knowing what to make of her outburst. But as he made another mug of tea, he decided it would be better for his career and his safety to forget what she said.

Just the ramblings of an old woman, he thought.

Matej crept back into the office. He wouldn't forget what she said and started to make notes about what he heard. After what he had learned from the Italians, nothing would surprise him anymore.

And only minutes after the old woman left, they heard whistling through the front door. The boss seemed to be very happy with how events had turned out.

"Zlatko, is that tea you have just made?"

"Yes captain."

"Why don't you and Matej take a proper break? Go for a walk? Have a coffee in town."

"Sure, Captain. Thank you, Captain!"

"Matej, are you coming?"

Zlatko didn't wait for him to change his mind as Matej slowly lumbered down the stairs.

The kitchen table conversations went well into the morning and there was no point going out in the boat to fish at this late time. Besides, there was planning to do.

Rosa's feet seemed to glide across the floor as she worked around the three men. Her singing and Dinko's smiles made the home seem much warmer than it had been for many years.

What joy, and pain, these young men have brought into our house, she thought, listening as she worked.

"But how can we find out about the boat?" Luka pressed Tom and Dinko for solutions.

"Something made the police in Zadar confirm the drowning. Do they know more than they are telling anyone?" Dinko said, working through possibilities.

"We could get a message to someone to find out for us. Dinko, could we try one of our parents?"

"That's a good thought, but we need to be careful who we ask in the police."

"And who should do the asking."

Something was sitting at the back of Luka's mind that he couldn't quite remember. Someone that might be able to help.

Suddenly he had it.

"There was a policeman in our house when they took my father away."

"Not that bastard, Dragan!" Dinko quick to react.

"No, I think his name was Matej. He came back the day after to apologise to us for what happened. It didn't make any difference what he said to us at the time, but he did say, if there was ever anything he could do to help, we should ask," Luka said trying to remember what he looked like.

"Actually, I think he was at the vigil. He was speaking to the priest." Luka was now putting the pieces together.

"Do you think we can trust him, Luka?" Tom asked, feeling nervous.

"I don't know. But who else can we ask at the station? At least it's a start."

"I think Luka is right, added Dinko. I wonder if your mama or aunt will come with me? I could say I am a family friend."

"Which you are, Dinko." Luka put his hand on the big man's shoulder.

"Well, um, yes," Dinko said, feeling overwhelmed at the boy's show of affection. "Rosa, I think we will make another trip to Zadar soon. Luka. Tom. I think you need to stay here for now.

We will go the day after tomorrow. Let's say we are paying our respects. If anyone asks."

Matej and Zlatko had made it as far as the harbour. Seated on the rock wall, facing the sea with plumes of smoke rising as they took advantage of their boss's good humour.

"Do you believe it, Matej?"

"Believe what, Zlatko?"

"Believe that those boys drowned?"

"Why do you ask?"

"Well. I'd never say this to the boss, but we never really had enough evidence to say they had. I think it was too soon to close the investigation."

Matej thought about whether he should share his information from the Italians but decided against it. He didn't know how much he could trust that his younger colleague could keep it quiet from the captain.

"Whether it was or not, the decision was made way above our pay grade. Zlatko," Matej said, trying to feign disinterest when his stomach was churning over the same thing. Of course it was too soon, he thought.

"Should we start to investigate the missing girl now? I don't think that crazy old woman was right to make those accusations about the boss, but we really haven't even started to look."

"Maybe we just do this quietly, Zlatko. For some reason, the boss thinks she has left on purpose, or the mother has had something to do with it. I don't agree with either. Even though some families do send their girls sent away to work. Cooking, cleaning or looking after children. It helps bring in money. But this is different."

"So, where do we start?"

"I don't know. Let me think about it. Let's go back. We still have our reports to finish, and I don't want Dragan thinking we are taking advantage of his good mood."

They entered the station and climbed the stairs to the office, only to overhear the captain in a loud and obviously pleasant conversation on the phone.

"But of course, Inspector. Thank you for taking the time to make this call. Yes, I was suspicious right from the start and followed my instinct all the way. We knew exactly where those boys were going, it was only a matter of time."

Matej's eyes nearly got stuck in the back of his head he rolled them so hard.

"I will have my final report to you as soon as possible. Yes, the case is closed to my satisfaction and all leads were investigated. This was obviously an act of theft and deception carried out by the six boys and a clear threat to the state."

God, he hated the back slapping. Matej went to go down the stairs but stopped after hearing the final words from his captain.

"A promotion, sir? Well, I'm not sure I deserve this, but it would be a great honour. Of course, I understand you need to speak to the senior administration at police headquarters. Thank you, sir."

Mm. I wonder what will happen to that promotion when he finds out that three boys are very much alive in Ancona, mused Matej. I will keep that up my sleeve. Then I can retire.

"I'm going out, Zlatko. You stay and finish the report. If the boss asks where I am, tell him I had to run an errand."

"Sure, Matej."

Matej had to think. Where could he start without opening wounds any more than they already were.

Suddenly it came to him. He would start to make discreet enquiries about the missing girl, Mira. Maybe that would lead to something that they missed.

He made his way towards Mira's home first. They need to know we are taking this seriously, he thought. Maybe the mother or aunt can shed more light.

As he came up the steps, he swore he could hear two women talking. But they seemed to be talking happily, not what he would expect at this time.

That's strange, he thought. We have just held a big vigil after her son's remains have been confirmed and, her daughter is missing. They seem so happy. Something didn't feel right.

He stood next to the kitchen window. While he couldn't make the words out clearly, they weren't the words of a grieving family.

He cleared his throat loudly.

Silence.

Then he knocked at the door.

It seemed to take longer than normal for the door to open but Matej was a patient man.

"Who is it?" Ana's voice came from the other side of the door.

"It is Matej. From the police. I was wondering if I could speak with Mara?"

The door opened slightly, and Ana peeked through.

"Why do you want to speak with her. Haven't you brought enough misery to our family?"

"I would like to ask some questions about Mira's disappearance."

The door closed again. He waited.

Then Ana opened the door fully. "Come in."

Something is different, he thought as he looked at Mara.

A policeman's instincts can be very useful, especially when he is surrounded by emotions. His were telling him that he should pay attention.

Deciding to get straight to the point.

"Do you know where your daughter is, Mara?"

"What kind of a stupid question is that? You are a bigger idiot than I thought." Ana flew at Matej.

"Ana. Stop. It's okay. Let him do his job. At least he is asking questions. Not like his boss." Mara was very aware that they had to maintain some control.

Some of the local women had shared some of the things they had heard Dragan say about the disappearance of Mira.

"To think that he might say you sent the girl away to work. And only ten years old. He must be stupid."

And among themselves, "Yes, but maybe it's for the girls own safety. We all remember what happened to Marko. That captain always seemed to take an interest in Mira. Maybe she had to."

Matej pressed on.

"So, you can confirm you know nothing about where she is."

"Yes."

"Can you describe how she was behaving the last time you saw her?"

The questions kept coming. Some were repeated but phrased slightly differently, as if to catch them off guard.

They were keeping up the façade until Matej announced he only had a few more things to add.

"So, you never saw Mira leave. Didn't see where she went. And you said she never arrived home from school."

"That's correct."

"And you are certain she didn't follow or go with Luka."

'To Sibenik? Are you kidding?" Ana's hand flew to her mouth as Mara looked in horror.

"Sibenik?"

"No. I meant out in the boat. They must have headed down that way." Ana unable to disguise her dismay at her own stupidity.

"But you said 'Sibenik'. That must mean you must know something more about Luka. Why did you say that? "Matej had hit the jackpot.

Matej thought about this for a moment then decided to go with his gut. "Did Luka go to Sibenik?"

"I have nothing more to say. It was a mistake. Now you must leave. Enough with all of your questions." Ana stood and guided him to the door.

He saw Mara look away and knew that he was onto something. He could feel it gnawing at him.

As she held the door open, he turned back to them.

"Mara. I remember the night when Marko was taken. I came back to see you the next day because I was truly sorry for what Dragan had done. I understood why you must have hated me too. But back then I was too scared to challenge him. For my job and for my own safety. I have regretted that ever since. Now, with all that has happened, I want to help in any way I can. I meant what I said back then, and I mean it even more now."

Mara turned and looked up at him.

"No one knows that I am here today. If the captain knew, I would lose my job and maybe even be sent away. But I am near retirement anyway and I don't care anymore. I know enough about him to think that he can't touch me anyway. Please. Think about what I have said."

And with that, he turned and slowly made his way down the steps. The door closed behind him.

Why did she say 'Sibenik', he thought. That was an odd response to the question.

Some way further down the path, he stopped and sat against a rock wall and took out his notepad and pencil to write notes so he could review them later.

He wrote three headings and jotted points under each. Hoping that something might jump out.

<u>Information from Italians</u>
- Three boys from Zadar
- Escaped by boat
- Three but maybe four. Is someone lying to cover something up?
- No other evidence

<u>Outcome of Zadar investigation</u>
- Six boys escaped.
- Stolen boat.
- Human remains washed up on beach.
- Red shirt

<u>Additional information—Mara and Ana</u>
- Deny knowing anything about Mira
- Sibenik. What does that have to do with anything?

He read and re-read his notes with the gnawing feeling still bothering him, becoming more intense each time he looked.

Then it hit him. Of course, that was it! He slapped the book against his leg, sprang to his feet and marched back towards the house.

Knocking so loudly that they had to answer.

"What now?" Ana stood back in shock as he charged past her without stopping to be invited in.

He slapped the notepad onto the table and placed his two hands on top. Leaning towards Mara, he started to share what he believed he had discovered.

"There were never six boys in the boat, was there! That's why all of this has become so confusing. I knew there was something strange, but it wasn't until you mentioned Sibenik that I knew the Italians were onto something!"

They had no idea why he was rambling on about the Italians, but they stayed frozen with their eyes locked on each other. He seemed to be telling all of this to himself, oblivious of their presence.

"Only some of the boys were in that boat. And some escaped by land. They must have done that to throw us off the track. Of course! It's brilliant. And that's why, senora, you let it slip about Sibenik. And why you both seem to be acting differently now. I think you know that Luka wasn't in that boat and that maybe, you know he is still alive."

Ana's legs started to shake, and she quickly sat down next to Mara.

He continued to reveal his suspicions noting that there wasn't any resistance to what he was describing.

"How am I doing?" he said finally as he sat down at the table. Stimulated but exhausted at the same time.

Mara stared at him for what seemed to be the longest time. Willing herself to place trust in a man who was responsible for the disappearance of Marko.

Then finally she spoke. "You say you want to help us."

"Mara. No. Don't do this." Ana pleading with her.

"This is my decision, Ana. I can't keep living like this. We need help. For Mira and for Luka."

"I give you my word. Whatever you tell me stays between us. I want to help. You must believe me."

"Ana. Please bring another plate and fork. Matej, you will stay for a meal. I will tell you everything you need to know."

She put her hand on top of his and squeezed it.

"I knew back then that you were truly sorry for what happened to my Marko, but I had to hate you. It was the only way I could stay strong. I will trust you now but please don't hurt us again."

And for the next few hours, they spoke about what she knew.

Matej felt the relief of someone who had been pardoned for some great wrong and almost felt taller and lighter when he left their house.

His chin raised and chest puffed out, he took the path back to the station.

He did not care one bit what his boss had to say when he returned.

This was his investigation now.

CHAPTER 16

Paulo had returned and brought in some sandwiches and a glass of milk for Roko, placing them on the desk in front of him. Roko hadn't lifted his head at all since Josip had been asked to leave.

"My boss, Gino, will be joining us soon, Roko. Please eat something."

Roko, still with his head down, muffled a snotty reply, "No thank you. I'm not hungry."

The older officer returned, placing some documents on the desk and shuffling them around.

"I see you have calmed down Roko. That is good. I hope we can continue our conversation without any more trouble. Do you think you can do that?"

"Yes, sir."

"Now sit up please so we can hear what you are saying. I have something I want you to hear, then I will ask you some questions. Is it okay to proceed?"

"I suppose so."

"I have been speaking with your police in Zadar."

This caught Roko's attention immediately. It didn't go unnoticed by either officer.

"They have reported some interesting information that I would like to share with you."

Roko wiped his nose and eyes with his sleeve and looked at the man as he began to outline the key points. He made no mention of the remains, thinking this might be useful later.

"They have confirmed that six boys escaped after stealing a boat. After completing an investigation, which included checking if there had been any reported sightings of these six boys at sea, they concluded that all boys must have perished."

"But how could they know that if there wasn't any evidence?" Roko taking a new interest in the discussion.

"I will get to that later. But in the initial call, they were clear that there were six boys, so we had no reason to disclose your arrival. Until now."

"Why now?" Roko hoping for more information.

"Well, your friend, it seems, accidentally mentioned four of you and not the three that we were initially led to believe were in your boat. This caused us to go back to your police to ask further questions. It was then that we were told of the final conclusion that the Zadar police had made. Do you follow me yet, Roko?"

"Not really. No"

"I asked them the names of the six boys and they said," he referred to his documents on the desk, "Luka. Sam. Tom," then he waited for a moment while looking directly at Roko, "Josip, Bruno and ... Roko."

Roko continued staring at him. Not saying a word.

"I thought to myself, Roko. It is too much of a coincidence that I happen to have three boys in my building who have also escaped around the same time and their names are also Josip, Bruno and Roko. Do you agree that this is too much of a coincidence?"

Roko knew they had been beaten. It didn't matter which of his friends made a slip by saying that there were four of them, not three in the boat. What mattered was why only three of them made it to Ancona.

He took a deep breath in, then exhaled loudly.

"I think you want to talk, don't you, Roko. After all, it must be hurting you to keep everything inside. We can see that you are upset," Gino said trying the soft approach now.

Roko slumped into the chair.

"I will tell you everything but first, I would like my friends to be here when I do."

Paulo whispered something into the older man's ear as he was shaking his head. Roko could see that he wasn't in agreement with the request.

The older man waved him away.

"I think we should hear what you have to say. My colleague is concerned that you might be trying to influence your friends in some way by having them here while you tell us what happened. I am going to allow it. But Roko, I will be asking them to confirm what you say is correct. And to be clear, your ability to be approved for a visa to stay here, relies on the truth. Do you understand?"

"Yes, sir. I do."

Two other chairs were brought in along with the other boys.

"Please sit down, boys. I am going to tell you what I have shared with Roko. Then Roko has agreed to tell the truth about what happened."

Gino repeated the story to them as they sat quietly listening. Josip and Bruno gasped upon hearing that they had all been declared dead by the police in Zadar.

"But our families? They think we are dead. God, how can they have said that sir?"

'That is something that we still need to find out. But for now, I want to get to the truth about what happened. This will be very important for your future here," Gino said, not wanting there to be any misunderstanding.

"Now we come to the discrepancy about who was in your boat. Were there three, or in fact. four boys? Roko?"

Another deep breath but this time trying to stifle the tears that threatened to come again.

"There were four of us," he replied softly. The officers nodded at what they had suspected to be the truth.

"Please continue, Roko."

"Four of us left in the boat. Me, Josip, Bruno and Sam."

"And where is Sam now?"

Gasping to speak now. "It was an accident. Sam was drinking all of the water from the can, and we were running out. None of us knew how long we would last out at sea or if anyone would come and rescue us." The tears wouldn't be stopped as Roko struggled to speak.

"Please go on, Roko." Another gentle nudge.

"I told him to stop …"

"And then Sam stood up and wanted to fight Roko but when he did, the boat started rocking." Josip interrupted, catching Roko by surprise.

"And Sam fell, hitting his head on the oarlock. There was blood everywhere and we couldn't do anything." Bruno also started to cry.

Roko looked from one to the other, not believing what he was hearing.

"What did you do then?"

"Well, sir. Roko was so upset at what happened, he just held Sam, and we all took turns trying to wake him and hope he was going to be okay. But he wasn't. And then he died." Josip chipped in again.

"What did you do with the body?"

"We were so scared that we would get into trouble if we had a dead body. So, we talked about it, and all agreed."

"Agreed what?"

This time Roko took over.

"We agreed that we should bury him at sea, sir. I was the one who lifted him and put him overboard." Roko dropped his head again. The shame came not from what he did with Sam but for doubting and getting angry with Josip and Bruno.

They had come to his rescue now.

"Is this what happened, Josip and Bruno? Are you telling the truth?"

"Yes, it is," they responded together. "But Roko also said prayers for him too."

Both officers sat looking at the boys.

"Well, I must say that this is one of the most tragic stories we have heard. And we do hear many stories of refugees who want to come here but are lost at sea. But none as young, or as brave as you. I can understand why you couldn't say anything. I am sorry that you have lost a friend."

"What are you going to do now? You can't send us back." All of them now plead with Gino.

"I will need to review everything that we have. Including how we deal with your police now that they have declared you to be dead. Clearly your families need to be told that you are safe, and I am not sure how your authorities will deal with that. We all know how your country treats its people." The man worked through possible scenarios as he spoke.

"The one thing I can assure you is that we will not put you in harm's way. But this may take time and some sensitive negotiations. While we work through these, you will stay here with us."

"And if you can get agreement from the Zadar Police? What will happen then?" Roko trying to find hope.

"We will arrange for you to be taken by train to an immigration camp. You will be given jobs and looked after until you decide what you would like to do next. There are a number of countries who are accepting migrants, such as Canada, the United States and Australia. We can arrange for you to visit those embassies to arrange visas. That is the best outcome that I can see for you, but it is a long way off. Let's take one day at a time." He stood to leave, shuffling the papers again. "For now, go back to the dormitory and get some rest. It has been a tough day for you."

Deciding that there was no point waiting another day, and with the insistence of Luka and Tom, Dinko and Rosa set out for Zadar the following morning.

"I will bring some crostoli with me, Dinko. Then it looks like we are paying our respects. We need to remember that we can't look happy."

The trip took just over an hour and apart from some cursory glances from some of the other fishermen at the harbour, they went unnoticed as they walked towards the row of houses that Luka had described.

This time, when they knocked, Mara opened the door. She had to stop herself from hugging them with glee for taking care of her boy. Instead, once they were inside, they greeted each other warmly with Ana also joining in on the reunion.

"What news of Luka? Is he alright? And Tom?" Mara was eager to hear everything that they had to tell. Even as far as what he had eaten the day before.

"Maybe we should let Tom's parents know you are here? They can also visit?"

"Let's wait for the moment. We have some things to discuss with you first," Dinko said, not wanting to stir up too much excitement at this stage.

They went over everything that had happened from the time that the boys escaped up to Mara and Ana reliving the moment that Luka came back that evening during the vigil.

"My heart was filled with so much joy," Mara said almost singing, "it was the most wonderful feeling. But then I had to think about my Mira, and I had to suffer again."

Dinko and Rosa couldn't imagine what that must have been like as a parent, but they could certainly understand the loss. They had both grown very fond of Luka and Tom. Their home felt so much different now they were sharing it.

"The boys want to find out what happened to their friends," Dinko said, shifting the conversation now. "But we need to have help to do this. It seems very strange that without any other evidence, the police have declared them to have drowned?"

"Yes, I agree. And who do the remains belong to now? Thank God, they are not my Luka." Mara was starting to see a way forward.

"We had a visitor last night." Mara relayed to them the conversation with Matej and his offer to help them.

"Wasn't he the one that Luka mentioned, Dinko?" Rosa inserted herself into the discussion.

"Yes, he was, but do you think we can trust him to help us, Mara?"

"I don't think we have a choice. Ana, maybe we can see if he can meet with us today? You could go to the station and ask for news about Mira?"

Ana still wasn't one hundred percent sure that they were doing the right thing by involving the policeman, but even she couldn't argue that there wasn't any other option.

She hurried out of the door to go to the station.

Matej was surprised to see the old woman so soon after they had met. He sensed her apprehension about him and thought she may have persuaded Mara to decline his offer to help.

Just as he agreed to meet, Dragan came down the stairs, hearing the voices from his office.

"What did she want?" he demanded.

"They are still asking about our investigation into the missing girl, sir." Matej decided to needle his boss at every opportunity to see his reaction.

"How many times do I have to say it? There is no investigation." He huffed and puffed as he yelled back.

"I will go and speak to them, sir. It may be that they just need to be told more than once. Don't worry, I'll go straight away."

"Good. Maybe they need to be better parents and stop their children from running away," he said as he turned and climbed back up the stairs. He mumbled something else that Matej couldn't make out, but it didn't sound good.

I will write that in my notes too, he thought. Why is he so adamant that we ignore this?

Matej couldn't describe the reception he was given as welcoming, but it was definitely an improvement on the day before.

The big, bearded man known as Dinko pressed Matej on everything that Mara had said about him. He even mentioned how badly he had been treated by the police when he was arrested all those years before and then saved by Marko.

"This is not a threat, but a promise, Matej. If you betray me or this family, I will make your life hell. Do you understand?" Dinko said, now standing nose to nose with Matej.

Matej stood tall and did not move. He kept hold of Dinko's gaze. "I also made a promise last evening and I do not intend breaking it."

"Good. I think you need to tell us what the police know about this whole mess. And don't leave anything out."

Matej described their response from the very first day when the boat was reported stolen, up to and including the vigil. He described his captain's insistence on closing the investigation, despite the fact that it was too soon. He told them about making contact with the Italian Coastguard and customs office in Ancona.

"The initial calls did not result in anything," he said, "the Italians reported that no one had seen six boys in a rowing boat or found any evidence of them. But then, I took a call that was meant for the captain." Matej proceeded, unsure whether he should disclose this to them.

"Yes, go on." Dinko said, sensing that he needed encouragement.

"First, I need to say that no one else knows about this, not even Dragan. And I don't want to tell him yet."

Matej then filled them in on his call from the senior customs officer.

Wide eyes and looks of amazement greeted him as he revealed that five of the six boys were in fact alive.

"But that is incredible. Roko, Josip and Bruno made it. Luka and Tom will be ecstatic!" Rosa couldn't contain her joy for the two boys. She couldn't wait to get home and tell them.

"But the remains. If no one knows where Sam is, do they belong to him?" Dinko was puzzled.

"All I know is that the Italian authorities were still questioning the three boys. I said I needed some time to think about everything, especially how we would inform the parents. And even worse, how the captain reacts when he finds out that he was wrong."

"You are right. This is a very delicate situation and the fewer people that know, the better. But thank you, Matej, for trusting us also. It seems we each have something that will ensure we have mutual trust."

"What do we do now?" Ana pressed.

"We can't do anything until I hear back from Italy. At least until, we are certain we have all the facts. But you must tell Luka and Tom the great news. I just hope we can also find out where Sam is." Matej felt part of something good for a change.

"But what about Mira?" Mara said after they had all spoken of the positive news.

Matej felt the as though the wind had been taken out of his sails on hearing her name.

"I haven't forgotten about her, Mara. It's just that we don't have anything to go on at the moment. But I am sure that something will come along. I promise to keep looking." Matej still felt uneasy about how Dragan was acting in response to the missing girl, but it would have to wait until this was sorted. Or if any evidence came to light.

Matej left them with a promise that he would make contact if he heard any new information from the Italian authorities.

Dinko and Rosa, eager to tell the boys the news about their friends, also left soon after.

"It should be me telling Luka," Mara said sadly.

"Yes, Mara it should be you, but how wonderful it is to know that he has Dinko and Rosa to keep him safe for us now." Ana squeezed Mara's hand as they smiled at each other.

CHAPTER 17

They heard the truck rumbling up the gravel road in the distance and both boys rushed outside to greet them. Luka ran to the driver side door to open it.

"How is Mama? What did you find out? Is there any news about Mira?" Luka hardly took a breath between questions.

"Slow down, Luka! Let's go inside first. There are many things to tell you."

"Did you see my parents too?"

"Not this time, Tom. But Luka's mother or aunt will get a message to them to say that we had visited. After what we heard today, we all decided it was better to keep it as quiet as we can. At least for now."

"Tell us then. Please."

"Rosa, let's have some wine and food." Dinko felt like they should celebrate.

"After you tell them, husband. Do you think I want to miss out on seeing their faces?"

"Okay. You might want to sit down first. Roko, Josip and Bruno," the boys took in a deep breath as Dinko mentioned their names, "they are alive. They made it across to Italy."

"What? Are you kidding Dinko?" Their faces were aghast at what they were hearing.

"Yes. They are alive."

Rosa hugged each of them and in turn, they hugged Dinko as well. "I don't believe it! But how?" Tom struggled to figure it out.

Dinko told them everything they had been told by Matej. Almost word for word as each boy kept checking with him to see if what they were hearing was true.

When he finished, they all fell silent.

"So, what happened to Sam then? Are they his remains they found on the beach?"

"They don't know Luka. And as far as everyone else still thinks, the remains are yours. And we need to keep them thinking that way, especially Captain Dragan. God knows what he will do if he finds out."

Matej eventually made his way back to the station to find Zlatko and Dragan waiting for him.

"Well? Did you sort that mess out once and for all?"

"I think so, sir. But I don't think they like the police very much. I was only allowed in the house for a brief moment before they asked me to leave."

"We can't do anything about that. This is not a popularity contest after all. Now, I was just telling Zlatko that I have been summoned to a meeting with my superiors. I expect it is something to do with the promotion they want to give me for solving this case," Dragan said, beaming at them.

"Well, congratulations, sir. That is a great honour." Matej felt the bile rise in his throat at the thought of it.

"Yes it is, Matej. I will be out of the office tomorrow and I'm not sure when I will be back. You will take charge in my absence."

"Yes, sir. Thank you, sir."

I will contact the Italians while he is away, thought Matej. Hopefully they can give me an update on what they have found out.

"If you have nothing further to finish today, go home. I am going to find somewhere to have a drink and celebrate my success. It's not every day you get a promotion!"

They watched him leave.

"You don't look very happy for the boss, Matej?"

"That's because I'm not sure any of this is over yet, Zlatko. I'm going home. See you tomorrow."

Later that night, Dragan stumbled his way up the narrow stairs to his tiny room. He felt for the lock and fumbled for his keys in the dark. He could hardly stop himself from swaying. The taste of rakjie was still in his mouth.

His necktie hung loosely around his unbuttoned shirt and his waistband seemed to have given up trying to keep his shirt tucked in.

The woman that he had spent the last hour with, after he had finished drinking, had done little to satisfy him.

She was too old anyway, he thought. He conjured up the images of who he really desired and felt the familiar stirring.

He stumbled to the mirror, taking some time to focus on his reflection. "Inspector Dragan," he said slurring his words. "Not bad for a kid with a hare lip. Too bad that bitch isn't here to see me now. Then she would think differently about Dragan," he yelled with his fist raised.

He laughed loudly, repeating, "Inspector Dragan. Inspector Dragan." A loud bang at his door was followed by an equally loud voice. "Hey, shut up in there you drunk idiot. No one cares who you are at this time of night. Keep the noise down."

With that, Dragan lunged at the door and flung it open to find an old man standing there, fists at the ready.

"Come on. Fight me," the old man challenged.

Dragan took one look and laughed before pushing the man with all his weight, sending the man backwards as he screamed at Dragan. A door opened and a woman rushed out to the man's side. Helping him to get to his feet.

"Leave my husband alone. Can't you see he is an old man?"

"Then keep him inside, or else the next time he wants to fight Dragan, he won't be able to get up! Ever."

Dragan turned and went back to his room, slamming the door behind him.

"Fucking peasants. When I get this promotion, it will be time to find somewhere else to live. Somewhere that is better suited to an inspector!"

Within minutes, he was on his back, still fully clothed and lying on his bed. And there will be many more privileges for an inspector, he thought as his hand started to move south.

There was a significant change in Roko, Josip and Bruno at breakfast the following morning.

"Hey, remember that magazine we saw under the jetty that day?" Josip remembered it all very clearly.

"Yeah, I remember," said Roko laughing, "your kurac was very interested Josip!"

"So was yours! Especially at the size of those breasts!" They all started to laugh at the memories.

Roko stopped suddenly and put his spoon down, before looking at them both.

In a whisper that only they could hear, "I don't know how to thank you for what you did yesterday. And I feel terrible for thinking that you would be any different."

Bruno spoke first. "We decided that we couldn't let them send you back, Roko. Not to what you left behind. All of us have seen what your father does to you and to your mama. You have had more punishment in your life than all of us together."

"Bruno is right, Roko. When we talked about it, while they were interviewing you, neither of us wanted it any other way. What happened out on the boat was an accident. We know you didn't mean for anything bad to happen to Sam."

For the first time, Roko's tears fell in joy and friendship rather than in pain and suffering. His friends had helped him out this time, but he knew he would still have to live with what he had done.

"I wonder where Tom and Luka are?" Josip said, changing the subject.

"Yeah. I wonder if they made it very far. Or if they are even here yet?"

"Do you think we will be able to find out?"

"I don't know but maybe we can ask after that officer has spoken to the police back home."

"But they think we are all dead? And that the body parts belong to Luka."

"Do you really think they are Sam's?" Bruno questioned it now.

"It's hard to know for sure but I guess they have to be with Luka's red shirt in the netting as well." Roko went silent again.

"Let's stop talking about this now. There's nothing we can do. Hey, maybe they have a football we can kick around outside?" Josip said.

It took three attempts before the woman at the customs office in Ancona answered the phone.

"I am sorry, sir, but the senior officer is not in today. Can I take a message for him?"

"Yes. I am with the police in Zadar. He knows who I am. My name is Matej. If you could please ask him to call me back as soon as he is able, I would be grateful."

"Certainly, Officer. I will personally see that he gets this message."

As Matej hung up the phone, he thought he should have emphasised that the call should only be to Matej. Heaven forbid if the captain took the call. But after recalling their last conversation, he felt satisfied that the customs officer understood the possible implications if that happened and gave it no further thought.

Luka and Tom raised their glasses to Roko, Josip and Bruno surviving the crossing. Luka couldn't help but feel relieved and happy for Roko. At least he will have a better chance being away from his father, he thought to himself.

As they talked about their three friends, Luka decided it was time to ask Dinko for the biggest favour. He hoped that he wasn't stretching their friendship.

"Dinko. Can you take us to Italy?" The original plan that

Luka had thought when they first met Dinko, seemed even more important to them now.

Rosa grabbed her husband's hand as if to show her support of Luka's request.

"We need to see our friends and I need to know what happened to Sam," Luka said, pleading.

"I made a promise to your Mama and the others that we would wait to hear back from the policeman first. The great news is that we know they are alive. I will be happy to take you across to Ancona but only after we hear back from Matej. I hope that you understand the position that we are in, Luka."

'We do, Dinko," Tom answered for them both. "And we could never repay you for what you are doing for us."

"Luka's father saved my life. I don't think there is anything you need to do to repay me. That is more than enough. We should hear something any day. Rosa can make a call to Matej at the police station from the church. I am sure the priest will say it's okay."

Matej sat at his desk, working his way through the notes he had taken. He couldn't believe how big this mess had become. The scenarios that he had run through his mind, from telling his captain, through to the parents finding out that their boys were alive were all nearly impossible to plan.

And in every one of them, he saw the reaction of his captain. And that was only the ones he could predict. Matej couldn't imagine the desperate lengths that Dragan would take to protect his reputation, and now his promotion.

"I don't want to be a part of this," he muttered under his breath. It can only end badly. But what can I do?"

He reached for his typewriter and started to type out his notes. As the sentences formed, the path started to emerge for him and he knew what he needed to do.

When he was satisfied with the final document, it was already the middle of the afternoon.

It doesn't look like I will hear back from Italy today, he thought as he folded the paper and placed it in an envelope.

Maybe I will leave this with Zlatko, he thought as he slipped it into the pocket of his jacket.

Zlatko was just entering the building as Matej was leaving.

"Where have you been all day?"

Zlatko looked slightly guilty.

"Well, I thought with the boss away, I could start asking some questions around town. About the little girl, Mira."

"Oh? And did you find anything?"

Zlatko's head dropped. "Nothing, Matej. But it is bothering me that there isn't anything."

"It's good that you are trying, Zlatko. Just remember what the boss said, okay? You don't want to get yourself into trouble with him over this. I'll see you tomorrow."

The panel of suits sat across one side of the long table. Dragan was frozen in a salute on the opposite side.

The room was large and palatial with heavy velvet drapes secured with gold tassels across the imposing windows. The view from behind them stretched along manicured gardens with ponds dotted between them. Dragan took it all in before the formalities began.

The police headquarters building was impressive and the time that it had taken to make the journey from Zadar to Split had been worth it, thought Dragan.

One day, this will be the view I see every morning, he thought, smiling as he anticipated the future he had been dreaming of since becoming a policeman.

Lots of paper shuffled and throats cleared before the chairman introduced those present.

"Please be seated, Captain."

There were questions from each of them, ranging from enquiring as to why Dragan had joined the police force through to his achievements as a captain over recent years. He congratulated himself for making sure that his reports through to his seniors captured his actions in a positive light. There was never any doubt about where he wanted his career to head.

As his audience with the senior ranks was closing, the final comments were made by the chairperson.

"Captain Dragan, please stand."

Dragan's knees wobbled as he nervously stood, hoping to hear what he had been waiting to hear.

"The panel will now consider everything that has been discussed today. As you are aware, the decision to promote any officer to the senior rank of inspector must be unanimous. We will therefore review this information carefully. We also need to be satisfied that a rank of this importance will be able to be occupied appropriately. You will receive our decision in writing at the earliest convenience. Thank you for attending today."

Dragan felt slightly let down by the lack of an immediate outcome. Without letting his shoulders drop as he stood to attention, he thought that they could have invited him back the following day, especially as he had travelled far to attend.

Oh well, he thought. There is no chance that I will miss out after everything they heard today. I am sure that I will be wearing the suit on an inspector very soon.

He relaxed after the last man left. The next train back to Zadar wouldn't be until early the next morning. I can at least start the celebrations here tonight, he thought as he almost skipped down the winding marble staircase to the front reception.

Believing that his boss wouldn't be back that day, Matej decided to sit for coffee in one of the small shops in town before heading to the office. Zlatko can be charge for this morning, he thought. It will give the boy some responsibility.

Zlatko heard the phone ringing as he approached the front door to the building, just catching it as the caller was about to hang up. Breathless, he answered.

"This is the Zadar Police. Zlatko speaking."

"This is the customs office in Ancona. My name is Paulo. A message was left by one of your officers, Matej? It was left for my senior officer, Gino, but he has been called away and has asked me to follow this up."

"I am sorry, sir, but Matej isn't in the office yet. I am Zlatko, his colleague. Can I take a message?"

"Um. No. I was informed by my boss that I was to only speak with Matej."

That's funny, Zlatko thought. Why would Matej only want them to speak with him?

"I can leave him a message, Paulo. I am sure he will be here soon. Are you sure you can't give me some idea for the call?"

Just then, he heard footsteps coming from behind, "Wait.

I think I heard him coming," Zlatko turned to the door only to see it wasn't Matej but his captain returning early from his trip away.

"Who is it, Zlatko?"

He placed his hand over the mouthpiece, "It's the customs people from Ancona sir. They want to speak with Matej."

Dragan grabbed the phone from the unsuspecting officer.

"Yes. This is Dragan. I am the captain of the Zadar Police. Whatever you want to tell Matej, you can tell me. We have no secrets between us in this office."

Zlatko stood as Dragan waved at him to get up so he could sit on the chair.

"Boys? What boys are you talking about?" Dragan's face contorting and grimacing as he listened.

"Rescued by the coastguard? There were four, but only three made it? Escaped?" The realisation of what he was hearing, along with the fact that Matej had kept this from made him apoplectic.

Zlatko couldn't move as he watched his boss's face turn purple with rage. Dragan's hand become a tight ball as he banged it several times on the desk.

He picked up the phone and tore it away from its cord, throwing it across the room. Then he slowly turned to Zlatko, with a look of pure hatred.

Zlatko shivered, unable to move quickly enough as Dragan lunged at him with arms outstretched and grabbed his collar with both hands. The captain slammed him against the wall and shook him violently. Zlatko's head hit the wall hard. Dragan's face was only inches from his, which forced him to look away.

"Did you know about this?"

"No, sir. Please. I knew nothing, sir." Zlatko was terrified of what might happen next.

"How long has Matej been talking to the Italians behind my back!"

Zlatko was still pinned to the wall.

"I don't know. Please believe me. Today was the first I knew of any of it, sir."

He felt the captain's hands relax and when they let go, he reached for something to hold onto, for fear he would faint.

"Find that bastard, Zlatko. Arrest him and bring him to me. No one deceives Dragan and gets away with it. I will make him pay for what he did."

Zlatko looked at Dragan with wide-eyed shock at the command he had been given.

"But why, captain? What am I arresting him for?"

"For withholding evidence. Deceit. And insubordination. That should keep him locked up till he is just rotting flesh. Now!"

Zlatko walked quickly out of the building as Dragan made his way slowly up the stairs to his office.

Matej started to walk towards the office. He was enjoying the autumn sun and the respite from constantly feeling as though they were walking on eggshells around the boss. It was nice to have some peace, he thought.

He even started to whistle as he turned the last corner that would take him down the street to the police station. In the distance, he saw Zlatko sprinting towards him and immediately sensed something was wrong.

Zlatko kept turning his head back as if he was being followed. He seemed to be waving for Matej to turn around and go back.

Matej stopped as the young man caught him under the arm and started to lead him back around the corner from where he came.

"What is it, Zlatko? You look like you've seen a ghost. What's wrong?" Matej became very worried for his colleague.

Breathing hard for the second time that day, Zlatko tried to sound coherent, but the words kept falling over each other leaving Matej grasping to make sense of them.

"The captain! Phone call. Ancona. The missing boys …"

Matej went pale.

"He wants me to arrest you, Matej!" Zlatko said, now very distressed.

Matej now led the young man out of sight, understanding what must have happened to lead to the captain wanting his head on a plate.

"So, Dragan knows?" He had anticipated that this would happen sooner or later. "Zlatko. Listen to me. I know what I am doing but I can't involve you. It's too dangerous and if the boss even suspects you know something, you will end up in the same place as I might."

"But Matej," he tried to say, "why does he want to arrest you?"

"Because he is a madman, Zlatko. This will ruin his chances at a promotion because it will be an embarrassment to the government. Not to mention that it looks like we were trying to cover it up."

"Now, this is what you are going to do. You will go back and say that you couldn't find me. And that you thought I would be back in the morning. Make something up. Like I had to follow up on a report about a stolen bike. Just try to reassure him that everything is normal."

Zlatko nodded furiously.

"You can say that I was definitely coming back into the office as I expected to hear back from Ancona."

"But I had no idea you had even called them, Matej. Otherwise, I wouldn't have let him take the phone off me. I could have lied for you." He sniffed back the tears, feeling guilty for the innocent part he played.

"It doesn't matter now, Zlatko. Its better you didn't know." Matej placed his arm around Zlatko's shoulders.

Reaching into his jacket pocket, Matej withdrew two envelopes. "But there is something you can do for me, my friend."

"Anything, Matej. You know you can trust me."

"Get in early tomorrow morning. Before Dragan. Leave one envelope on his desk. Let him think that I left it there."

"What's in it?"

"Just the outcome of my investigation and something for him. I am going away for a while, Zlatko. Don't worry, it will all work out. I hope."

"And the second envelope?"

"If anything happens to me, promise me you will send it to the police headquarters. It explains everything they need to know."

He hugged the young man then walked away quickly.

Taking a few deep breaths and placing the envelopes in his pocket, Zlatko walked back to the station, rehearsing his lines for the captain. I just hope he believes me, he thought. For all our sakes.

CHAPTER 18

Matej folded his uniform neatly and placed it on his bed next to the other two sets that were issued every couple of years. He held his cap and badge up to look at them for one last time. Fifty years, he thought. I have given service to my community through many troubles and wars.

I am finished now. He placed the cap on top of the folded uniforms and put his badge in his pocket. Just in case, he thought.

Packing a light bag, he quickly surveyed his small flat before closing and locking the door. He didn't want to be seen by any of his neighbours, so he crawled through the open window at the end of the landing and climbed down the narrow fire escape to the tiny lane below. Past the piles of rubbish and through the rickety wooden gate that would take him to the back of town.

Once on the road, he planned to catch a ride to the place where he could finish what he had planned to do.

He would go to Sibenik and convince Dinko to take him to Ancona.

Zlatko crept back into the police station. Careful not to alert Dragan that he had returned. He felt for the envelope in his pocket and decided to sneak up the stairs. Maybe he could leave it on the desk now rather than wait for the morning.

As he reached the top, he could see that the door to the boss's office was ajar and could just make out the captain speaking with someone on the phone.

"Yes, that is correct, commodore. We have been informed that the fugitives have been apprehended and are being held in Ancona. Yes sir, that is what I am requesting. Any assistance that the navy can give me, and my men to repatriate them back to Yugoslavian soil, is most appreciated. As you can understand, this could be a major embarrassment for our government if this is not done discreetly. Yes, I can confirm that I will be accompanying your officers to make the arrests myself. Thank you, sir. I will expect to see your men, and the boat, first thing in the morning."

Dragan was about to hang up the call. "Just one more thing, commodore, the fugitives will not be returning to Zadar. Yes, that's correct. I will confirm their final destination with you later today."

Shit, thought Zlatko. He's going over there himself. But how can I warn Matej?

Just then the door flew open, and Dragan stormed out.

"Well? What are you standing there for? Where is he?"

Zlatko drew a deep breath. Be brave, he thought. For Matej.

Standing to attention and saluting, "I could not find him anywhere, sir. But I do recall that he said that he needed to be back in the office tomorrow as he was expecting that very important phone call. I believe it was the one you took." He felt the sweat from his armpits.

"But he doesn't know that I took the call, does he Zlatko?" Dragan saw how this might unfold to his advantage.

"No, sir!" Zlatko saluted again and clicked his heels. Don't overdo it, Zlatko, he thought to himself, you'll give it away by stupidity.

"Very well then. I will tell you exactly what I want you to do, Zlatko. And be warned, this is a direct order. If you disobey me, just like your traitorous colleague has done, you will experience the same fate. Do I make myself clear?"

Zlatko walked away with the orders he had been given, feeling a sense of dread but also grateful that he knew that Matej wouldn't be back the following day.

How could the captain expect him to arrest his friend and colleague, then take him to the gaol until Dragan returned?

Zlatko sat on the bench outside, rolling tobacco slowly in his fingers with a cigarette paper stuck to his lip.

He hoped whatever Matej had written for the boss would put an end to this and maybe he wouldn't need to be arrested. He slipped it out of his pocket again. For a split second, he thought of opening it.

No. Matej trusted me to do one thing. I can't let him down now, he thought as it went back into his pocket.

Dragan spent the next few hours making the necessary arrangements for how he would deal with Roko, Josip and Bruno. For all intents and purposes, they will stay dead, he thought. Or near enough after I have finished with them.

The final call he made before confirming the next day's arrangements with the commodore of the navy and then his captain-in-charge, was to an old friend who worked as the prison warden at the notorious labour camp on the island of Goli Otok. The island was situated one hundred and thirty-seven kilometres to the north of Zadar in the Kvarner Bay.

From Ancona, it was about one hundred and ninety-five kilometres. A powerful boat, like a navy cruiser, could cover the distance in around four hours in calm weather conditions.

Goli Otok had been established in 1949 and was used to detain political prisoners. Particularly those who supported Josef Stalin, after the split between Stalin and Tito. Whilst the brutality of the prison was well known, its purpose changed as time passed, but it still took all manner of criminals, from those who committed serious crimes to common thieves.

Prisoners were treated harshly, with forced labour, limited sanitation, malnutrition and psychological abuse.

Not only did it treat its prisoners badly, but it was a stark reminder to the population of what would happen if there was dissent. It created as much fear externally as it imposed internally.

"Yes, I hope to have them in your custody by nightfall tomorrow. I can't see any difficulties with the hand over from the Italians. They are fugitives. I imagine the Italians will be glad to be rid of them and the trouble they have caused. Yes, I have the necessary authority to act. I met with the senior administration yesterday and they are aware of the sensitivity of the situation. Discretion is the key here my friend."

"You are a master, Dragan. Come and work up here. We could do with someone like you."

Dragan didn't want to disappoint his friend by saying what he really thought of the north of the country, especially the prison islands. It was the last place on earth he would want to be.

"Thank you, my friend. But you are the expert up there. There wouldn't be enough room for the two of us."

"I would always make room, Dragan." He laughed as he hung up the phone.

Pleased with his skills of manipulation, Dragan almost thought this was better than the previous outcome had been. Why settle for them being dead by drowning, when he could instigate their slow deaths to his satisfaction.

Even better that his old friend at the prison would see to it. He needed to finish this, or his promotion would definitely be at risk. And that would not be acceptable. At all.

I will notify the Italians in the morning, just before we leave, he was thinking as he turned his office lights out. That will give them enough time to finish processing what they need to finalise in the four hours it will take for us to arrive. Those boys will be in my custody by early afternoon and then in the camp by evening.

He walked past Zlatko without even a sideways glance, as he left the building.

Only another twenty-four hours and I will be celebrating, he mused. It will be Inspector Dragan then, he thought, laughing loudly as he walked home.

The large truck took about fifty meters to stop, forcing Matej to jog towards it. Climbing into the cabin, he asked the driver if he could take him somewhere near the harbour in Sibenik.

"That's exactly where I am heading, friend! Are you meeting someone there?"

"I hope to. He doesn't know I am coming but its urgent that I speak with him. Maybe you know of him? Big bearded fisherman, named Dinko?"

"That podlac! Of course I know him. I think he can almost drink more rakjie than me." The driver laughed to himself.

Probably remembering the drinking competitions, thought Matej.

"I will take you to him. Maybe you can also buy me a drink afterwards for giving you a ride?"

Matej wasn't keen to get into a drinking session with either man, but if it meant he could convince Dinko, he would happily oblige.

Arriving at the harbour, his new friend decided to come with him to look for Dinko's boat. Matej had offered him two kuna to buy himself a drink, but the man refused.

"It's been too long since I have seen Dinko. We will have a drink together."

Matej sighed and followed the man to where Dinko's boat was moored.

"Mm. He's not here."

"Are you sure this is his boat?" asked Matej.

"Of course I'm sure! The boat is named *Rosa*, after his wife."

The man was clearly disappointed at missing out on seeing Dinko. "I tell you what, friend. Give me the two kuna, and I will drive you out to his place. It's not that far and I can drop you at the end of the road and be back for a drink in no time."

My luck seems to be changing, thought Matej. "I am very grateful for your help, my friend," he said slipping another kuna into the man's hand.

"Anyone who is a friend of the big man, is a friend of mine!"

"What is your name, so I can tell Dinko and Rosa?"

"I am Sime. They know me well. I sometimes take Rosa into town."

"Thank you, Sime. You have no idea how much this will help."

The truck stopped and Sime pointed to the house, which was about a hundred metres up.

Matej calculated he'd had more exercise today than he'd had in the past week, as he trudged along the gravel road.

The knock at the door startled them but as soon as they saw it was Matej, they couldn't have ushered him in quick enough, with a plate, fork and glass of wine on the table even before he'd sat down.

"This is a surprise, Matej. What brings you here? You must have news?" Dinko said, forgetting that Luka and Tom had yet to meet him.

Matej looked at Luka, remembering the first time they had met very briefly many years before. They seemed to acknowledge that time without needing to speak further about it, but Matej understood the trauma that Luka must have felt, seeing his father being taken away. He hoped that what he was doing now, may alleviate the guilt he still felt.

After the warm handshakes all around, Matej sat down and started to tell them what had transpired over the past day.

"And you are sure that he knows that Roko, Josip and Bruno are alive?" Tom asked.

"There is no doubt about that. What I don't know, is, if he was told about Luka and Tom."

"But they might only know that they escaped on foot. Only we know where they are," Dinko said, plotting the information out.

"That is what I'm hoping. But if Dragan is true to his word, he will do anything to make sure those boys stay dead. He has too much to lose if they suddenly reappear." Matej was mindful of how harsh he sounded, but the situation was now desperate.

"What do you think he will do?" asked Luka tentatively.

"It wouldn't surprise me if he handles this himself. He has powerful friends everywhere. I wouldn't put it past him to do something terrible to be certain this whole mess goes away. Quickly and quietly."

Dinko sat deep in thought, taking in everything that Matej was saying.

Dinko then spoke with a strength that Rosa had long forgotten but it was one of the reasons she had fallen for this big, rough bearded man. When Dinko made up his mind to do something, it would be done. And heaven help anyone who stood in his way.

"We will go to Ancona. We will leave first thing in the morning. If this Dragan knows that they are alive, anything could happen to them. You are right, Matej."

"I will pack some food for us," Rosa offered.

"Us? What do you mean us, Draga? It might be dangerous for you to come." Dinko was unsure about how to respond.

She drew herself up to her full height and strode over to where he was sitting. Pointing a finger in his face she spoke, "I promised to take you in sickness and health in front of God, my husband. This also includes dangerous boat trips. You will not be leaving Rosa behind!"

The look of terror on Dinko's face as he bore the full impact of Rosa's reaction was enough to break the tension and they all laughed at how she had reduced him to her size.

And as if he knew he wouldn't win the argument, he laughed along with them.

"There is only one more thing," Matej said, thinking aloud.

"We need to notify the customs officers that we are coming. I don't want to risk us arriving and they are unprepared.

"Good thinking, Matej. We will call before we leave. It will take around four hours if the sea is good to us, so that should give them plenty of time."

It had not gone unnoticed, that Luka and Tom had been silent as they discussed what they would do.

"Tom. Luka. Are you alright?" Rosa asked softly.

This time Luka stood and spoke. "Many weeks ago, my friends and I made our plan to escape. We wanted to find a better life. We all knew the risks, but we never thought we would cause this much trouble. I am so sorry to have brought this to your home."

"This may have been started by what you and your friends decided, Luka," Matej said now reassuring them, "but this means something to all of us in different ways. We are in this together now."

As they all headed to their beds, Rosa wrapped the loaves of bread in cloth and placed them in a bag on the table. The cured meat and cheese would be added in the morning. Nodding with satisfaction at what had been agreed, she blew out the flame in the oil lamp and hummed. This is a good thing, she thought to herself, a very good thing.

CHAPTER 19

It is going to be a beautiful day today, the customs officer thought, as he looked out across the azure waters. He was glad to be going home. I have a feeling this might be a very interesting day, he mused as he started to write up his nightshift report.

The phone in his office was switched over from the main reception at the end of each day. There was the occasional call but unless there was a boat carrying refugees intercepted by the coastguard or a suspicion of contraband, nothing too much happened.

So, when the phone rang again, he was taken by surprise.

"Hello. Ancona Customs, can I help you?"

"Yes. Good morning. My name is Matej and I am a police officer with the Zadar Police. I have been communicating with Gino, your senior officer. Am I able to speak with him please?"

"Well, the police in Zadar must start very early in the day," came the reply, "this is the second call I have received from your office already."

Matej's mouth dropped open, trying to think of what to say

next. "Oh. I am sorry to disturb you again. Did another officer call too?"

"Yes. I imagine he may have been your boss. His name was Dragan." The man started to wonder if the police in Zadar communicate with each other.

"Did he call about the boys that are with you?" Matej was now feeling ill at what might be unfolding.

"Yes. Although he called them fugitives and that they were wanted by your authorities. My understanding is that he will be coming on a navy cruiser today, to take them into custody."

Oh God, thought Matej, this can't be happening. What do I do now? He turned to his friends waiting by the truck.

"I must go. Thank you." There was no point trying to explain to someone who knew nothing.

"We need to leave. Now!"

Seeing the frantic look on Matej's face as he ran towards them, they all climbed into the truck.

"What happened, Matej? What's wrong?"

"Dragan is going to Ancona to arrest them!"

"But when?" demanded Dinko.

"Today."

Dinko had the accelerator flat to the floor as they drove down to the harbour from the church.

"When we get to the boat, remove everything from the deck." Dinko shouted loud enough for the boys to hear in the rear. "We need to get all the unnecessary ballast out. It will give us more speed."

The truck ground to a halt and he had barely pulled on the handbrake as they all got out.

Racing down to the boat, Luka, Tom and Matej formed a line

between the boat and the jetty as Dinko started to decant the large tubs and left them next to the metal cleats.

"That's enough. Get in. Let's go!"

The engine roared as Dinko reversed it away from its moorings, before putting it into gear and taking off at speed.

Come on, old girl, he thought, don't let me down. That naval cruiser will be much faster than us, I just hope we have a head start.

Dragan closed the door to his office just enough to look in the small mirror that was hanging on the back.

Smoothing his moustache and adjusting his cap, he was feeling very confident about how things were panning out. He was certain that he had communicated the gravity of the situation to the customs officer when he had called earlier, and he had little doubt that they would comply with his request.

He made his way down the stairs as Zlatko walked in the door.

"Good morning, sir," he said, standing to attention again and somewhat surprised to see his boss in early.

"Zlatko, I am going to Ancona today to arrest those boys. I won't be back until later tonight."

Zlatko gulped at what he was hearing. Oh no, he thought, this is bad.

"You will be in charge. Remember what I told you to do when Matej arrives. And remember what I also said will happen if you fail." And with that, he turned and strode away.

Zlatko went up the stairs to the captain's office and placed the envelope on the leather writing pad on his desk.

"Whatever you are doing, Matej, I pray that it will rid us of this monster," he uttered under his breath.

The cruiser was waiting for Dragan at the harbour jetty. He spent the first few minutes repeating what he had discussed with their commodore to ensure they understood the importance of this mission.

Yes, this was going to be a very good day, he thought as he sat on deck with his feet up on a handrail.

The sea was calm, and the sun was shining, giving some warmth to the cool morning. And once I have finished today, this whole mess will be behind me, he thought. Inspector Dragan. He smiled as they slowly headed south before crossing into the channel to go through the Kornati islands and into the open sea.

Then dropping his cap over his eyes, he nodded off.

Gino was surprised to see his nightshift officer waiting for him in the reception area of the Customs building as he arrived at work.

"Something must be wrong if you are still here?" he said as the officer followed him through the glass doors to the office area.

The officer briefed him on the two calls that he had received earlier that morning.

"And you are sure he said they were coming to arrest the boys today?" Gino said, looking perplexed.

"That's what the officer said, sir. He didn't give me a chance to ask any questions, just that he would be coming."

"How long ago did he call?"

"Maybe a little more than an hour ago."

"Okay, so that gives us about three hours. Thank you, Officer. Go home and rest. I will need to make some calls."

Zlatko picked up the phone at the first ring.

"Hello, This Zadar Police."

"This is Ancona Customs. My name is Gino, and I am the senior officer."

"Oh, thank God!" exclaimed Zlatko as he started to tell Gino what had happened but was soon cut off.

"There is no time for this, I already have enough information to understand the position we are in. I need to speak with Matej urgently. Is he available?"

"He's not here sir," he said and explained his predicament about his colleague.

"Mm, that is unfortunate. But he did contact our office this morning, so he must be somewhere.?"

"Wait a minute. Hold the line, I will be right back sir. Please don't hang up."

Zlatko bounded up the stairs to the boss's office and grabbed the letter that he had left for him as instructed by Matej. Tearing it open as he came back down, he took the handset and started to read out aloud.

To Captain Dragan
Report into the investigation of the Six Missing Boys.

He skimmed through the details of Matej's recent findings which included the confirmation from the Ancona Customs that three boys had been intercepted by the Coastguard.

His eyes widened when he reached the part about Luka and Tom in Sibenik.

"We already knew this officer. The boys were interviewed and gave a full account of how they managed to successfully escape. It is just unfortunate about the accident and the sixth boy, Sam."

"The remains." It was falling into place for Zlatko now.

"Yes. It appears they may have belonged to their friend Sam. Although without any further forensic testing, no one can be one hundred percent sure."

Zlatko kept reading until he came to the salient part.

I am going to travel to Ancona, with Luka and Tom, to meet with Roko, Josip and Bruno. It has been confirmed that the remains are highly likely to belong to their friend Sam, not Luka as initially concluded.

My movements after I have visited Ancona will not be clear until I can be certain that the boys and I will be safe.

The only way that I believe I can achieve this is by resigning my position, effective immediately.

He read on uninterrupted.

I have made a copy of this report. If anything happens to me or those boys, my instructions are that it is delivered to the senior administration office for police.

"Signed from Matej, "Zlatko breathing out heavily.

Gino was trying to think what this might mean after Matej had called that day.

"We know that Matej is aware of your captain's plans for today because my man told him earlier. But does your captain know about Matej?"

"He hasn't seen the letter, sir. He left before I could give it to him." Zlatko was pleased that he had failed to carry out the one job that Matej had given him.

"Thank you, Zlatko. If Matej is on his way, lets pray that he gets here first." And then he hung up.

The only other call that Gino made was to the Italian Coastguard.

CHAPTER 20

The naval cruiser carved through the gentle waters with speed and ease.

"It shouldn't be much longer now, Captain!" the seaman shouted. "Probably only an hour to go!"

Dragan gave the man a wave in acknowledgement and turned back to look at the sea behind them.

I can't believe they made it this far in a wooden boat, he thought. Under any other circumstances, I would be impressed.

"We will be there soon," Dragan muttered to himself and salivated at the thought of the boys' faces when he would tell them they were being taken into his custody.

The *Rosa* bumped along at full throttle. It wasn't a smooth trip, despite the calm sea but she was giving it her best. Dinko stood in the wheelhouse with Rosa and Matej, while Tom and Luka looked back at the disappearing coastline of their homeland.

"I don't think I ever realised just how far it was, Tom."

"I know. I can't believe they made it either."

"How much longer till we get there Dinko?" yelled Luka.

"Maybe an hour or so," he yelled back. "We have made good time."

"I haven't seen any naval vessels either," Matej added. Keeping his fingers crossed that they wouldn't.

Just offshore from the port of Ancona, two coastguard cutters were cruising out to the open sea after the urgent briefing they had received from the commodore.

The crackle of the radio alerted the cutter's helmsman immediately.

"This is Coastguard One to Coastguard Two. Do you copy, Coastguard Two?"

"This is Coastguard Two. We copy you, Coastguard One."

"Do you have any sightings of the target vessels as yet?"

"Negative, Coastguard One. Nothing to report yet."

The helmsman and navigator were on the operating deck keeping watch as instructed. Suddenly the navigator spied a vessel through the long-range binoculars and gave a nudge and thumbs up to the helmsman.

"Wait! Coastguard One. We have a vessel in the distance. We are going to make our approach now."

"Copy that, Two. Just remember your instructions. Once you have established and confirmed their papers, you will report back to me. Copy?"

'Yes, One. Copy that. Over and out."

The cutter took off at speed and then slowed to pull alongside the vessel.

"Shit. What do they want?"

Everyone congregated on deck to hear the loudhailer.

"This is the Italian Coastguard. Please switch off your engines. We are coming aboard."

Once the rope had been tossed to secure the vessels, an officer from the coastguard leapt onto the deck.

"You are in Italian waters. What business do you have to be here?"

"We are on official police business from Zadar. We have been in communication with the Ancona Customs Office."

"I need to see your papers." The coastguard looked through each of them as he eyed each owner carefully. "Please wait here," he said as he turned and climbed back up to the cutter.

They heard the crackle of the radio but couldn't make out what was being said.

"This is Coastguard Two to Coastguard One. Do you copy Coastguard One?"

"We copy Two. Go ahead."

"We can confirm the vessel and its occupants, One. Awaiting next instructions."

"Please hold, Two. I need to confirm with Base. Over and out."

He shouted from the cutters cabin window to the increasingly impatient audience on the other vessel.

"I am waiting further instructions. Please hold there."

Not far away from where Coastguard Two was holding its target, Coastguard One had also intercepted the other vessel that they had been briefed about earlier.

The two vessels were being questioned closely by the Italian authorities as to their reason for being in foreign waters.

Finally, the crackle of the radio again.

"Coastguard One to Coastguard Two. Do you copy, Two?"

"We copy, One."

"You are clear to escort the vessel into port. Please go directly to the customs building where you will be greeted by the senior customs officer, Gino. Do you copy?"

"Copy that, One. On our way."

There were sighs of relief as the vessel's occupants were advised that they had clear passage into the port. The added touch of an official welcome made them feel even more confident of a positive outcome.

Meanwhile, Coastguard One was advising the occupants of the other vessel.

"We have been informed that we must hold you here until further instructions. I am advised that it will only be for another few minutes. We appreciate your patience."

More deep sighs and swearing under their breaths as they wondered why they were kept waiting.

It took about thirty minutes before they would be given an update, adding to the frustration. As the crackle of another radio alert came through, the helmsman opened the side window from the cabin and yelled out to them.

"We have been given the all-clear to escort you into port where you will be met by a customs officer. Please follow us."

The vessel started its engine and moved in concert with the cutter boat.

The sight of the port made them relax immediately.

"Phew! I thought they were going to keep us waiting for hours."

But then horror struck.

"Oh no. I don't believe this! Are you seeing what I'm seeing?" someone exclaimed.

They looked on to see a group of men standing on the pier in uniform, shaking hands and appearing to greet each other warmly.

And right in the middle, slapping the backs of the others, was the familiar black moustache of Captain Dragan. He appeared to be enjoying the attention and, clearly, there was a mutual recognition between the uniformed men.

The naval vessel had arrived first.

"Do you think they kept us waiting so the other boat could arrive first, Dinko?" Rosa now very worried.

"It looks that way." Dinko's shoulders slumped over the wheel as he manoeuvred his boat with the instructions of the coast-guard.

"What do think they will do with us Luka?" Tom said, wiping the perspiration from his palms on his trousers.

"I don't know, Tom. We've come so far. I can't believe they are so friendly with that prick, Dragan." Luka's fists were clenched into a ball. How great it would feel to be able to knock him out, he thought.

As Dinko edged his boat close to the far side of the pier, a young customs officer took the rope he had thrown and secured it around the bollard on the pier, before asking to come aboard.

"My name is Paulo. I am a customs officer. Can you please come with me."

Crestfallen at the site of the warm greeting that Dragan had received, they followed Paulo in silence.

The lump in Matej's throat was so big, he thought he wouldn't be able to breathe.

It's over, he thought to himself. The bastard has won.

While the uniformed party were led through the large front door into the reception area of the customs building, Dinko, Rosa, Matej, Luka and Tom were taken down a narrow concrete path between the side of the building and a high fence with barbed wire curled along the top.

"This is not looking good," muttered Dinko, "I don't like this at all."

They were led to an office at the rear of the building. The door had a window that was reinforced by wire. Inside, there was a formica topped table with six chairs. On the table was a jug of water and some glasses.

"Please wait here. Someone will be with you shortly. I will bring back some sandwiches."

"Can you tell us what is happening, please Paulo?" Luka asked anxiously.

"You will find out as soon as my senior officer lets me know his decision. This is a very complicated matter, and it is important that we consider all outcomes. Not to mention that we must maintain good international relations," he said and left.

They heard the door click behind him.

"God. We are locked in. What are we going to do now?"

"It sounds to me as though they will make the relationship with our country a priority over what happens to us." Tom was becoming despondent.

"Yeah, it will be easier for us to just disappear if they take us back." Luka dreaded the next few hours of waiting.

Dinko's big arms wrapped around Rosa's shoulders as she drew the black beads from under her collar and began to pray.

Matej hunched forward and stared at the floor as Tom and Luka sat in silence.

The sandwiches came and stayed untouched on the table.

On the other side of the building, Dragan and the naval officers were being led by Gino into a grand meeting room with a huge, polished oak table in the middle.

"Gentlemen, please make yourselves comfortable. I have arranged for refreshments to be brought in for you after your long journey." Gino alerted one of the receptionists that their guests were ready.

"We are truly grateful for your welcome and for your hospitality, sir, it is most kind." Dragan was beginning to think that this was something that would become a regular occurrence once he had been promoted.

"Can I please enquire about how long this situation might take? As you can imagine we are very keen to return the boys to their home. Of course, we will need to complete our own criminal investigations once we return. The wonderful part for me, is knowing how happy their families will be to see them alive." Dragan was enjoying every scintilla of the lie he had created.

"Of course, Captain. It is my pleasure, on behalf of the Ancona Customs to be of service to our friends from Yugoslavia. But first, please eat."

Dragan wasn't hungry at all and would have preferred to get it sorted and get out of there quickly. But thinking that it wouldn't harm diplomatic relations to accept their hospitality, he soon forgot his impatience and began enjoying the offerings.

"Oh. I won't be able to join you gentlemen, I have another matter to attend. Captain Dragan, if you could just present the official request to take the boys into custody to my officer here, I will see that it is expedited post haste."

Dragan almost choked on his food. Official request? But he didn't have one. He thought it was enough to say that his seniors were fully aware. Shit. I need to think of something, he thought, panicking.

"Um. Gino. It was my understanding, when we spoke on the phone, that the awareness of my seniors would be satisfactory in this matter. After all, I am a sworn officer. Surely that is enough?" Beads of sweat started appearing on his brow.

"Yes. Well. It would be most unusual for there not to be some written documentation, Dragan. Whilst I appreciate that you are a sworn officer in your country, that doesn't mean anything here."

Gino could see that his response had upset his guest and quickly clarified his response.

"But under these circumstances, I am sure we can find a satisfactory path forward. I will need to make a couple of calls first. Please be assured that we will do everything in our power to help."

Dragan sighed in relief, but he wouldn't relax until he had those boys locked in the secure cabin on the naval boat and on their way to Goli Otok. At this rate they wouldn't get there till late, and he was hoping that the navy officers wouldn't leave him there to find his own way back. But on second thoughts, if that did happen, he and his prison mate might have some fun with the boys overnight. And no one will ever know.

This was turning from a good day into an excellent day.

After leaving the official party, Gino met with Paulo in their office area.

"You have the others in the back meeting room?"

"Yes, Gino. They have some refreshments, and they won't be able to get out." Paulo felt very uncomfortable at the level of security his boss had instructed him to apply.

"Okay, you know what to do next. I need to contact my superiors to confirm the documentation. After you have finished, meet me back in my office."

"Yes, sir."

Paulo walked through the office space and down the long corridor to where the sleeping quarters and meals area were located. There was a large outdoor courtyard in the centre and as he passed by the long windows that surrounded the external area, he saw the three boys playing kick to kick in the sun.

How much different they look now, he thought. I just hope that the Zadar Police understand that there really isn't any criminal case for them to answer.

Paulo walked into the yard just as the ball came flying towards him. He deftly caught it on his chest and let it roll to his foot before kicking it back to Roko.

"Hey! Great shot Paulo. Come and join us. We can play two on two!" Josip and Bruno were dribbling around the officer as they goaded him to play.

"Sorry guys," he said, starting to feel the sadness wash over him as he knew what was coming next. "Not now. But I do need you to come with me."

"Where are we going?" Roko queried.

"You need to meet some people. Gino and I will be with you. It's okay."

Trusting Paulo fully, they followed him without hesitation.

They made their way through the long corridor until Paulo stopped.

"Okay. Before we go in, I must inform you that my boss will be coming back with me as soon as he finalises some things. Please be patient."

The boys wondered why Paulo made them wait outside but it wasn't until the door opened that they realised.

CHAPTER 21

"Tom! Luka!" The boys rushed inside, surprise and shock on their faces.

"You are here! And you are safe!" They hugged and cried together as Dinko, Rosa and Matej watched on.

They fought over each other to speak as they laughed and cried all at the same time.

Dinko, Rosa and Matej were overwhelmed at the sight of the reunion, and it was only then that they realised the impact this had on the young men.

"My God. What these boys have risked being here today," Dinko muttered as they nodded in agreement.

"Yes. Not to mention what we have had to do as well. I just hope this works out for them," Matej said, sounding nervous.

Once the initial shock had passed, each of them tried to reason what might happen next. But with each assumption came an equal challenge. There was nothing left to do but wait, and as the time passed, no one was feeling confident at all.

Paulo had left them at the height of their excitement. He could only speculate what would happen next.

"How did it go?" his boss enquired when he walked in.

"They were ecstatic, Gino. It's such a shame that they can't enjoy the moment for longer. I just wish there was another way, and we didn't have to do what we must do now."

"I know, Paulo. But this is the right outcome for everyone involved. I have the documentation. Let's go and do this together."

Paulo sighed as walked alongside Gino. He would have loved to open the doors and told them to run but losing his job wasn't worth it.

As they approached, they could hear the talking coming from inside. Gino stopped for a moment to listen before knocking gently at the door.

They stopped as he entered the room with Paulo. The tension in the room was palpable as the men sat down.

"My name is Gino. I am the senior customs officer in Ancona. I am sorry to have to inform you that your reunion must be cut short."

The group gave a collective gasp at hearing this. Rosa grabbed Dinko's hand. Matej sat and waited for the inevitable instruction that the customs service would be handing the boys over to Dragan.

Gino continued.

"Boys, I imagine by now you are aware that the captain of the police in Zadar has travelled here today seeking your extradition back to Yugoslavia to face allegations of criminal behaviour."

Roko could feel the tears come as Luka put his arm around him.

"I have some documents here that I am required to show you. Once you have seen them, you will be taken away from here."

Rosa gasped.

He read each of their names out and then handed them their individual document to review. Their hands shook as they tried to make out what they meant.

Gino then smiled as he said, "Welcome to Italy and congratulations on becoming temporary citizens."

A collective cheer rose up as the moment had sunk in.

"Now. I apologise but I must move you to a safe place immediately. It is a refugee camp that is located about fifty kilometres from here. You will be looked after and be given work until a permanent place is decided. As I did advise you, the Italian government will assist you. Paulo will accompany you to the train. It departs in thirty minutes, so you will need to hurry."

Dinko couldn't believe what he was hearing and almost shook Gino's arm from its socket in gratitude.

"I must also ask you to also leave immediately, Dinko. My men have left a can of fuel on the deck of your boat so you can make the journey back. It's the least we can do for what you have done for these boys."

"But what about Dragan?" Matej asked.

"Yes, leave him to me. I need to deal with that situation but not until the boys are safely on the train and you have left. I don't know how much time I can give you as a start, but I will try to delay them as much as possible."

Luka stepped forward. "We can never thank you enough for what you have done for us, sir."

"Yes, you can Luka. Live the best lives you can. This opportunity may not happen again. Make the most of it."

Matej caught Gino as he started to walk out of the office, shook his hand and whispered something in the man's ear.

Gino looked down at what was in his hand and understood what he was saying.

"It would be my pleasure, Matej."

He turned back to the office to see Luka and Tom hugging Dinko and Rosa, hearing them promise that they will meet again.

He stood back and waited until Paulo arrived. They watched and waved to the five boys as they hurried to the waiting car.

Dinko wiped his eyes with his sleeve as he slapped Matej on the back with his other hand.

"So, what did you say to Gino?"

Matej told them as they walked back down the concrete path that they came. They laughed all the way to the boat.

Gino strode back to the large meeting room where Dragan and some of his navy colleagues were waiting. Making sure that the security guards were standing nearby in case things went awry, he tucked his shirt into his trousers and adjusted his cap before entering the room.

"Gino," Dragan started to say, "I am afraid this is taking too long. I must insist that the boys are handed over to us so we can leave."

"I understand, my friend. As I did say to you, the customs service provided assurances that we would help in any way we can."

Dragan started to shuffle in his seat, sensing he was about to be dealt an unexpected blow.

"I made the necessary calls to my superiors as I was keen to represent your situation to them for their due consideration. Unfortunately, in the time that it took for those representations to be made, the boys were already granted temporary visas to remain in Italy. They are now, temporary Italians which gives them permission to stay."

"They what?" Dragan said in almost whisper unable to conceal his disgust at what he was told.

"I am sorry, but there was nothing else I could do. It was a matter of timing. And as we speak, they are on their way to temporary accommodation.

Please accept my apologies on behalf on my government."

"Do you have any idea what this means for me?" Dragan said, just keeping himself from exploding.

"No, I don't but how about you return and inform the parents that you were singularly responsible for establishing that their sons are in fact, alive and, that they have secured temporary citizenship in our wonderful country. My responsibility is finished now, Captain. You may tell the story as you wish. I advise that this would be the better course of action in relation to your future. Would you agree?"

"You bastard. You tricked me. You never intended to hand them over. I won't forget this. Friend!"

Dragan's chair was knocked backwards to the floor as he stood and stormed out. The naval men following, completely confused at what they had witnessed.

"My security men will escort you to your vessel. I have also asked the coastguard to provide you safe passage until you have left Italian waters. Please heed my advice, Dragan. Nothing good can come from revenge."

Gino followed behind the security guards until they reached the naval vessel.

"Oh, I almost forgot Dragan. Someone asked me to give you this." Gino handed the object to Dragan.

Dragan, looking confused, said, "It's a badge. So what?"

"Your man, Matej asked me to give it you."

"Matej? But how?"

"He was here. And he said, 'Tell Dragan, I quit.'"

Dragan looked at the badge again and then at Gino before spitting on it. Then he drew his arm back as far as he could and tossed it into the water.

"He might quit, but he can't hide." Dragan turned away to climb into the boat as the seaman loosened the rope and rolled it back into the boat.

Gino stood on the pier watching it leave with the two coast-guard cutters in escort, one leading and one close behind.

They would see the boat out to sea as far as they could, making sure that it wasn't able to make any ground on Dinko who had already had a good head start.

"If I ever see you again, Captain Dragan, it will be too soon," Gino muttered under his breath as he wandered back to his office. "This will be a very satisfying report to write."

CHAPTER 22

Dragan was oblivious to the question from the helmsman as he considered how to recover from this absolute betrayal. He was still seething.

"Sir!" The man yelled this time.

Dragan jumped.

"What?"

"Where are we going now? Our orders were to take you north, to the island."

"No. Forget that. We will go back to Zadar. Now leave me alone. I need time to think."

I'm very happy to leave you alone, the seaman thought as he returned to the boat's operations room. Dragan watched the helmsman and his navigator talking.

They are talking about me, he thought. This is humiliating. How dare anyone do this to me?

Just then Gino's words came back to mind.

How the hell am I going to turn this mess around? he thought, feeling more and more irritated. And how did Matej get here? Who was he with? Dragan now believed that there were invisible forces conspiring against him.

And then as swiftly as his conundrum had arrived, it dissipated.

Save yourself, Dragan, he thought. You are still in line for a promotion and as that bastard, Gino said, no good can come from revenge. Well, maybe not this time.

He would arrange to meet with the priest when he returned and tell him of the miraculous news. That the boys were safe and well. Then they would meet with each of the parents, leaving Sam's to last. He would just have to deal with the questions as they arose.

Maybe a town celebration would help them forget the original outcome of the investigation. Anyway, what other conclusion could they draw? They had human remains as evidence.

Yes, this could work in my favour, he thought with increasing confidence.

I could be a hero in all of this.

⚓

With a mixture of sadness and joy, the others on the *Rosa* watched as the Italian shore disappeared.

"I can't believe how they pulled that off. I wish I could have been there to see the look on his face when Gino told him!" Matej took immense pleasure at the thought.

"I hope they'll be okay," Rosa added wistfully. "They may have come a long way to now but there is still a long way to go."

"They are safe, draga," Dinko said, chiming in to reassure her. "This danger is over for now. And I can say I wouldn't have missed being a part of it for anything in the world."

"Me too, dragi, me too."

"So, what are you going to do now that you have no job, Matej?" Dinko asked, looking ahead.

"I really don't know, my friend. The police force has been my life, and I had never thought I would finish, let alone be driven to quitting. But that monster. I couldn't stand working another day with him as my boss."

"What are you like at hauling fish?" Dinko winked at Rosa as she smiled knowingly back at him.

"Well. I've never had to," Matej was uncertain of where this question was taking him.

"I've just lost two good workers and while two old men like us won't be nearly as good as them, I think it could work. What do you say, Matej?"

"You won't be able to go back to Zadar while Dragan is still there. Not yet anyway. And we have room for you to stay. Besides, my husband is right. Neither of you is getting any younger!" Rosa said and laughed, clearly in support of Dinko's proposal.

Matej's eyes glistened as he looked at his new friends.

"Thank you both. Maybe just for a while, but I do have to make sure of a couple of things when I am back." Matej was thinking about the impact of his letter and wanted to ensure that Dragan understood its implications.

"Great! Then it is agreed."

The train station in Ancona had opened in 1861 and was the most important station within the region. However, it had received substantial damage during World War II and had only recently undergone reconstruction work. The boys' train would be heading towards Rome as the camp they had been assigned to was situated about eighty kilometres from the Italian capital.

Once aboard, they didn't have to wait long before the train

pulled slowly out of the station. The five boys waved back at Paulo through the windows as it drew away. There had been two officers assigned to escort them through to the army, just to make certain they arrived.

"I've never been on a train before," Josip said, completely in awe of the experience as the others acknowledged it was their first time as well.

They sat facing each other, none were sure of what to say especially as they hadn't been alone together since saying their farewells from Sam's house.

"What do you think the camp will be like?" Roko asked, keen to break the silence.

"I guess it will be like Gino said. We will have our own beds and food but will be able to work as well. Maybe we can even learn a trade?" Bruno said.

"I wonder how long we will have to stay there?" Heads shook and shoulders shrugged at the question.

"Do you think there will be Italian girls there?" Grins formed at each other at Josip's question, followed by laughter.

"Josip! Those pictures are still in your head! Of course, there will be Italian girls but why would they look at your ugly face?" Josip lurched at them all as they set on him, still laughing.

"What's going on here? Settle down. There will be no fooling around on the train." the conductor said, keeping his eye on the young group.

"Sorry, sir!" The boys grinned and shuffled back into their seats.

"We are just very happy to be here in your beautiful country," Luka responded. Hoping that this would appease the train official.

"Humph," came the response. "Just don't let me catch you fooling around again."

"I am so happy we are here. What would have happened if …" Josip started to say before being cut off.

"Don't even think about it, Josip. We are lucky to have made it this far." Luka said trying to keep the conversation positive.

"Yes, but we wouldn't be here if it wasn't for you, Luka," Roko said looking directly at his friend.

The train made several stops before arriving at the station where they were taken to the former army camp known as Le Franshcete Di Alatri.

The camp was surrounded by high walls with numerous barracks on the large site. There were guard towers at each point and a tall guard tower at the centre of the internal yard, supposedly to keep watch over some of the residents who were convicts rather than escapees and refugees.

They were led to the main administration building. It was built from large pale concrete blocks and sat right in the middle of the camp. The accommodations were barrack-like with large dormitories of eighty beds with a shower block and toilet facilities and were lined up in rows. There were two sections of these buildings known as N1 and N2.

A large guard greeted them and showed them into a small office while he conferred with the two officers to confirm their transfer and accompanying paperwork.

"I wonder if they will let us stay together," whispered Bruno.

"I don't see why not. It's not like we are criminals," Tom responded.

The guard and the two officers shook hands as the official processing had concluded.

"Good luck to all of you," the officers said and shook their hands one by one. "You are safe here, they will take good care of you."

The boys thanked them as they left.

"Come with me," said the guard, "I am taking you to Section N1 where you will be allocated a bed in the dormitory. Just leave anything you have under your beds. I will keep your visa documents locked in the office so that they are secured. You can shower first if you like, then I will take you on a tour of the facility."

On the first night, an older man, who was from Greece, moved in to be near them under instruction from the guards. As they were new, it was practice to have someone who knew the facility to keep an eye out for them.

"There are people here from everywhere," the Greek informed them. "Many have escaped from Corsica, and even Abyssinia, Eritrea and Libya. All of these are seeking asylum after what happened to their countries during the war."

"Does everyone get to stay in Italy?" Roko asked.

"Not everyone wants to stay here. Some will apply to the United States, Canada or Australia and others might stay for a few years to get citizenship. But enough questions for tonight. You must be tired from everything that has happened today. Get some sleep."

Luka and Roko had chosen beds that were next to each other and neither found it easy to go to sleep. The others were soon snoring while they both lay staring at the high ceilings.

Luka had something he had been wanting to ask Roko since they left Ancona but didn't want to ask until then.

"Hey, Roko."

"Yeah. What?"

"What happened to Sam? Really."

No answer.

"Roko?"

"As they said. He fell and hit his head. Then he died. That's all." Roko rolled over away from Luka.

"Okay."

"Now go to sleep. Goodnight, Luka."

"Goodnight, Roko."

The scream that echoed off the concrete walls in the large dormitory woke everyone up. The Greek man and Luka were sitting either side of Roko when they finally helped him to wake and to realise it was just a nightmare.

"Roko! It's okay. We are here," Luka said, soothing his friend.

"Sorry. I'm sorry to wake you," Roko said in a lather of sweat and still shaking.

"It's alright, Roko, there are many who scream at night from the trauma and war they have seen. It's not just you." the Greek man said demonstrating his worth to them on their first night.

"Did I say anything bad?" Roko seemed eager to know.

"Nothing, Roko, it's okay. Go back to sleep," Luka reassured his friend. He didn't want to tell him what he had thought he heard. Roko kept repeating, "I'm sorry, Sam. Sam, I'm sorry," before letting out the piercing scream.

After everything his friend had been through with his father's cruelty, Luka had hoped he would find peace, now that he was free of him.

But it didn't appear to be the case. Not yet.

CHAPTER 23

The phone rang at the police station just as Zlatko was about to leave. It didn't seem as though he would see his boss come back so he decided to call it a day. It was past his finishing time anyway.

He caught it just in time.

"Hello. Zadar Police, can I help you?"

"Yes. I am the chief warden at the Goli Otok prison, and I was expecting five prisoners this afternoon, but they have not yet arrived. I am calling to see if anything has happened?"

"I'm sorry, sir," Zlatko said not understanding this at all. "I am not aware that you were receiving any prisoners from us."

"Yes. Dragan called me. They were coming directly from Ancona."

"Oh God. What has he done?" Zlatko muttered with his hand over the mouthpiece. I have not had any briefing or update sir. Perhaps they have been delayed."

"Mm. Well if you do hear from him, tell him I cannot possibly process them this evening. It will have to wait until tomorrow," the warden said and promptly hung up.

Zlatko took the copy of Matej's letter and read over it again.

Maybe it is the right time for this to be posted, he thought as he rushed out of the door.

The naval boat arrived in Zadar just as dusk was setting in. It was late for Dragan to go into the office, but he needed to make sure he had a story that was believable to share in the morning. Zlatko would be asking for a result and he also had to plan for how he would notify the parents.

As Dragan walked from the harbour in the dimming light, he failed to notice that he was being watched.

Zlatko was equally confused seeing Dragan on his own.

After the call from the warden, he thought he would wait and see if the boat did return with the boys, as he had been expecting. What was the captain thinking by arranging for them to be taken to that hell hole in Kvarner Bay? He had only heard about its reputation, and no one had ever been reported leaving it alive. In fact, the stories about torture made it the worst prison in the entire country.

"So where are they? And where is Matej?" Zlatko mumbled as he walked some distance behind the captain.

He followed the captain until he saw him approach the police station, then turned to walk home.

Deciding that there wasn't anything he could do that night, Zlatko thought he would wait until he heard whatever story Dragan would tell him in the morning. Then he would decide what to do with the letter.

He wished he knew where Matej was. He would know what to do.

The door was still unlocked to the building when Dragan arrived.

"Bloody Zlatko. I leave him in charge, and he can't even make the building safe. What good is he," he mumbled as he climbed the stairs.

He found the light switch on the wall and thought it felt like he had been away for weeks, not just a day.

The scattered papers on his desk caught his attention. I didn't leave these here, he thought as he picked them up. Must be Zlatko again, careless and messy.

Then he saw his name at the top of the first page and sat in the chair, the leather seat breathing out with his weight.

To Captain Dragan, he started to read.

He took a deep breath, but it didn't stop the rage boiling up inside as he read the last lines again.

I have made a copy of this report. If anything happens to me or those boys, my instructions are that it is delivered to the senior administration office for police.

He dares to threaten me, now breathing heavily. The tightness in his chest made him dizzy as he tried taking bigger gulps of air. He sat back in his chair, trying to calm himself down.

In moments, his breathing returned to normal, and the dizziness had passed.

He took the papers and folded them neatly before he spied the torn envelope on the floor under his desk.

Someone has already read this, he thought. Shit. This could mean trouble.

Throwing the envelope in the bin, he stood and placed the papers in his pocket before switching off the light and heading down the stairs.

I need to talk to the priest, he thought. He will help me.

Locking the large wooden door behind him, Dragan made his way to the church. The sanctity of confession would protect him. And it seemed as though he might need it.

I can't lie. I can't lie. I can't lie, Dragan repeated the words over and over in his head as he entered the narrow wooden door and sat down. Waiting for the familiar sound of the door clicking in the adjacent chamber and then the window between them sliding open.

"Bless me Father for I have sinned." He crossed himself and listened to the familiar response from the priest.

"What is troubling you, Dragan?" came the gentle words from the priest.

He took a deep breath and then thought, well, what's the worst that could happen?

"Well, Father. I am here because I want to confess that I made a big mistake and want to ask forgiveness."

"That is good, Dragan. Please tell me what happened."

"It is about the boys who escaped."

"Go on." The priest's attention had well and truly been captured.

"Well father, the truth is, if I didn't follow up on a slim lead that was given to me by the people in the Ancona Customs Office, the boys may still have been thought to be dead." He let the priest take this bit of information in.

"What? They are alive?" The priest was incredulous.

It had the desired impact, which gave Dragan courage to continue with his story.

"They are indeed, Father." He went on to describe how he intervened when the customs officer advised them of locating three boys in a boat just off the Italian Coast. And it was Dragan who thought the coincidence was too great and went to Ancona to investigate.

The fabrication continued and Dragan became even more animated.

"I gave them my blessing to stay in Italy, if that's what they had truly wished. It was the least I could do after everything they had endured."

"But this is wonderful news Dragan. I can't believe this! What is your reason for wanting me to hear a confession?"

"I made a mistake by rushing to close the case after we found those remains at the beach. And I feel terrible that my decision caused such distress for the families. I wish I had waited." Dragan was pleased with how this was coming together.

The priest stayed silent. Not knowing how to process what he had been told.

"Father. I would like your help to meet with the families and give them the news."

"But of course, Dragan. This is truly a miracle for them."

"If we can make a start first thing tomorrow morning, then I can meet with the journalist. Everyone should hear about this miracle, Father." Dragan congratulated himself for turning his day around.

The priest issued the penance that Dragan needed to make to absolve himself, not thinking it was needed anyway.

Dragan said his farewells as the priest continued to laud him for the great work he had accomplished for the families and in lifting the spirits of the town.

Dragan left the church. What a day, he thought. "Maybe I have come out even better than I had originally planned," he muttered, "this could be very good indeed, Inspector Dragan."

All he needed to do to now was to deal with the letter that had been left for him. Zlatko must know something, he thought. I will meet with him first thing in the morning and then I can put this whole mess behind me.

The next morning, Zlatko arrived to find his boss was already in the office.

"Is that you, Zlatko? Come to my office now. I have the most wonderful news to tell you!"

Wonderful? Zlatko thought, scratching his head. What can be so wonderful about planning to send five boys to rot on Goli Otok?

He climbed the stairs slowly and waited at the office door to be invited in.

"What are you standing there for, Zlatko? Come in! Sit down."

Dragan repeated the story he told to the priest the night before. Zlatko couldn't believe what he was hearing.

"This will surely confirm that I will become an inspector, Zlatko. There is more than enough to say that a higher-ranking officer is absolutely necessary here. They can't ignore this!" he exclaimed.

Zlatko was about to mention the phone call from the prison, when his boss took the letter from his pocket and placed it on the desk in front of Zlatko. His tone changed immediately. He was sinister and menacing.

"Do you know anything about this, Zlatko?"

Zlatko took the letter and pretended to read it, already aware of its contents. He needed the time that it took to read to calm his insides and think of a passable response.

"Yes, sir. I was made aware of its contents."

"By Matej?"

Zlatko nodded.

"And did you open this letter that was addressed to me?" Dragan's suspicion was increasing.

Zlatko felt the need to stand and salute as he spoke. He wasn't going to cower to Dragan any longer.

"I felt it was my duty, as the officer in charge in your absence, to be aware of relevant information pertaining to the growing situation between Zadar and Ancona. I had received a call from the senior customs officer in Ancona and was able to fully brief him. Sir!" He clicked his heels together and saluted once again.

He continued, "I am delighted to hear that despite the risk of the situation deteriorating, you were able to intervene and turn it around. This is a very good outcome for the boys and their families, and it will improve our reputation with our community." Zlatko didn't believe a word he was hearing himself say to Dragan.

"Do you know where the copy of the letter is, Zlatko?" Dragan wasn't falling for the officer's sycophantic reaction. He wanted that copy.

"No, sir. I did read that there was a copy, but I have no idea where it might be. Should I look in Matej's desk, sir?" He tried to stop himself from shaking.

Dragan didn't buy it. If Matej had shared that he had written the document, then he was sure Zlatko would have been told where the copy might be. He may have even been the one to deliver it to head office under different circumstances.

"Yes. Go through his desk." Zlatko locked eyes with his captain and tried not to give anything away.

"And Zlatko," Dragan said as the officer started to leave.

"Yes, sir?"

"Without your ex-colleague here to protect you, things could become very difficult for you if you think you can deceive me. Do you understand what I am saying?" Dragan forced a more sinister tone on the officer.

Zlatko knew exactly what he meant and swallowed hard.

"Yes. I do, sir" he said as he left the office to the sound of paper being torn.

Dragan closed the door behind Zlatko and stood looking at himself in the small mirror. There were only a few more things he had to do before he could finalise the whole situation. He smiled at his reflection. For a moment his disfigurement was invisible, and he imagined looking at Inspector Dragan.

"No. Nothing can stop me now."

Not long after, Dragan descended the stairs, his temperament had completely changed, which caught the officer off guard. He had been anticipating a bad day getting worse. Especially without Matej's support.

"We need to make this wonderful news public, Zlatko. But first, I will meet with the priest and visit each of the families to inform them. We will leave the young man, Sam's family until last. It will not be good news for them."

"Yes, sir."

How could this monster have gotten away with this, Zlatko thought. Surely fate will make him pay in some way.

"I want you to visit the newspaper office and ask the journalist to meet me here this afternoon. Don't say anything either. I want to be the first to break the news, but you can tell him it will be the biggest story of his career." Dragan was now getting even more enjoyment out of his change in fortune.

Going from house to house, each of the families were not only in complete shock at what they had been told, but Dragan had become an overnight sensation. From villain to hero on a complete fabrication.

The priest had offered Sam's family a memorial service and after some protesting from his stepfather, Sam's mother surprisingly stood her ground and said that she was grateful for the offer.

And for the entire community, it had been the story of the year as the copy was rushed to print.

> ## MIRACLE IN ZADAR! DEAD BOYS FOUND ALIVE IN ITALY! OUR HERO CAPTAIN!
>
> Five of the six boys who were believed to have perished as they tried to escape to Italy in a stolen boat, have been miraculously located in Ancona.
>
> Following a tip off from the Italian customs authorities, the captain of police in Zadar, personally undertook an investigation into the claim that a group of boys were apprehended by the Italian Coastguard and taken to the customs office in Ancona.
>
> "It was just a gut feeling," the captain reported. "My conscience wouldn't let me rest until I could establish the truth, one way or another. This is a wonderful time for their families." The Captain went on to report that the remains that were found were almost certainly of a young man new to town and that he was the victim of an accidental death at sea.
>
> "The family have been informed and have been offered a memorial service for this brave young man."
>
> The captain then finished by reporting

that he had, in fact, decided not to pursue any criminal charges in relation to the theft of the boat.

"They, and their families have been through enough," he said.

The details of the memorial service will be forthcoming.

Dragan stood admiring the headlines as his back was slapped by people wandering past the police station.

I should send a copy of this to head office, he thought. Maybe they will fast track my promotion. Or maybe when I am summonsed there, I will happen to have it under my arm by sheer coincidence.

His smile had not left his face.

Matej and Dinko were making their way into the market after a reasonable haul that morning. It had felt like months since they had made their journey to Ancona, but it had only been a week and Matej had quickly become accustomed to his change in career. He loved being on the open sea and did not miss the stress that policing had given him over many years.

Sibenik was now his second home and while he was conscious that he didn't want to overstay his welcome with his new friends, Dinko and Rosa, he felt more at home with them than he could remember.

There had not been any news from Zadar since they had returned, and Matej decided it was best if he stayed away until things settled. Although knowing his former boss, he knew he would always have to watch his back if he ever returned.

Once they had set up their stall with the day's catch on display, Matej wandered off. He was enjoying the banter with the other traders and looked forward to hearing the many stories they would share.

Dinko was busy with customers until he saw his friend out of the corner of his eye. Matej was pacing furiously and shaking some papers in his hands.

He stopped what he was doing and lumbered over to him as quickly as his large frame could carry him.

"Hey, Matej! What is it? Has something happened?"

"That bastard! How can this be allowed to happen?" Matej's face was beet red, and it looked like smoke would come from his ears at any minute.

He pushed the newspaper at Dinko's chest.

"Read this rubbish," he said as his legs gave way beneath him and he fell onto the bench.

MIRACLE IN ZADAR! DEAD BOYS FOUND ALIVE IN ITALY! OUR HERO CAPTAIN!

"How does he keep going? He's a cockroach. He doesn't die," Matej continued as Dinko tried to figure out what he was reading.

Dinko slumped down next to Matej.

"This doesn't make sense, Matej. How can they say he is a hero?" Dinko was at a loss to understand anything about the article.

"I think he is a master at looking after himself, Dinko. I am sure there are things he has done that no one even knows about, let alone the things that we do. He is a man who will have secrets, and I would bet that none of them are good." Matej felt as though all they had achieved was in vain.

"At least the boys are safe, Matej. We can be thankful for that," Dinko's shoulders slumped, and he let out a deep breath. "Maybe it is time to let this one go, my friend."

Matej felt Dinko's large hand on his shoulder.

"Let us now have a peaceful life," said Dinko.

"I wish I could Dinko, but this is not finished yet for me. I need to make a phone call."

CHAPTER 24

The boys discovered that the camp had been operating since 1942 and was initially designed to house prisoners of war during World War II.

There were many people of different nationalities interned at the camp and numbers swelled to over five thousand at the beginning of 1943.

Owing to the overcrowding and the haste with which the structures were built, those who stayed there endured poor sanitation, inadequate medical assistance and unless you were the subject of the Geneva Convention "guarantees", the camp was a dismal and challenging place.

After the war had finished, the accommodation was converted although reportedly, there was little improvement in conditions.

But none of this dulled their enthusiasm.

"Did you hear that the camp manager is looking for help to keep the garden and paths maintained?" Josip reported back to the group at lunch.

"I think they wanted us to be occupied and besides, maybe we can learn some new things." Luka chipped in.

Whilst each one of them managed to find a routine, they knew they needed to decide on where they would go after leaving the camp.

"I found out that we can start the process of filing applications to migrate," Bruno added as they ate the sandwiches in the large mess hall.

"Where will you go Bruno?" Josip was hoping they might apply to go to the same place.

"I don't know. There are a lot of choices, but I guess it depends on what jobs are available and where we will live."

"Yes, but what is your first choice?"

"Maybe Canada. Or even South America?" Bruno replied.

"What about you, Tom? Where would you go?"

"Definitely the United States. If I can get into university to start engineering, I think it will give me the most opportunities."

"Luka and Roko? Do you know yet?"

"I want to go to Australia," replied Roko, "That's about as far as I can get from him. Even then it's not far enough." Roko eyed Luka as he spoke.

"Luka? What about you?" Roko was hoping too that his friend would apply to Australia.

Luka thought for a moment.

"I don't know. With Mira still missing, I don't know if I can be too far away from Mama. I am all she has right now."

"But you can't go back, Luka That is still too dangerous!" They all spoke over each other trying to encourage Luka away from that idea.

Luka shrugged his shoulders. Before he found out about Mira, he was one hundred percent committed to finding a new life away from his home. But now, indecision had crept in, and he felt torn between his own desires and the responsibility he felt for his mother.

"I'm going for a walk," he said quietly.

He could hear them talking among themselves as he left.

The decision about their applications, could take as long as two years, depending on which country they chose. But for some of the boys, getting the process started as soon as possible was important.

Luka found his way to the camp library where they could access paper and pens to write to their families.

He found himself a table on his own and started to write a letter to his aunty. She would know what to do.

Dear Teta Ana,

He was stuck for what to say as soon as he wrote her name.

"Maybe I will write to Mama first," he muttered to himself. "I don't want to worry either of them but..."

Luka had trouble finding any words but after he described their first week in the camp and what they'd been doing, he found the words came more easily.

Mama, we were talking today about which countries each of us would like to go. Tom is definite about applying to the United States. He thinks it will be easier for him to apply to university to take an engineering course there. I think his mind is made up.

Bruno has said he wants to go to Canada or South America, and I think that Josip will apply to go there with him. Although I don't know if Bruno is happy about that. Anyway, they will decide between themselves. It looks like it will take about two years anyway. A lot of people want to go there so it will take a long time.

Roko says he wants to be as far away from his father as he can, and I don't blame him. He is applying for Australia, and I think that will be quicker.

Is there any news from Zadar? Is there any news about Mira, Mama? And how is Teta Ana?

I have a lot to think about and it is hard to know what to do but I wish I could be there for you.

I miss you, Mama.

Love Luka

He leaned against the back of his chair and held the letter up to read over what he had written.

How am I going to make this decision, he thought.

Zlatko laid the paper in front of him. Still in shock at how Dragan had managed to manipulate the situation in his favour. The captain hadn't come into the office that day, so he was left on his own to think about what he was going to do without his colleague and mentor, Matej to advise him.

The days that had passed between the boss's return, the pointed conversation about the letter written by Matej and what might lay ahead for him were a blur for Zlatko. And there had been several times that he had thought of quitting the police force.

The shrill ring of the phone startled him.

"Hello. Zadar Police. Can I help you?"

"Zlatko. It's me."

Barely able to say the name before, "Ssh! Don't say my name!"

"He's not here today, Matej. It's okay." Zlatko was delighted to hear his friend's voice.

"Good! Now tell me why that bastard is a hero."

Zlatko relayed the events that led up to Dragan's trip to Ancona and then what had happened since his return.

Matej also filled him in on what had happened with the boys when they were reunited and the intervention of the customs officers.

"Their boss, Gino, was incredible," he said. "I don't know how he managed to stop an international incident that day, but Dragan would have been furious."

"I can't believe he got away with it, Matej. I spoke to the prison warden at Goli Otok, and he confirmed that the boys were due to be sent there. And by Dragan himself!"

"What? Goli Otok! But that place would have killed them. I need to sort this bastard out. Is there any chance we can meet, Zlatko? Somewhere in private? I need your help."

Zlatko didn't need to give this much thought. He was still annoyed at being directed away from investigating the disappearance of the little girl.

"I'm in, Matej," he thought for a moment where a safe place might be. "Can I come to you? Where are you anyway?" He realised he still didn't know where Matej was.

'I'm in Sibenik. When is he due back into the office?"

"I don't know. But I do know he has been waiting to meet at head office about his promotion."

Zlatko thought for a moment. "How about the day after tomorrow. Then, if he does come into the office tomorrow, I can make some excuse."

They made the necessary arrangements and eventually thought that the church would be the safest place in Sibenik.

They were about to hang up when Zlatko remembered. "Wait, Matej! I forgot to tell you about the letter."

Matej listened as Zlatko told him about the lie he told to Dragan.

"Have you still got the copy?"

'Yes, it's at home. I will bring it with me."

"Good. See you at the church." A plan started to form in Matej's mind. "And Zlatko?"

"Yes?"

"Be careful. We have seen what he can be capable of. Say nothing to anyone."

Zlatko placed the handset gently on the receiver. He felt sick at the thought of what his boss could do to him if he found out.

Now I need my own plan too.

Matej thanked the priest for the use of the phone and made his way back to where Dinko had parked the truck. Just near the market.

"How did it go?" Plumes of smoke rose as Dinko leant out of the cabin, enjoying his cigarette.

"He said he will help. Now I just have to figure out what to do," he said as he climbed into the passenger side of the bench seat.

"What do you mean 'I'? This is still a joint operation my friend!"

"I can't ask you and Rosa to do more, Dinko. You have done so much already." Matej tried to be sensitive yet, firm.

"You forget that I also have a past with Dragan, Matej." He put his foot on the accelerator as he flicked the cigarette butt away.

Matej looked out of the window, thinking through the options.

"Okay Dinko. But if there is any risk, it will be me who takes it. Zlatko is still young and has a future ahead of him. And Rosa would never forgive me if anything happened to you. I won't involve you unless you agree to that condition," he said, appealing to his friend's conservative side.

"Agreed. It's a deal."

Dinko smiled at the thought of making plans for Dragan's demise. *This won't be easy*, he thought. *He might be a monster, but he's not stupid.*

The truck rolled on in silence, both men lost in thought.

The captain arrived at the office later that day. He didn't say where he had been, and Zlatko didn't ask.

"Are there any messages, Zlatko?"

"No, sir. Are you expecting any?"

"I am waiting for my meeting at police headquarters in Split to discuss my promotion. It should be coming any day now."

"Yes, sir."

"Maybe I should send them a copy of the newspaper, Zlatko? They will be more impressed then!"

"They certainly will, sir. It is a fantastic outcome."

"Oh, by the way. I am looking at some houses closer to town. I don't think that an inspector, living in a small apartment is fitting for the position. Do you, Zlatko?"

Feeling even sicker in the stomach, Zlatko replied. "I think something grander is warranted, sir. Will you be doing this soon?"

"Over the next few days. Why?"

"I was hoping that I could take a day off sir. The day after tomorrow. I want to visit a cousin who is ill."

"Mm. I guess that's okay," Dragan said, slightly suspicious, "Where is this cousin?"

Zlatko gulped again.

"Just inland from Sibenik." Shit, I should have planned this better. It slipped out.

"And does this cousin have a name?" Dragan fished, thinking he would catch him out.

"Yes, it's Matej." Zlatko thought this would catch him off guard. Two could play at this game.

Dragan looked shocked, then started to laugh.

"What's so funny, sir?" seeing he had fallen into the trap.

"I was thinking that you couldn't be so stupid to tell me you were meeting with your ex-colleague!"

"Don't you think I know what would happen to me if I did, sir?"

"That's what I thought too!"

"Of course. Take the day. But you will need to make up the time."

"Of course, sir." Zlatko was more determined than ever to help to bring him down.

"The tight bastard," he mumbled. "Can't even see it within himself to give me a day off." But he was also smiling too, as he went back to his desk.

CHAPTER 25

By the time the day had arrived for Matej, Dinko and Zlatko to meet, Matej had shared all his suspicions about the captain. Whether he could prove it or not, he felt strongly about the hunches he had regarding Dragan's behaviours.

As they drove into town, with Rosa cramped between the two men in the truck's cabin, the questions continued about Dragan.

"But I was there, Dinko. When Luka's father, Marko, tried to defend his family, only to be dragged away for trying to assault a policeman, Dragan couldn't help himself with the little girl. It was disgusting the way he looked at her."

"So, you think he had something to do with her disappearance?"

"There was an old woman who came to report him for loitering around the school. Zlatko didn't take it seriously at the time, for obvious reasons. He was afraid."

"But you don't have any other evidence?"

"No. Nothing at all. It's like she has vanished into thin air."

"Mm. I don't think there is any point stirring him up if we don't have evidence. It will only end up with someone else being hurt. We need to outsmart him, and I think I know how." Dinko was taking great pleasure in thinking about ways to deal with Dragan. Once and for all.

They arrived at the church to find Zlatko waiting on the steps, enjoying a cigarette and watching the passing traffic.

"Hey, Zlatko. Doing nothing as usual?" Matej yelled as he climbed down from the truck's cabin to greet his friend.

"I was taught by the best!" Zlatko's quick-thinking response made them both laugh as they embraced.

After quick introductions, Rosa made her way into the church to perform her daily tasks, but not before warning them about planning anything too risky.

"This captain of yours is a dangerous man," she said. "If you are going to come up with something to outsmart him, you better have a back-up plan in case something goes wrong." She wagged her finger as she disappeared through the large wooden door.

"Did you bring the letter, Zlatko?" Matej checked as they started to walk towards the town square. They would find a quiet kafana where they would have some privacy but also a good coffee.

Zlatko nodded as he took it from the inside of his jacket and handed it to Matej. "Dragan tore up the other one, so this is the only copy."

They found a place where they would have the privacy they needed and waited until Dinko had finished reading the letter.

"So, Matej. What did you think your 'Head Office' would do when they receive the letter? Can you trust that they would support you? Or him? If something happened and you weren't there to tell your side of the story, then it might be his word only." Matej and Zlatko could see that he was making sense.

"What do you think we should do Dinko?" Zlatko asked.

Dinko was smiling now as if he been waiting for this moment to arrive.

"I think the only way to get this bastard is by using his arrogance to our advantage." Quizzical looks came from the others as Dinko spoke.

Dinko took them through his plan. The more that they explored it with him, the more they understood that this would potentially hurt him, but it would also spare them, if it backfired.

Matej rubbed his stubbled chin as Dinko spoke. "I'm not sure about this. I don't think he understands anything other than violence and hurting people. That's why I think we need to use the same tactic on him." Matej couldn't see how Dinko's idea would work.

"But that's the whole idea, Matej. That's what he expects. And he knows how to respond. If we do the opposite, we might have a better chance at succeeding." Dinko could almost see the whirring of his friend's mind.

"Maybe you are right, Dinko. It might just work if we catch him off guard. And what's most important is that we don't look like the bad guys." Matej felt more enthusiastic now.

The only thing was that it relied heavily on Zlatko to carry it out.

"Zlatko, are you sure you can handle this? If you are at all worried, then tell us now." Matej wanted his less experienced colleague to feel supported.

"I've been waiting for this opportunity, Matej. If nothing was going to change at the station, I had decided to quit anyway. I can't work like this any longer. You can depend on me." Zlatko's resolve was getting stronger with the thought that something would change either way this went.

Happy with their plan, they wandered to a gostionica near the water to have lunch, accompanied by some locally made red wine.

"How do you think the boys are going?" Dinko asked.

"I don't know," replied Matej.

"At least it has to be better than that prison Dragan was going to send them to," Zlatko reminded them.

"What prison?" Dinko asked.

"I didn't want to say anything to you Dinko. Zlatko intercepted a phone from the warden at Goli Otok. He was looking for Dragan to find out why the five prisoners he had been expecting had not yet arrived." Matej let it sink in for Dinko.

"My God." Dinko shook his head. "He is a monster."

Dinko thought further. "Did you say that the warden and Dragan know each other, Zlatko?"

"I believe they may be friends." Zlatko replied.

"Maybe we can use this as well." Dinko went on to explain how this could all come together.

They finished lunch and walked to the jetty to help Zlatko find a boat to take him back home.

"You are welcome to stay tonight, Zlatko."

"Thanks, but, as it is, I have to work extra hours to make up for today. If I am late tomorrow, it will just be worse. Anyway, he is not suspicious now but that could change if I'm not at the office first thing tomorrow morning."

They said their farewells and reminded Zlatko to leave a message with Rosa at the church once everything was in place. Then it was a waiting game.

"And remember, Zlatko, the more praise and adulation he receives, the greater his downfall. You just need to plant the seed," Dinko said, encouraging the young officer.

"I understand, Dinko." Zlatko said as he leapt onto the boat and waved goodbye.

Later that evening, Matej and Dinko shared their plan with Rosa.

"This is good," she said knowingly, "I knew you would see a way to do this, my husband," she said as she took his face in her hands and kissed him on both cheeks.

Back in Zadar, Zlatko sat at home and planned the phone calls he needed to make the next morning. Hoping that his boss would not be in the office.

"Hopefully he is out looking for his palace," he muttered to himself. He found himself smiling again.

Just plant the seed, Zlatko, he thought. Just the seed.

The next morning, Zlatko arrived at the office just as dawn broke. He had found it hard to sleep with the ideas swimming around in his head, but an early start meant he could get his thoughts in order before his boss arrived.

Dragan had also decided to make an early start and was surprised to see his officer already at work.

Zlatko could see that he was still basking in the afterglow of his self-assumed triumph.

"You are here early, Zlatko. Is there something happening that I should know about?" His suspicions were heightened at any change in routine.

"I am making up time as you ordered, sir. With all the activity in the past weeks, there are still reports to complete."

"Mm. I did say that didn't I. Very well. Continue. I am only here briefly, then I am attending to some business. Stay here and take charge while I am gone."

"Yes, sir." He stayed seated. He had lost the urge to stand to attention and salute. That would only be shown out of respect and Zlatko had none left for his boss.

"Oh and Zlatko."

"Yes, sir"

"Put those reports on my desk when they are finished. I want to make sure they are accurate accounts," he said as he climbed the stairs to his office.

More like doctored accounts, Zlatko thought, as he watched him go.

The first call that Zlatko made, after he was sure that his boss had left, was to the senior administration office at police headquarters.

After a brief introduction to the receptionist, he was put through to the office where his captain's promotion was being handled. And owing to the unusual nature of the call, he was directed straight to the chairman of the interview panel who was undertaking the review.

"This is most unusual, Officer," the chairman replied after hearing Zlatko's proposal. "I don't recall any request in the past, where serving officers have made representations to a panel, in the event of a consideration for promotion."

Zlatko started to sweat as he heard the response. He would have hated for this to fail at the outset.

"But having said that, and as you have duly pointed out, it does demonstrate the positive impact on culture when officers have the confidence to make this approach. This will reflect very positively on the government policy for unity and consistency."

Zlatko breathed out in relief.

"Yes. I will agree to your request. And I am grateful that you have showed the maturity and initiative in ensuring our candidate selection for such senior positions is supported by our serving members."

"Thank you, sir." Zlatko couldn't help but stand on hearing this and saluting with his free hand. "When do you anticipate holding the next panel meeting sir?"

"Mm," he checked his diary. "As soon as possible, officer. It looks like I have an opening in one week which should give enough notice for those who need to attend. I will contact your captain tomorrow."

"Um, sir?" Not wanting to push his luck but hoping for one more request to be approved. "Knowing my captain, it may make him nervous or concerned if he knows that I will be there beforehand. He may try to talk me out of it, owing to his desire for all of us to share in our achievements."

"Yes. Go on."

"Could we keep this between ourselves sir? I am sure that my captain will then be able to attend without this as a distraction beforehand."

"Good idea officer. I will make sure you are given the meeting details separately and that also gives me time to discuss this with the other members of the panel. They can then hear directly from you, rather than me trying to brief them in advance. Will that be all, Officer?"

"Yes, sir. Thank you, sir."

"No. I should be thanking you. This is going above and beyond your duty to the state, Zlatko. I look forward to shaking your hand."

They both hung up as Zlatko slumped back in his chair in utter disbelief that he had succeeded.

No time to rest, Zlatko, he thought. There is one more call to make before I will leave a message at the church in Sibenik.

Matej will be proud of me, he thought with a smile.

The phone was answered on the second ring, and by the person he needed to speak to, much to Zlatko's surprise.

"Goli Otok prison, this is the chief warden speaking."

Zlatko made the requisite introductions and provided the reasons for his call. The warden nodding as he listened intently.

When he had finished, there was a moment's silence that prompted Zlatko to check if the warden was still on the line.

"Sir. Are you still there?"

"Yes. Yes, Officer. What you have shared has given me much to think about. I am not sure if I can give you an answer immediately."

Zlatko tried to contain his disappointment. After his previous call, he had thought this would be easy.

Then an idea came to mind.

"Of course, I understand, sir. I would be happy to communicate your hesitation to the senior administration at police headquarters. They were very pleased at the opportunity for a positive reflection on the government's work around unity and consistency. I am sure they could contact your superiors and ask them to provide you with support and advice."

Silence again but this time Zlatko allowed his response to sink in.

"No, Officer, that won't be necessary. Of course, I would be happy to provide a supportive reference for Dragan as you have outlined. In fact, please give me the contact details and I will call them now. I imagine they will be even more pleased when they hear that the department of security is working closely with the police."

"That is most kind of you, sir. I am sure that the outcome will be of great benefit for Captain Dragan." Not to mention, us, Zlatko thought.

They hung up the call. Zlatko had planted the seed as he had been instructed and had thoroughly enjoyed the role he played.

He left a message for Rosa at the church to pass onto his friends and it wasn't until later in the afternoon that he received a call back, just as his captain returned.

"Hello, Zadar police, can I help you?" The pre-prepared speech all ready if Matej called while his captain was in the office.

"It's me. Matej. Can you talk?"

"Certainly, sir. Can you tell me what you need, and I will try to help you."

"He's there isn't he. Did you call headquarters? Did they agree to our plan?"

"Yes, that's correct."

"Great, Zlatko. Did you call the warden?"

"Of course, sir. I understand what you are saying and can reassure you that everything that had to be done has been done. The Zadar police does its job, all the time."

"Don't go overboard, Zlatko," Matej said, sensing his former colleague's ego was growing. "This is us you are talking about, not the bloody CIA."

Zlatko giggled. "Well, sir. I am anticipating we will find out over the next week. Please call back then."

Zlatko hung up.

Matej scratched his head. That boy was enjoying this game too much he thought. *You are just jealous, you old fool,* he thought as he smiled to himself.

The waiting game had commenced.

"Who was that, Zlatko?"

"No one, sir. A wrong number."

"Okay. I'm leaving for the day. I am expecting a call from headquarters regarding my promotion any day now. I need you to remain in the office to make sure it isn't missed."

"Yes, sir. I will make sure you get any messages."

The following morning, the call came that Dragan had been waiting for, but what he didn't know was that Zlatko was equally excited, and anxious, to receive it.

The details of the meeting to discuss his boss's promotion would be held in a week's time. The location and time were confirmed, twice, by Zlatko before he took the message upstairs to the captain's office.

"Excellent, Zlatko. Things will be very different around here after I have been made an inspector, he said with conviction, "No one will disrespect me then." He leant back in his chair with one hand rubbing his paunch as the other went to his groin.

"I look forward to that, sir," as he left the room.

CHAPTER 26

The week passed quickly, and Zlatko had to work extra hard to contain his anxiety at what he needed to do next. His presentation to the panel went around and around in his head, to the point that he was able to construct the entire scenario.

"Take it easy, Zlatko," Matej had cautioned him in, the only time he was able to speak freely before the day arrived. "You have done well to get us this far. Just present the information as we discussed. Write it down and read it if you have to but stick to script."

Zlatko understood exactly what Matej was saying.

He was ready.

The day before the meeting was due, Dragan announced that he would be travelling to headquarters in Split that afternoon. Zlatko was relieved to hear it as he had no idea how we would create a story about his own absence on the day.

The next morning, Zlatko arrived in Split after an almost two-hour trip by bus. It was his first time at headquarters and on arrival he was immediately overawed by the sheer opulence of the building and its surrounds. The grand arches at the top of the steps to the entrance, along with the ornate columns surrounding a first-floor walkway.

As he wandered into the grand reception area, the marbled staircase and polished tiles caught his breath.

"Wow," he said under his breath, "this is spectacular."

He approached the receptionist and was given the details to where the panel meeting would take place.

He walked around and then waited outside, taking in the beautiful gardens, until the time had arrived.

As he walked back in, he caught a glimpse of his captain at the top of the stairs, shaking hands with men in highly decorated uniforms. He guessed that this would be his audience.

Waiting until they disappeared, he climbed the winding staircase to the designated room, where he waited outside until the exact time. He didn't want to spoil anything by risking an explanation to his boss as to why he was present.

The door creaked as he opened it slowly. Dragan had his back to him, standing alongside a chair that was facing a group of men. A long wooden table divided them.

Zlatko looked around for the only other chair in the room, that happened to be just inside the door. He sat down quietly and waited to be called.

The chairman struck the gavel on its wooden block before calling the meeting to order.

"Please be seated, Captain."

Zlatko's hands went to his trembling knees, and he wished he had visited the bathroom earlier.

The chairman introduced the panel members before refreshing the group on the task at hand.

"As you are aware, we are here to decide on Captain Dragan's potential promotion to inspector. But, in a most unusual twist, I have agreed for representations to be made to the panel regarding this promotion."

Dragan shuffled in his chair. This had come as a surprise.

"I do acknowledge that you weren't briefed on this prior to today, Dragan, but under the circumstances, I felt it was of greater benefit for you and the panel to hear this directly. Without any further comment from me, I would like to invite an officer from the Zadar Police to please step forward."

Zlatko needed the edge of the chair to help him stand as Dragan's face went pale watching his officer walk towards him.

Zlatko extended his arm to Dragan and felt the moist palm as shock was etched on his boss's face.

What the hell is this, thought Dragan. What is he up to?

Zlatko stated his name and rank before giving a brief introduction about himself and his time as a police officer.

"Now, Zlatko. Can you please outline the reasons you are here?" the chairman asked.

Dragan swallowed hard as Zlatko took a deep breath.

"I am here to report to the panel on captain Dragan's excellent leadership whilst he has been our captain. He has been instrumental in developing a culture of working together, respect, gratitude that is based on the ideals and policies of our government."

Dragan couldn't believe what he was hearing.

"He is an experienced investigator, who is highly skilled at solving crimes." Zlatko continued to the nods and smiles of the panel members.

Dragan was speechless.

After referencing several examples of his boss's skills, most notably the successful discovery that the five escaped boys were alive in Italy, he read his final statement.

"As Captain Dragan has embedded such high quality into our policing practice, we are almost able to operate without him being there at all."

The panel members clearly enjoying this as they whispered between themselves. So much so, the chairman had to strike the gavel to get their attention.

"Thank you, Zlatko. The panel is grateful, as Dragan must be, at hearing of the positive impact he has made in Zadar. Are there any questions for Zlatko?"

The chairman then started to address Dragan.

"The representation from your officer only confirmed what the panel had already decided Dragan. However, the one concern that was raised was whether there would be enough to support the position of inspector in Zadar. It is not lost on us that the impact you have made on your station, has allowed them to operate at a very high level."

Dragan sensed that something was about to go wrong as the chairman continued.

"It was therefore a timely surprise that we also received a reference from the prison warden on the island of Goli Otok. As you know, the relationship between our security and police forces is critical in the government's response to unity and the adherence with policy. The warden couldn't speak highly enough of you and how beneficial it would be to further integrate that relationship. He recalled a comment you made to him about there not being enough room for two experts. We think that the north of our country, including Goli Otok, would benefit greatly from two experts."

Dragan could feel his blood boil as it struck him what had happened.

"It is therefore the unanimous decision of this panel to promote you to inspector and to expedite your immediate transfer to the Primorje-Gorski Kotar County. We look forward to hearing how you will represent our government in the same way you have clearly done in Zadar."

And with that, he struck his gavel and produced the documents for the panel members to sign and approve the decision.

Zlatko wasn't sure whether he was being too cheeky, but he couldn't help himself when he strode up to Dragan and shook his hand vigorously.

"What an honour captain! And so well deserved!" He moved on to shake the hands of the panel members.

He couldn't wait to tell the others.

He took one more look at his former boss, before striding out of the room. That was the last time he would see the man he knew as Captain Dragan.

"He did what?" Matej couldn't believe what he was hearing as he, Dinko and Rosa huddled around the mouthpiece from the phone.

Zlatko had rushed back to the office and placed the call to Sibenik. It wasn't long at all before the call was returned.

"Tell me exactly how he looked again, Zlatko." Matej couldn't get enough of what he was hearing as Dinko and Rosa fired questions at him as well.

Zlatko was laughing into the phone as he regaled the events of that morning.

"They said it was effective immediately," he said. "I have no idea where he is now."

"Maybe you should lock up the office and stay away, Zlatko. At least until you know he won't come back in to see you." Dinko now taking over.

'I was hoping I could come to Sibenik. I could do with a drink."

"Or three!" yelled Matej. "You won't have to pay for any after what you did today."

Zlatko packed up his things as soon as he had hung up the phone and as he locked the front door, he couldn't help remembering what Dragan had said the week before.

"Things will be very different around here after I have been made an inspector."

He couldn't have been more right.

CHAPTER 27

Mara must have read Luka's letter a dozen times. Between tears, smiles and deep breaths, she couldn't help but be proud of her son.

"I wish Marko were here," she said to herself as she placed the letter back in the envelope.

She went into the room that he had shared with Mira. She ran her hands over their beds to smooth out the bed clothes, just as she did many times a day.

She glanced at the clock on the wall to see that she still had time. The black dress was already laid out on her bed with the sheer black veil beside it.

The deep sigh spoke of surrender. She needed to let her son know, but she didn't know how to say it.

She sat back down at the table to gather her thoughts.

My dear son,
How wonderful it was to get your letter. I must have read it a thousand times and each time I felt prouder of what you have been able to do. For you and for your friends.
I am glad that you are being treated well and that you can

start to make plans for where you want to go. Whatever you choose, my son, I will be happy for you.

She paused at this point. Not knowing how to proceed. She read the little that she had written.

"I can finish this later," she said aloud, leaving the letter lying on the table and went to change into the traditional clothes for mourning.

The procession to the church grew as mourners joined the slow walk. Mara's head was bowed in prayer. It was only as they got closer to the church steps that she raised her eyes, as if there might be a sign to say that the time had come, and it was right.

"Here, take my arm Mara," Matej said moving in beside her as she entered the church. Zlatko had sent word to Sibenik, and out of respect for everything that had happened to her family, Matej felt the need to be there for her. Dinko, Rosa and Zlatko walked behind them.

Solemn silence fell as each of them dipped their fingers in the holy water just inside the front door. They crossed themselves then they moved quietly to the long wooden benches. They deeply genuflected before sliding across to kneel in prayer.

The family always moved to the front rows.

Mara sat there alone.

Matej, Dinko, Zlatko and Rosa in the row behind her.

Only weeks before, Mara had visited her sister-in-law noticing that her cough had worsened, and her breathing seemed to be more laboured.

"Ana. You must see the doctor," she urged her sister-in-law.

"What can he do? I'm old. I don't need the doctor to tell me that!"

Ana's stubbornness had meant that she had become Mara's champion and best friend when Mara had lost hope. She had forced her to keep going in her darkest moments. But it also meant that once she had made her mind up about something, nothing would shift her.

Over recent weeks, her health declined and along with a distinct mistrust of doctors, it meant that it was rapid.

"Why do you need to poison yourself with that rubbish?" she would argue about medicine. "Eat plenty of garlic and good food. That's the best medicine!"

And then, only three days ago, on the day that the letter arrived from Luka, Ana was found by one of her neighbours lying face down in her garden.

And as Mara rushed to share the letter with her, a neighbour stopped her in the street.

Ana had died before she could tell her that she had news from their boy, Luka.

The service finished and the priest waited at the door as the congregation filed out, shaking hands and blessing each of them as they passed.

Mara stayed seated.

Prayers for Ana.

Then prayers for Marko.

And prayers for Luka.

She still couldn't find the right ones for her Mira.

After the burial had taken place, they went back to her house where Rosa greeted each of the villagers as they brought a plate of food and paid their respects.

Once they were alone, Mara spoke.

"Where is Mira, Zlatko?"

The officer looked across at Matej, hoping his friend could provide the words he needed. Matej shook his head.

"We have found nothing, Mara. I have spoken to everyone again. The teachers, her friends and all the villagers. No one can tell me anything." He didn't want to mention the old woman who came to report Dragan's behaviour. With no evidence, it would be impossible to investigate.

It was the truth and that's all he had.

"It is time for us to go," Dinko said reluctantly.

"Come with is Mara," Rosa offered, "You shouldn't be alone now."

Mara shook her head.

"Okay but if you need anything, please let us know."

Matej was last to leave. "You should lock your door, Mara."

"No," she said. "I don't want Mira to be locked out."

He squeezed her hand as he left.

Two weeks later, as Luka was up on a rickety scaffold painting the external wall of one of the accommodation buildings, he heard his name called.

"Hey, Luka! You have a letter!"

He scampered down the wooden ladder and hurried to retrieve his mail. Many of the refugees didn't receive any contact from families. Some because they didn't know where they were and others, because there was no system of getting mail out due to ongoing conflict.

When anyone did get any news, they were quickly surrounded

by others, just wanting to have some contact with the outside world. Whether it had any relevance to them or not.

The cold of winter was upon them but there was still the occasional day that the sun shone. So, Luka found a quiet spot on the grass and started to read.

My dear son,

How wonderful it was to get your letter. I must have read it a thousand times and each time I felt prouder of what you have been able to do. For you and for your friends.

I am glad that you are being treated well and that you can start to make plans about where you want to go. Whatever you choose, my son, I will be happy for you.

She told him news of the village and then that she had seen Matej, Dinko and Rosa.

They were all keen to know how you were and send their love.

He turned over the page and suddenly gasped as he read her final paragraph.

I am so sorry to tell you like this, Luka, but Ana has died. Her health had become worse as the weather got colder. Matej, Dinko and Rosa came to her funeral and have been a wonderful support to me at this time.

And as if to soften the blow for her son, she decided to write a little white lie.

*In her last week, the one thing that made her happy was to hear
about you in your letter. She loved you very much, my son.*
*   I miss you very much,*
*   Mama*

And, as if a light had been turned on, Luka knew exactly what
he would do.

CHAPTER 28

"Who's in charge here?" said the thundering voice as a very junior officer came running from the tearoom.

The police station had remained unchanged except for a change in personnel. The junior officer had only started three months prior and was still learning what to do.

"Can I help you, sir. I am sorry, but the captain has just stepped out of the office for a moment."

"What sort of policing do you call that! He has probably found a place for coffee and a cigarette! Typical lazy bastards!"

A hand landed heavily on his shoulder from behind, making him jump.

"You forget that I learned from the best, Matej!" Zlatko said as he walked in. The two men laughed and embraced.

"So, you have made captain now? There must have only been one application!" He laughed.

"It was only recent, Matej," he said as they settled down. "I was completely surprised but apparently after the meeting about Dragan, they decided that I should take charge. It has taken this long for my papers to come through." Zlatko was still feeling uncertain about the added responsibility.

"Well, they haven't made a mistake, Zlatko. You will make a fine captain."

"You could always come back, Matej. I could do with some help to train my young apprentice."

"Nah. My days in uniform are finished, Zlatko. I am happy working on the boat and have even become used to smelling like fish," he joked. "But I am always happy to help out. But no uniform."

"It's a deal." Zlatko turned to his junior officer. "Show respect for this man. You will learn much from him if you do."

Matej grinned as the officer stood to attention, clicked his heels and gave him a salute.

"Exactly as I taught you, Zlatko. He will do very well."

The young officer let out a deep breath.

"Now. Where will we go for coffee?"

The letters from Luka had been regular and Mara's spirits lifted each time they came.

It was now over twelve months since the boys had arrived at the camp. Luka had written about where each of the boys had applied to emigrate, and it seemed as though they were getting closer to a final decision.

Tom had already had his visa accepted to travel to the United States and was due to leave once the documents were signed.

Josip and Bruno had visited the Canadian and Venezuelan embassies and were waiting for confirmation that they had been accepted. It seemed that Bruno had developed an interest in South America after speaking with some of their fellow refugees, but Josip thought that Canada seemed a better option.

And Roko was going to Australia. It had been confirmed and, he too, was just waiting for his papers.

Mara opened the latest letter and began to read. Apart from the news from the camp, her heart lifted when she read his final lines.

I have had my application to stay in Italy accepted, Mama. I decided that I want to be near my home and maybe once I have full citizenship, I will be able to return to Zadar. This is what I want to do, Mama.

I am very happy.

Love,

Luka.

CHAPTER 29

2016

Another restless sleep for Roko and as usual, the same nightmares were responsible.

Maria had woken up in the spare room. They had spent more time sleeping apart in recent years than in the same bed. If Roko fell asleep in his chair, the main bed was hers. But when the nightmares were bad, she would creep into the spare bed.

She heard him struggling out of bed the morning after his birthday. The groans were almost always followed by the hacking cough to clear his throat. Then a final spit into the basin before the tap was turned on.

Then the clunk, clunk, clunk of the walking frame as he made his way to the kitchen.

Roko was glad that his eightieth birthday was behind him. Not owing to his ageing years but because was just tired and wouldn't care if he didn't see another one.

However, today was something to look forward to and the one thing that made him smile was watching his grandson play football. It reminded him of the days in Zadar and for one day a month, when his eldest son would pick him up, he felt good.

He heard the car arrive in the driveway followed by the familiar slam of the door.

"How many times do I have to tell you? Don't slam the car door!" his eldest yelled. Falling on the deaf ears of his son.

"Hurry up, Dido! We have to go!" Roko smiled each time he heard his grandson with the same call on football days.

"Don't hurry an old man. I am eighty years now," he said as he made his way out the door.

Maria hugged her grandson, nibbling his cheek as she always did.

"Baba, stop!" he said laughing and wiping his cheek as he ran to the idling car. She almost didn't hear the phone ring as she stood in the porch waving goodbye and couldn't quite collect her breath from rushing to answer.

"Hello," she said, still breathing hard.

"Hello," a male voice she didn't recognise, "I am hoping I have the correct number. I would like to speak to Roko please." The accent was foreign.

"I am sorry, but he is not here now. I am his wife, Maria. Who is speaking please?"

"I am, or was, a friend of his from many years ago. My name is Luka."

Maria put a hand on the kitchen bench to steady herself. "Luka?" she said, "My God. Please wait a minute."

Luka could hear the scraping of something along the floor as she reached out for a chair.

"Is this really Luka? From Zadar?" she said, still in shock.

"Yes, it is. So, Roko has spoken about me?"

"He spoke of no one else when we first met, Luka. I feel like I already know you."

"How is he?"

"He is getting old. He was eighty only yesterday. He has difficulty walking and complains a lot, but other than that, he is still my Roko," Maria said starting to feel comfortable sharing this with Luka.

They spoke for some time, each feeling more at ease.

Then a question came to mind for Maria. One that she hoped Luka could answer and easier to ask without Roko being present.

"Luka. Do you know that Roko has bad nightmares?" She hoped that she hadn't wandered into something that was difficult for Luka to answer.

"What kind of nightmares, Maria?"

"Well, sometimes they are just mumblings and restlessness but other times they are very bad. He thrashes about and keeps yelling out the same name." Before she could say it, Luka interjected.

"Sam."

"Yes. But how do you know?"

"Because I heard it when we arrived at the immigration camp. On the first night we were sleeping in the dormitory, I was awoken by it. It took ages to calm him down. I was hoping we could talk about it. But we never did."

"But where are you calling from Luka? I seem to remember Roko saying that you had stayed in Italy?"

"Yes, I did. But I am making one last trip with my wife to see one of our children who now lives in Australia. It has taken me some time, but I finally found out where Roko was living. I was really hoping I could see him or least speak over the phone."

"Where in Australia?"

"We are in Melbourne, Maria. My son tells me it is only a short drive to Ballarat. That is where you are living? Would it be alright for me to visit?"

"Oh, Luka," Maria couldn't stop the tears. "I think this would be the best present that Roko has ever had."

"Will tomorrow be okay?"

"That will be perfect. And I will make it a surprise for him." Maria started to giggle.

"I hope it doesn't give him a heart attack!" Luka replied, laughing.

They finalised arrangements as Maria began to think about what she would need to prepare.

"Thank you, Luka. This will be a very special visit."

Later that afternoon, she heard the car pull into the driveway and rushed to the porch to see her grandson helping Roko out of the car. He stood with his grandfather's walking frame as Roko reached out to grab it.

"How did you go?" she called out.

"We had a draw, Baba. It was one all." He was disappointed as he walked alongside Roko.

"Dido said that I should have tried for a goal, but the coach yelled for me to pass it, and my teammate missed. Then the siren went."

"Of course you should have kicked it! In my day, if you were in a good position, you take the shot." Roko said, giving his coaching advice.

"It's not like that these days Papa," his son joining in. "The boys need to learn how to share the ball around and play as a team."

"Bullshit. That's why they came a draw. No one has winning on the mind. What's the point of playing if you don't play to win!" His hand ruffled his grandson's hair, and he continued the same argument with his son. His son rolled his eyes.

"Come inside boys. I have made fritters."

"Fritters, Maria? You never make fritters after football." Roko looked at her quizzically as she let out a giggle, "Are you sick, Maria?" The only thing he could think of saying.

"I just thought it would make a nice treat," she replied.

"Sorry Mama but we can't stay. We are going out for dinner tonight." Their son said apologetically.

"What's wrong with eating at home?" Roko replied.

"Oh, Dad. This again? Just because you and Mama don't go out, doesn't mean everyone else should stay at home."

Roko turned to go inside, shaking his grandson's hand as he did. "Next time, take the shot," he whispered into his ear. "Your coach doesn't know what she is talking about."

'Yes, Dido," he called and walked back to the car.

Roko looked at his wife. Something about the look in her eyes put him on edge.

"Has something happened Maria?" Roko asked, feeling a little concerned.

"No, my husband. Why?"

"Because you look different for some reason."

'You are imagining things, Roko. Go and sit in the lounge and I will make dinner."

By the time Maria went back into the lounge with his dinner, his head had fallen back onto the chair and his mouth was wide open, fast asleep.

She left the tray on the side table in case he woke up and she went back to the kitchen to finish preparing for their visitor the next day.

Roko didn't stir all night and woke up the following morning with a blanket around him and a stiff neck.

"Good morning, husband," Maria chirped, "Why don't you have a shower?"

"I don't need one. I had one on my birthday," he said stubbornly.

"If it was up to you, that would be the only day you would have one." She knew she needed a reason for him to relent. "We might get visitors today and I would hate for them to leave early because you hadn't showered."

"Who is coming? Haven't we had enough this week." Roko was losing his patience now. She was acting strangely, and he wanted to know why.

"It's a surprise," she said, now losing her patience. "Go and have a shower. You'll find out soon enough."

He could tell she meant business and he couldn't be bothered arguing so he slowly did as he was told.

When he had finished, he went back to the lounge. Exhausted from what should be a normal daily routine. He heard her humming in the kitchen and then the sound of a car pulling up. A car door slammed shut and Roko could just make out an old man walking towards the front porch.

Who is he, he thought.

There was a knock at the door and then Maria rushed to open it.

"Hello Maria," a voice said that he didn't recognise.

She walked into the lounge with a grin from ear to ear, the old man followed behind her.

Roko adjusted his eyes to see. She was waiting for a hint of recognition.

"Hello, old friend," the man said.

Roko gasped as his eyes lit up. "No. It can't be," he said. "Luka?"

Maria's hand went to her mouth.

One minute, Roko was wedged in his chair, the next he was embracing his old friend. His head buried into his friend's shoulder, weeping. He couldn't even recall how he moved without his walking frame such was the power of that moment.

He let go and leaned back to look at his friend's face. "You are an old man!" he exclaimed, laughing.

"Just like you!" came the quick response.

After much back slapping and arms wrapping around shoulders, Maria told them to sit at the table. She had laid out a feast for them, knowing that they would probably be there talking for hours.

She stood by as they began their journey back in time. She knew they would hardly know she was there, but she sat and listened, mesmerised by the stories they told.

"So, you lived in Italy all this time?" asked Roko. "Did you ever go back to Zadar?"

"Yes. I was able to visit Mama but not for about ten years after we left."

"What about you, Roko?" Luka could have guessed what his answer would be.

"I never went back. What would I go back for, Luka?"

They stayed silent, both knowing what he meant.

"And the others? Do you know what happened to them?" Roko asked.

"I know that Tom went to university and studied engineering. I saw his parents once and they said he had visited. I haven't heard anything else about him since. Bruno went to Venezuela and that's the last I know. And Josip was in Canada. I met up with him many years ago when I was on a visit to Zadar. It was a coincidence that we were both there at the same time. We had coffee and talked but I got the impression we wouldn't see each other again."

"Mm. I guess it was always going to happen. Once we had all gone our separate ways, things would change. We wouldn't have much in common anymore."

Both men went quiet.

Roko dared to ask, "Did you ever find Mira?"

Luka shook his head. "We finally had a mass for her in the year before Mama died. She had waited in hope all those years. She just vanished, Roko."

It seemed as though the conversation was taking them into the painful times and Luka took the opportunity to ask the question he most wanted to ask his friend.

"So how are you really, my friend," he asked, looking directly at Roko.

As if he knew what was coming, Roko looked back at Luka.

"What are you asking, Luka?"

"How are you sleeping?" Luka asked gently. "Do you still have those nightmares?"

Roko swallowed hard as he felt his eyes getting moist. He looked at his wife. Her stare locked on him, hoping that he could let go of whatever it was that was haunting him.

For over sixty years he had maintained his silence, as his two other friends had done for him as well.

He took a deep breath.

"It was an accident Luka. But it was my fault it happened." The flood gates opened, and he buried his head into his folded arms on the table in front.

Maria was also crying as Luka put his hand on his friends back. The relief she saw in his face as the words came out was palpable and once, he had calmed down, they just poured out.

Luka just listened. His hand never left Roko.

Roko slumped back in the chair when he finished, wiping his eyes and nose with his sleeve.

"I could never say anything, Luka. What would you think of me?"

Luka knew exactly what he thought of his friend. "You are not him, Roko. You were never like him. That's what I think. And what I know."

Luka stayed until late evening and when they heard the taxi arrive in the driveway, it felt too soon.

"Thank you, Luka," Roko said embracing his friend. They both made commitments to stay in contact with each other.

As the taxi pulled away, Luka looked back to see Maria with her arm around her husband as they waved.

Roko slept that night. And for the first time in over sixty years, nothing woke him.

CHAPTER 30

1954

Families had returned to the beaches on the Dalmatian Coast once the summer had arrived and Zadar seemed more popular than ever before.

People fished off the jetty and the children collected shells and pebbles from the shore.

As parents looked for the right spot to set up for a picnic lunch, their djeca, searched for souvenirs to take back home.

"Don't go too far," came the familiar warning. "Stay where we can see you."

"We are just going near that old house on the water," shouted the young boy and girl.

"Okay but don't go in the water without your papa or me!"

They ran towards the dilapidated wooden structure. The poles that held it up seemed as though they were struggling under the weight.

"Let's dig for treasure," said the girl "and who ever finds it gets to keep it!"

They fossicked through the sand beneath the pebbles, digging holes and leaving mounds of sand behind.

Suddenly, the girl gasped. She looked up quickly to see where her brother was, hoping he wasn't nearby.

Then using her hand, she dusted the sand away to reveal a thin gold broken chain with a small cross dangling from the clasp at one end.

Looking around again, she tried not to squeal. It's buried treasure, she thought.

She held it tightly in her hand and ran back to where her parents had laid out the picnic rug.

"Where are my shoes and socks, Mama?"

"I have put them in my bag. It's over there, Vesna."

Very pleased with her find, Vesna wondered who it might have belonged to. She sat thinking it might be a beautiful princess or a mermaid.

Well, it is mine now, she thought.

Finders keepers.

THE END

AFTERWORD

Many thanks to Ann Dettori at Dettori Publishing and to Lucy for her fantastic editing. To my wonderful husband Paul for encouraging me to take this leap and follow my passion for writing. To all of my friends who have provided frank and fearless feedback and encouragement over my writing journey-a very big thank you!

Thank you to the Australian Writers Centre for their great course, "Fiction Essentials" that helped start my writing education.

And to Mum and Dad and their families for having the courage to make a life in a new country. Thank you.

ABOUT THE AUTHOR

Tricia Bulic has wide experience working in healthcare as a nurse and has also held executive roles in mental health, disability and local government. She is a keen rower, active cyclist and is a devoted door opener to her adorable Staffy, Bonnie. Born in Ballarat, she has lived up and down the east coast of Australia and is now living in Geelong with her amazing husband, Paul.